THE WAR
AGAINST CHAOS

By the same author

Bethany
The Illusionist

THE WAR
AGAINST CHAOS

by

Anita Mason

HAMISH HAMILTON · LONDON

HAMISH HAMILTON LTD

Published by the Penguin Group
27 Wrights Lane, London w8 5TZ, England
Viking Penguin Inc., 40 West 23rd Street, New York, New York 10010, USA
Penguin Books Australia Ltd, Ringwood, Victoria, Australia
Penguin Books Canada Ltd, 2801 John Street, Markham, Ontario, Canada L3R 1B4
Penguin Books (NZ) Ltd, 182–190 Wairau Road, Auckland 10, New Zealand
Penguin Books Ltd, Registered Offices: Harmondsworth, Middlesex, England

First published in Great Britain 1988 by
Hamish Hamilton Ltd

British Library Cataloguing in Publication Data
Mason, Anita
The war against chaos.
I. Title
823'.914 [F]   PS3563.A7874

ISBN 0-241-12176-0

Typeset in 12/13 Sabon by
Centracet, Cambridge
Printed and bound in Great Britain by
Richard Clay Ltd, Bungay, Suffolk

Acknowledgement

This novel was largely worked out, and partly written, during an Arts Council Writer's Fellowship at Trinity and All Saints' College, Leeds. I should like to record here my appreciation of the encouragement, hospitality and stimulating talk from which I benefited during my two years at that college.

A.M.

1

Hare was walking home from a faith party the first time he saw the creature in the tail coat rooting among the dustbins, and for a moment he thought someone had been playing tricks with his drink. It was dwarfish in height, with something misshapen about the head, and it was picking through the rubbish with a speed and ferocity that reminded him of a rat. Then it turned, hearing footsteps, and Hare saw its face. It was a mild and human face, wearing old-fashioned round-rimmed spectacles, behind which the eyes blinked frequently as if the light of the street lamp was hard for them to bear.

They stood looking at each other, Hare's heart pounding. An interrogatory expression crossed the creature's face and it moved forward, making a little sound in its throat.

Hare raised his fist. The thing backed off, and disappeared with a scuttling gait down an alleyway, its frayed black coat lifting and falling on its posterior as if that was what propelled it.

Hare leaned against the lamp post, shaken as he always was by such contacts. Other people seemed able to laugh off these irruptions of the irrational and chaotic, but they disturbed him profoundly. With an effort he called back to mind the rousing songs they had been singing at the party, hoping their warmth would dispel the chill the encounter had caused him. But the songs sounded lifeless, and the alcohol fumes that had so pleasantly clouded his brain had already settled into the metallic flatness of tomorrow's hangover.

Hare had a room in a decaying house in a district which nobody lived in who could help it. The room, advertised as 'Single-bedroom flat, suit professional person', was in fact a bedsitter off which opened a cupboard containing a twenty-year-old gas cooker and two saucepans. Hare ate most of his meals in the small cafés round about; cheap, garish places which he liked because they offered undemanding company.

The house belonged to Mrs Raptor, who possessed a bullying manner and a screeching voice. All the tenants were afraid of her, which was why no-one ever complained about the fact that the window frames were falling out of the walls. She had a fifteen-year-old daughter, Jacinth, who from time to time came to Hare's room and took off her clothes. Hare's feelings towards Mrs Raptor amounted therefore to terror. Sometimes he wondered if he was the only person in the building thus visited by Jacinth, but it did not seem a good idea to enquire.

Hare was forty-five, and on bad days looked fifty. The bad days came increasingly often, but perhaps that was part of being forty-five. Another part of it was that, as more and more of his life slipped away, he knew less and less what he had done with it. There seemed nothing to show for all those years doggedly undertaken: no achievement in career or personal life, no rewarding friendships, no poems written, trees planted, children begotten – especially none of the last, they being the way most people solved the problem. His wife had left him, one uncomprehended February afternoon, and everything had been stitched-together ever since.

He had been lucky to get the room. Often he told himself so, as he climbed the ill-lit stairway, with its cracked lino, brown walls and smell of cabbage, to his door on the second landing. He had been lucky to get a room in a respectable house (he supposed it was respectable: Mrs Raptor laid much stress on the point), luckier still to keep his job. The job had many qualities in common with the house, but no-one else knew that. Appearance was nearly everything. For a man who had come as close as he had to being marginal, it was everything.

Hare worked in Universal Goods, that monolithic organisation which some said was a department of the Council (and certainly the men who went in and out of the top floor offices of Universal Goods could not be distinguished from the men who went in and out of the ground-floor Council offices). Being employed by Universal Goods was in itself almost a guarantee of solidity. There were rotten apples in every barrel, of course, as Jacobs had twice said recently in Hare's hearing. Hare thought Jacobs had given him a funny look when he made this remark: hostile, Hare thought. Jacobs was his immediate superior, a fleshy, fruity man with a fleshy, fruity laugh, usually heard in appreciation of his own jokes. That he had a vicious side, and that Hare was just the sort to arouse it, as mice arouse cats, Hare did not doubt.

All in all, therefore, it was a bad omen that he had seen the dwarf in the tail coat on the way home from the party. It was always dangerous to see a marginal. The contact seemed to stay with you, so that for some time afterwards you could not quite get your moral balance, and were prone to deviant thoughts. Most people who became marginal had seen one not long previously. (Such, at any rate, was popular belief. Hare did not know if it was true. To find out if it was true you would have to enquire closely among people who were or had been associated with marginals; thus becoming one of them yourself. The risk was hideously high. Curiosity, in any case, was discouraged.)

*

9

He had been late for the party. He was nearly always late these days. He would be ready to set out at the time necessary to arrive promptly for an engagement, and at the last moment would find something to do. Hand raised to take his coat from the peg, he would remember a faulty plug, and turn to investigate it, or his eye would fall on a newspaper and he would start to read it, or he would decide that after all he should wear a clean shirt, and then find a button was missing on the one he chose. He knew he was doing it, and his insides grew leaden at the thought of the frantic journey and the unconcealed disapproval that lay ahead, but he could not stop doing it. Something had changed in him. He would rather be fifteen minutes late, and bear the cost, than one minute early and pass a minute of his life unnecessarily in a place where he did not want to be.

He was ten minutes late for Mrs Lovejoy's faith party. It was the eighth in the current series of faith parties and he had been late for seven of them. In the large bright drawing room about twenty people were already seated in a circle.

The vogue for faith parties had begun about twelve years ago as part of the drive for national regeneration, and Mrs Lovejoy had taken them up with the energy that character-ised all her doings. Her group held parties monthly at members' houses in rotation, and no-one felt able to drop out for fear of being thought unwilling to provide his or her share of hospitality. In the two years Hare had been attend-ing, there had been only three defections: two owing to death and one caused by madness.

Hare was not expected to host a party: it was known that he lived in lodgings and could not entertain more than a few people. The circle's forbearance towards him in this respect was of a piece with the way they treated him in general. He was thought eccentric, but harmlessly so. Thus he was not under the same obligation as the others to continue attend-ing. Yet the very fact that he was freer than they to drop out of the circle meant that he could not take advantage of his freedom. To do so would confirm the suspicion that he was not sound. He could not afford that, because it was true.

Mrs Lovejoy was an overbearing woman with small restless eyes which, while powerful instruments of coercion, were seldom fixed for long on the person to whom she was talking. She talked a great deal. She appeared, discoursing on morality and family life, on television and radio programmes. She had been one of the founders of the Decent Read campaign, and was apt to recount its early battles with an indignation that would have suggested rather that the battle was still to be fought than that it had long ago been won. She sat on many committees. The cause was never a surprising one. Her photograph appeared from time to time in the Government press.

Of Mr Lovejoy nothing was known save that he existed. He had been seen once on the stairs, a small dome-headed man dressed in flannels and a blazer and carrying a pile of journals. Mrs Lovejoy had hinted that he was a scientist of a rare type.

Hare knew everyone in the room except a surly-looking young man in a raincoat. The others were the usual circle. Hare was regularly astonished by them. None of them had ever given the slightest sign of boredom or embarrassment, of being amused at the expense of other members, or of wanting a drink (until the drinks were served). Was it really possible that they enjoyed each other's contributions (he did not doubt that they admired their own), and took seriously the stated purpose of the faith parties, 'The strengthening of the nation through the spiritual efforts of its citizens, gathered in small groups'? Glancing round the room, he experienced a familiar sinking feeling: yes, it was possible, and he forgot it every time he was not with them.

The proceedings opened with a prayer.

Religion had declined since Hare's boyhood – necessarily,

with the shift of the focus of piety to the beleaguered State. Even before that, it had ceased to work as a system of incentives: it was simply not possible to believe in Heaven any longer, however much you wished to, just as an earlier generation had had to stop believing that the sun circled the earth, whatever their eyes told them. The rewards of virtue these days were the approbation of your fellows and a solid position in society.

In the new scheme there was less space for God than there had been before, but still there was some. God was the senior partner of the State: old, old-fashioned and long due for retirement, he yet had about him the aura of vanished power and vast experience. He lent weight to any undertaking, and in this capacity he was now invoked by Mrs Lovejoy. 'Amen,' chorused the flock.

A curious word, thought Hare, and wished it was still possible to get hold of a good dictionary.

There followed a patriotic song, after which the proceedings proper began.

Mr Auckland was first. A smallish man with a nervous smile, he fished in his inside pocket and the smile died. Further fumbling in other pockets produced only coins and tickets. He sat crimsoning under his wife's stare.

Mrs Auckland knew exactly where her contribution was. It was in her handbag. She brought it out and read it in a tone of accusation. It was a verse cut from a magazine. It rhymed thumpingly and was loudly applauded.

They continued round the circle. Miss Minching had written a dialogue between Faith and Reason which went on for twenty minutes. The Spencers, a devoted elderly couple, sang a duet about the virtues of constancy. The sullen-looking young man pulled from his pocket a scrap of paper from which he read, with pride, a description of his state of mind. The man on Hare's right, smiling complacently, unfolded eight sheets of paper.

12

Hare let his eyelids droop just a little (just a little was not noticeable) and slid forward fractionally in his chair. If you did it properly it looked as though you were concentrating; it helped if you furrowed your brow. Furrowed, Hare dozed lightly while the man on his right read an allegorical short story of his own composition. Instinct alerted him on the last page, and he was awake and nodding with appreciation two sentences before the end. It was his turn. He drew from his pocket a small book.

Hare was the only member of the gathering who ever read from a book. That he should bring a book, and that this should pass without comment, was appropriate to his role as the group's eccentric. Hare enjoyed this licence, but did not push his luck. What he read was always the purest inanity. His offering this evening had been chosen with the help of his friend Solomon, from whose shop the book had come. It was in praise of freedom of speech. Solomon had hugged himself with glee. Hare read it solemnly. No-one smiled.

It took another hour to get through the remaining contributions. Finally, after a few minutes' desultory chat and shuffling (it did not do to look too eager), the guests sauntered through to the adjoining room where drinks were set out. For a while there was little conversation; then gradually a convivial hum arose. It generally arose about the time Hare finished his third glass. Drinking was one thing he was not cautious about: caution was unnecessary. By the time he had reached the end of his third glass, everyone else would have reached the end of theirs too. Drinking would go on until well past midnight. People could no longer manage without it. All over the city, the faithful drank like fish.

Hare lived in the district of Dossdown, and worked in the commercial and banking quarter. This meant that he had to travel through the Zone, which required a special pass. The fact that this pass had been issued to him without trouble, and that his entitlement to it had never been questioned, gave Hare, in his darker moments, a feeling of reassurance. If serious doubts were entertained about him in higher quarters, he would not still hold his pass.

The Zone was a danger area, or an interdicted area: there were various ways of thinking about it. The best way was not to think about it at all. Much of the time there was an official pretence that it did not exist. However, its physical existence was never denied outright. It could hardly be, when the wall around it could be seen by anyone who took the trouble to walk through the boarded-up, deserted streets which led there. Not that anyone would have dreamed of doing so. From some parts of the city the wall could still be glimpsed in the distance, although all but a few of these vistas had now been blocked off. What made the Zone a daily reality to many citizens was that part of the underground rail system ran beneath it. The line had been laid many years ago, before the Zone had become what it now was, and it would have been uneconomic to reroute it; so the trains continued to shuttle at frightened speed through the echoing unlit stations where it was still just possible to see advertisement hoardings from a vanished age speaking a nearly forgotten language. The names of these stations were never uttered. They were there and not there. Their precise status, the status of the Zone itself, was a matter for theological debate, but certainly not for vulgar speculation. Out of respect, fear, a lively regard for survival and even a kind of embarrassment, the people who travelled on those trains averted their eyes from the windows as they passed under the Zone. It was obvious to commonsense that not all citizens could be trusted to behave with such circumspection. Hence the special pass, issued to those of proven reliability.

Hare had been reliable until his wife left him. It had ruined his career, naturally, and his social standing; but years of hard work and rectitude had saved him from the full severity of ostracism. He lost the pretty little flat overlooking the canal where he and Maria had lived, but he kept his job. For ten years he had been on probation. When he averted his eyes from the ghost-stations of the prohibited Zone, it was with a fear that one day he would be compelled to look at them, would be unable any longer to fight back the temptation to raise his head and stare. That would be the end of him. What caused him to tremble inwardly, though, was the sense of something fitting, the recognition of his own emptiness in the emptiness of the place that did not exist.

The door handle turned, slowly and surely, without a sound, propelled by a small but practised hand. As it ceased to turn, the door began to open inward. Here success was not complete: there was a single loud creak.

Hare sat transfixed in bed, praying. The door hesitated, then opened wide. Jacinth stood in the doorway, wearing tight black trousers and a low-cut blouse which showed the tops of her breasts. An unshaded light bulb haloed her head inappropriately and showed up the holes in the flowered wallpaper.

'Shut the door!' entreated Hare in something between a howl and a whisper.

She shut it. She came forward a little way onto the carpet and kicked her shoes off. Then for a few minutes she appeared not to notice him, but wandered round the room glancing at things, periodically rising on tiptoe with her hands clasped behind her back and a rapt expression on her face. She always did this, and it irritated Hare beyond measure.

As if he were not present, she began running her hand over the base of the reading lamp that stood on the bedside table. It was a cheap, garish, plastic thing masquerading as marble, but it had a curve which pleasingly fitted the palm of the hand. Hare was apt, in odd moments, to caress it himself. He was not aware of having done so in front of Jacinth, but as she smoothed her hand down and over it she gave him a mocking little smile. Then with a studied gesture she withdrew her hand, paused, and dropped it to the belt of her trousers.

The hand stayed where it was for a long time. Then she began to move her hips sinuously. It was a movement taken straight from the screen; everything about it was artificial, and performed by a girl of fifteen it looked ridiculous. It also looked very provocative.

Still undulating, she began to undo the buttons of her blouse. She did it very slowly. He watched her, as her hand glided from button to button while her hips continued to move in a rhythm suggestive of someone else's idea of lovemaking, and was rewarded at last by a wriggle, a flourish, and the sight of Jacinth's young, apple-round breasts, seen by no means for the first time and partially visible for the past ten minutes, but still very pleasing to behold. Although not, perhaps, for quite the length of time she stood there displaying them to his view.

The game was that he must now reach forward and attempt to touch them. He reached. She moved away, smiling, and to punish him drifted twice more round the room before coming to rest in front of him and slowly, very slowly, sliding down the zip of her trousers.

This was always the moment when Hare's excitement won, riding over his boredom, his irritation and his self-contempt. There was one perfect moment when she paused with her hand there, belt loose and zip open so that he could just see the young dark forest, and then she would drop her trousers and step out of them and stand there naked, and ever so slightly his phoenix would subside: Jacinth half-clothed was a schoolgirl into whom the devil had somehow

16

entered, Jacinth naked was simply a schoolgirl, and had spots on her back.

She came towards him. He flung back the bedclothes, removed his pyjamas. This was a ritual too. He lay down, she astride him. Hare found he could not concentrate, his mind kept wandering to incidents of the past few days; he vividly saw the dwarf's face, turned to him in the lamplight. 'What's the matter with you?' Jacinth demanded, and began to go up and down on him as if he were a footpump.

Under this methodical assault, Hare felt his interest begin to revive. He abandoned himself to pleasure.

There was a series of loud, tinny crashes on the landing, as if someone had dropped a lot of electric fires.

Jacinth unsheathed him like lightning and shot off the bed. Hare grabbed the blankets to cover himself.

'Sorry!' called the jovial voice of the man who lived upstairs and spent his weekends handing out uplifting moral tracts on street corners.

2

Hare was tall and thin, and had an unfinished look. His scalp had a tendency to dandruff, his shoelaces had a tendency to come undone, and buttons had a tendency to come off his shirt. He cultivated an air of abstraction, mainly as a defence. His eyes, small and blue, gleamed on either side of a high, beaky nose. Because of his abstracted air and because he was always untidy, it was not generally noticed that his eyes were shrewd.

Although assumed to be lonely, Hare was not, particularly. He was used to his own company and it bored him less than the company of most people he knew. Moreover, he found no trouble in filling his spare time. He read – real books, old ones, not the picture books that were now virtually all that was produced – and he went walking.

Much of the city these days was either undergoing some redevelopment scheme or other or in need of a redevelopment which it would not get. In the second category were the decaying housing estates where lived the poor who had not yet become marginal, hanging on with desperation to a job of a few hours a week and the shred of respectability it afforded. Hare avoided these ghettos, as at the other extreme he avoided the gaudy shopping precincts, and he found the Council's recommended pedestrian routes and leisure parks not to his taste.

There were still a few places worth walking to. Sometimes

he would stroll through the alleys and cobbled streets of the Shuttle, the artisans' quarter a few miles from Dossdown, and go into one of the wineshops for which the district was famous, and where trade until recently had relied on the fact that it was too dark to see what you were drinking. These wineshops, from being a haunt of alcoholics and the hopeless, had in recent months been taken up by the ruperts, as the young fashionable set were known, so that Hare, from being out of place in them for one reason, was now out of place in them for the opposite reason; but he still drank there occasionally because he liked the shabby voluptuousness of the decor.

He enjoyed the Shuttle; it was one of the few districts which still had its own atmosphere, and it always conveyed to him a feeling that something unexpected might happen. Twice it had: as he threaded his way through the alleys he had twice seen a woman in a tattered red dress walking in front of him. Something about her had aroused his curiosity. He had lacked the courage to catch her up and speak to her (what, in any case, would he say?), and on both occasions within a few minutes she had vanished into an alleyway and he had lost her, which puzzled him because he knew the winding little streets well.

Walking was as disreputable an activity as reading. There were several reasons for this. One was that it confronted the walker with a continual series of decisions as to which direction to take. This was not thought desirable either by the Council or by most of the citizens, who preferred to drive or go by public transport. Motor traffic was channelled in an efficient although complex network of routes, clearly signposted, with coloured symbols accompanying the place-names, for the benefit of those who could not read.

The traffic routes, it seemed to Hare, comparing them with knowledge gained from his walks, were often bizarre; but it was difficult even for him to piece together an overall picture of the city because so much of it was inaccessible – fenced off, dug up, or being turned into something else.

The idea that walking encouraged the dubious quality of initiative was, naturally, not mentioned. There was simply a feeling that you should not walk if you could reach your destination in any other way. Walking suggested curiosity, or introspectiveness, or a desire for solitude, or just plain poverty. In a word, it was marginal. The ruperts, as was to be expected, drove everywhere – at the moment in converted hearses.

Hare's third disreputable hobby was that he collected junk. At weekends he pored in musty little shops over the chipped relics of a despised past. He became something of an expert on the rubbish-tip end of the antiques trade. His room filled up with bits of glass, candlesticks, old photograph frames, cracked hand-painted plates, silhouette portraits of someone's great-grandmother, and boxes of things he had not yet had time to sort out.

Mrs Raptor complained bitterly about Hare's collection. She said it put too much weight on the floorboards, all that glass and metal and china. She was worried about her ceilings. Hare, in an uncharacteristic surge of defiance, said that if she was worried about ceilings she should look at the one in the bathroom, much of which had descended into the bath. Mrs Raptor was too astonished to think of a reply.

After a few weeks she returned to the attack. All that clutter was unhygienic, she said; it made it impossible to keep the place clean. Hare replied that he dusted and vacuumed regularly, and challenged her to find dirt. Her last complaint was curious: she said that the collection would attract burglars, as if they were a kind of rodent.

What was particularly satisfying about the junk collecting was that it could be combined with walking and the perusal of books, since it was in the musty little shops that books were usually to be found. What was particularly disreputable about both the junk collecting and the perusal of books was the people with whom it brought Hare into contact. Solomon, for instance. Solomon was old; how old it was impossible to tell, and he would not divulge. He had a matted beard which nearly touched his chest, and bright eyes that peered at you from surrounding folds of dirty flesh like diamonds from a coaly matrix. He had been many things – musician, banker, bicycle manufacturer, candle salesman – and had fathered seven children. Everything had gone, his family, the businesses, retreating from him like the tide, leaving him alone in a tiny shop in Morristown full of books piled one on top of the other from floor to ceiling, and a tiny room behind the shop in which he cooked and slept. Even this meagre haven was begrudged him: unnamed persecutors were always at his back, trying to evict him, but he would not go. He cursed them savagely, his thin old body shaking with passion.

Solomon knew more than anyone else Hare had met. He had about him the rags of a culture that could no longer be pieced together – at least, not in Hare's mind. He knew every book in his shop and where, in the ungraspable panorama of the world's literature, it fitted. When Hare visited him, he would make foul coffee on a paraffin stove in his back room, and serve it in tin mugs, and talk about books, the making and losing of money and the persecutors at his back.

Hare visited him often. He was fond of Solomon, and there was no-one else he trusted.

It was March. Blustery winds tossed the treetops and brought squalls of rain. Bits of paper blew along pavements and adhered to Hare's trouser legs. Pulling one off he found a doggerel verse written on it:

> Don't imagine, you up there,
> We don't get our bit of air.

We're wide awake when you're asleep.
Don't sleep too long, or dig too deep.

This was written in pencil on a torn piece of brown paper
bag and he had to puzzle over it for a few minutes before he
made it out. The writing was large and erratic, but not
childish. Hare could make no sense of it, but the impression
of menace was quite clear. A conviction that it came from
the Zone possessed him and in his fright he nearly dropped
it. But that would never do. There were people about: any
of them might have seen him studying the writing on the
paper. He put it in his pocket and hurried on, and when he
got home concealed it under the dirty sheets in his wardrobe.

He had just finished stowing it away when there was a
peremptory knock at the door. Mrs Raptor stood there,
emanating venom.

'A person called to see you,' she enunciated. 'This afternoon. A time when all honest folk are at work, as I told
him.'

It took a moment for this information to penetrate the
apprehension with which Hare always opened the door to
Mrs Raptor. Then he was puzzled, for he did not have many
friends and no-one would call on him at that time.

'Left no name, no message,' said Mrs Raptor. She looked
at him as if he had brought an unpleasant smell into the
house. 'Not a nice person at all. Very strangely dressed.'

She began to go down the stairs. Hare gathered himself
for what was necessary, but his voice squeaked. 'Was he a
tall man?'

'Tall?' The stairwell echoed with her bitter laughter. 'I
should say one thing he was *not*, Mr Hare, was tall!'

No-one seemed to know how long the Zone had been
hostile. It was difficult to get information, of course, because
people did not like talking about it and there were no books.

None that were helpful, anyway. He had combed through the books in Solomon's shop and there was no reference to the Zone. There were no books on modern history at all – nothing published more recently than a century ago, and those referring to an age which he could hardly imagine. It was as if the world had been swept clean of books by a great magnet. Perhaps the books he sought had never existed. He had to glean his understanding of the past from old novels, and it was like doing a jigsaw without having seen the picture, and without knowing whether the pieces even belonged to the same puzzle. For the past forty years no books of the traditional kind had been published at all. It was said that no-one wanted them. The nearest modern equivalent were the brightly-coloured 'information kits' that stood in racks in nearly every shop. Hare had never found in any of them any information which he wanted.

He had grown up in a world which had gaps in it. Through the gaps, the unknown and terrifying might at any moment rush. It had first done so when he was about five years old.

He had not known what was happening, naturally, but he was old enough to see that the adults around him did not know either. There was confusion and fear, and talking in whispers. The talk was of the Zone, and traitors. He didn't know what traitors were, and no-one gave him a satisfactory explanation. He knew what the Zone was: it was like a deep hole, and you stayed away from it lest you fell in. Presumably the traitors had fallen in. In that case, he thought, people ought to feel sorry for them, but nobody seemed to. There was also much talk about infection, which baffled him further.

Whatever it was passed, and after a time was no longer talked about. Hare's confusion persisted. One day, in his seventeenth year, he had realised that the confusion was not simply his, or even that of the people he knew, but was

23

attached to the subject itself – was part of its nature. This did not make anything easier to understand. By that time, perceptions of the Zone had already shifted several times within Hare's memory, and in the periodic welter of statements, forecasts and denunciations it was impossible to know what to believe. Nor had he ever known what to believe since.

Over the years, speculation about the Zone had risen and fallen in waves, each crest topping the one before in strength of condemnation and hysteria of language, each one accompanied by a whipping up of public fear. Hare was as prone to the fear as anyone; it would catch him suddenly as he read a paper or sat thinking about nothing in particular on the underground train. For, sceptic though he was, he knew that at the bottom of the pronouncements and warnings of the Council must be *something*, and that, although the reason everyone gave for being frightened might not convince him, there nevertheless *was* a reason for being frightened, and the further it departed from the reason given, the more frightening it became.

The most recent of the major crises had occurred about thirteen years ago. It had been set off by a press report that sounds of a sinister nature had been heard from the Zone at night. Other reports quickly followed. The noises were described variously as 'eerie', 'sickening', 'definitely human', 'definitely inhuman', and – in an access of poeticism – 'like the wailing of an abandoned tribe'. The reports appeared for a week and then stopped. By then questions had been asked in Council, statements denying that anything had been heard at all had been issued to calm the public, and there were again rumours of defections by highly-placed citizens.

After this, the Council took to issuing official statements about the Zone at roughly yearly intervals. The statements, if carefully considered, often contradicted one another, but no-one seemed to notice this, or to think it important when Hare pointed it out.

Hare's wife had been twenty-one when he met her. He had walked into a postcard shop and seen a lanky girl with hair like sunlight pricing cards at the desk. She worked there two afternoons a week to earn extra money: she was an art student.

Art had started to become not quite respectable. There had recently been several speeches about it in the Council. Art had an inherent tendency to subversion, the speakers claimed, which no society had ever quite been able to root out. It offered a natural field for the poisonous flowers of sedition, anarchy and decadence, as well as those of wholesome stock. That being so, and since the State could not afford to be internally weakened by the activity of subversives when it was having to gird itself for the greatest struggle in a generation, then the State should give thought to whether it should continue to tolerate, let alone encourage, the presence of artists in its midst.

No-one took much notice of these remarks at the time: they were made by councillors famous for the intemperance of their views. All the same, there was in the air a feeling that if you wanted to make it into the best society you would be advised not to take up painting.

Hare did not want to make it into the best society: he knew where he was going, a modest rung in the elaborate hierarchy of Universal Goods, where he was now serving his apprenticeship in the information department. He could see no danger in associating with an artist. Even if he had done it would not have stopped him, because he was in love.

He and Maria married six months after their meeting. He accepted her love as one of the miracles which occasionally befall the undeserving. In time he forgot that he did not deserve it, and also that it was miraculous; and then one day the miracle was withdrawn. She stopped loving him the morning he walked into the bedroom and found her looking through an old sketchbook: he had thought she had thrown them all away. By that time the intemperate speeches of the anti-art lobby had turned out to be an early indication of the way the wind was blowing. She reacted to his horrified stare with a look of steady contempt. He knew that look had been there all the time, waiting. After that they could not talk to each other about anything that mattered; the major channel of communication had been cut, and the remaining circuits could carry only bits and pieces, secondhand thoughts and cheap music.

They had then been married for seven years. Emerging from the cocoon in which they had wrapped themselves, they sniffed the air and found it changed. Life was very serious: even the popular songs reflected it. People endowed with a witty turn of speech had had to learn to curb their tongues, or at least to think faster than they spoke. An ill-judged jest could filter through the substrate of common intercourse and who-said-what until it came to rest in a place where it would destroy a career. But jokes must be made, and so they were, in batches, like cakes. The subjects changed every few months. The jokes circulated for a time, vanished, and came back a year or so later, repackaged.

Everything had become more difficult. There were dozens of forms to fill in. Changing your address required official permission, which might not be given. Personal identity numbers became essential to numerous trivial transactions such as borrowing tapes from the library. All these measures had been introduced because of events in the Zone. There was talk of a crisis.

More pervasive than the regulations was the constraint in the air: you felt watched. Everyone was being tested. The form-filling was only a token of what was really required of the citizen. If the state was to survive it must be sustained by

26

the unambiguous loyalty – more, the moral steadfastness – of everyone in it. The enemy sought weakness, so there must be none. A return to ancient, forsaken standards was called for: the sacredness of virginity, of paternal authority, of filial duty. Divorce was a disgrace, and cohabitation without marriage had become illegal.

It was at this time that the faith parties started. Maria had hated these parties: at first she had refused to go, but Hare had cajoled, threatened and begged, pleading his job and the social necessity, and so she had consented to go with him, and behaved with such spiky cleverness and scorn that it would have been better if he had left her alone. As, in the end, he did, but by then it was too late. Too late for the faith parties, from which he was gradually dropped, to be picked up again years later as one might pick up a stranded fish to see if it was still alive; too late for his job, which had become a labyrinth of blind turnings; too late for their marriage, which was in ruins.

How that had happened so completely without his realising it he did not know. Perhaps, as it was possible to sit for a long time through a winter's afternoon without realising that the light was fading, it was possible to walk daily through the ruined landscape of a relationship and not see that the structures had decayed. One does not see what one does not want to see. Hare still loved his wife, or thought he did. He had put her at the centre of his life and there she must stay. She did not want to. She wished to leave him. She said so, over breakfast.

Hare remembered sitting rigid while a piece of toast dropped from his open mouth to the carpet. The subsequent exchange was confused and vehement. He tried to hit her – it was pain, she had hurt him too much, he was not a violent man – but she dodged. He was not a quick man, either. He fell over a chair and sprained his wrist on the wall. That put a stop to whatever conversation there had been. Later, when he tried to talk to her about it, beginning on the lines of 'I must have misunderstood what you meant', he was told he had not misunderstood, not at all, that was precisely what she had meant and there was nothing more to be said. Hare's mind, in which universes clamoured to be said, reeled. Reel it might, she appeared not to care what effect her words had. He began to weep, unable to help himself. To his surprise his grief stopped her. She put an arm round his shaking shoulders and gave him a handkerchief. It seemed ridiculous and, through his tears, he laughed. She laughed too. He took this to mean he had won. There were no limits to his stupidity. A week later she left him.

Maria had hurled at him, during one of the random explosions of anger in which the wreckage of their relationship blew itself irretrievably apart, that the reason why he refused to let her go was that he feared the disgrace; and a part of him agreed with a sick smile that this was so and that he did not really love her. The day she left him, he knew the truth. This was love. Beside it, there was no other consideration.

Five years after the initial denunciatory speeches, the Council closed down the colleges of fine art and banned exhibitions of painting and sculpture. To encourage the talented to express themselves in approved ways, funds were diverted to the applied arts. For a time the shops were full of hand-woven textiles, pottery, printed silk and woodcuts, which nobody bought because the only people who could afford anything made by hand were not interested in buying it. After a while the applied artists were told they had better design wallpaper.

Hare's office had a dingy air, whatever you did with it in the way of calendars and plants, because the window looked out across a small yard to a high blank wall, and was

28

moreover barred, though why anyone should think of escaping by that route Hare could not imagine.

He had not always been in this office. He had started off on the first floor as an information clerk. His job had been to handle enquiries. It had perplexed him at first that this job should be given to a new employee who could be guaranteed not to know anything about the firm's business. In time he realised that his lack of knowledge was not an impediment, since most of the enquiries were complaints, or threats, or related to some other business entirely, or were disguised statements about the world made by one of the increasing number of mad people to be seen on the streets. It did not matter what he said in reply to these questions, as long as it was reassuring and said with authority. Occasionally there was a real enquiry, relating for instance to doormats, typewriters or fire extinguishers, but, again, it did not matter what answer he gave since the real answer was unknowable, there being no way of producing an estimate of the number of doormats, typewriters or fire extinguishers in the firm's numerous warehouses with which everyone with a say in the matter would agree.

To such questions Hare framed his answers according to a schedule, for he was orderly by nature and had a horror of the arbitrary: one week the answers would accord with what he thought to be the mathematical probabilities; the following week he would say the first thing that came into his head, on the principle that he might experience a moment of unwitting clairvoyance; and the third week he would use a system based on the clues in the crossword puzzle. He never received any rebuke for his answers, except once, when he had been with the firm about six months, when a typewritten slip of pink paper appeared on his desk bearing a reprimand for information he had given in response to an enquiry about paint rollers. The slip stated that the information had been confidential and should not have been divulged, that a

29

serious view was taken of the matter, and that the offence must in no circumstances be repeated. The following day a second, blue slip appeared on the desk saying that the previous slip had been issued in error.

He had enjoyed his time in Information. Most of his work was done on the telephone, which made him feel more in command of a conversation than he did face to face with someone, when he worried about his appearance and so lost the thread of what he was saying. He was well thought of by his superiors, received several pay rises, and was promoted to Senior Information Clerk. He had every hope of rising eventually to Information Officer Grade I and might even, if he fulfilled his early promise, have become Information Manager, one of the most influential posts in the Company. Then one day, without warning, he was transferred to another department.

There was never any explanation. Things did happen without warning in the Company: not infrequently Hare had passed a tragedy on the stairs. He had always pretended not to see. Now those with whom he had a few days earlier exchanged jokes pretended not to see him. Hare was desperate. He had been moved from his comfortable cubbyhole to a large, garishly-lit room full of clattering machines, where no-one smiled. He hoped for the first weeks that it would prove to be a mistake like the pink slip, but it wasn't.

He had to file pieces of paper. Some of them had to be filed according to a word typed at the top, some according to subject, and some according to who had written them, and there was no indication which was which. He realised after a few months that there was a system to it, a sort of hidden code, and applied himself to cracking it. He was good at that sort of thing, being logical and patient, but it took him nearly two years to work the system out completely. The day after he sat down at his desk and began distributing papers around him with barely a glance at their contents, he was moved to another department.

Since then he had been transferred eight times. He had tried to work out the system behind the transfers but had not been able to find one. There was no apparently progressive demotion, apart from his transfer out of Information, and sometimes he wondered whether even that had been a demotion, whether in fact he had ever had any prospects or had been destined from the start for a career consisting solely of changes of direction. Perhaps that was as valid a career as any other? Certainly the people who had been in the same office for twenty years did not seem to know more about anything than did he, who had been in ten offices in twenty years; and although he thought they earned more than he did, it was perfectly possible that *they* thought *he* earned more than *they* did, since nobody in that labyrinthine building had any idea what anybody else earned except the hunchback who operated the computer who, besides being a hunchback, was a deaf mute.

Hare's latest transfer had brought him to a small room in one of the innermost recesses of the building where pipes ran across the ceiling and interfered with a good deal of the wall. Presumably they were water pipes, although one of them was large enough, as an occupant of the room remarked to Hare the day before he was transferred away, to carry a chest of drawers without trouble, so goodness knows what it did carry. From time to time, indeed, the large pipe gave a surprisingly solid-sounding bump, which made Hare think of corpses.

In this room he sat and stamped dockets, or sometimes punched holes in them instead. The dockets recorded the transfer of goods from one warehouse to another. Hare stamped on them the date and the Company symbol, the latter depicting a man in armour holding a sword in one hand and a bird's nest in the other. If the dockets had a red serial number at the top he did not stamp them but punched them. Sometimes, carried away by the rhythm of his stamping or engrossed in what was going on in his head, he stamped ones he should have punched and then had to punch them as well, and Bolt, to whom he gave the dockets when he had finished with them, would snarl at him because it made his work untidy.

Bolt sorted the dockets into a set of trays on his desk, and gave them to the third occupant of the office, Blight. Blight went through the dockets marking them in pencil, and then packed them in a long, narrow cardboard box like a coffin. When the box was full he picked it up with a serious air and bore it away. Once, returning from the lavatory, Hare saw Blight setting off down the corridor with his box, and on impulse followed him. Blight's journey took him through nearly half a mile of passageway and stairs, and ended at a small, black-painted door in an obscure wing of the building. Blight set down his box, produced a key from his pocket and unlocked the door. As he stooped to pick up the box again, the door was ajar long enough for Hare, peering from behind a filing cabinet, to see the interior of the room. It was as big as a warehouse and entirely filled with shelves and storage racks containing dockets in cardboard coffins identical to the one carried by Blight.

Apart from 'Good morning' and 'Good night', Hare said very little to Bolt and Blight, and they said very little to him. What, thought Hare, was there to say? Yet Bolt and Blight conversed frequently. They conversed about the dockets. Bolt in particular found them exciting. Flushed, eyes glittering, he would point to a batch Hare had just placed on his desk and say to Blight, 'Wheelbarrows are experiencing record sales, which is very unusual at this time of year,' or 'There is a bottleneck in sink plungers at the Palace,' – the Palace being the largest and newest warehouse and mentioned always with great respect. Blight would nod, as if he

32

had expected it, and occasionally say, 'It is probably connected with the sunspots,' or 'If you remember, the same
thing happened seven years ago.' Because Bolt paused so
often to make these observations, and because Bolt's work
also took rather longer than Hare's, Bolt was always surrounded by a wall of unsorted dockets, above which he
would at intervals raise his head like a restive bull and
glower at Hare, who had developed a quick baring-of-the-
teeth smile in response.

Several times a week the door of the office would open
with peculiar forcefulness and Jacobs would enter. The room
would at once be galvanised by a current of activity and the
three of them would begin jerking.

'Morning Hare, everything in order?'

Jerk. 'Yes, Mr Jacobs, thank you.' *Jerk.*

'Good. Soon know what to do with you if it wasn't, eh?'

'Oh, yes, Mr Jacobs.'

'Everything all right, Bolt?'

Jerk jerk jerk. 'Thank you, sir, watering cans . . .'

'Watering cans, Bolt?'

'Getting critical, sir.'

'Getting critical, are they? As well you told me. We'll have
a leak on our hands next. Ha ha ha.'

'Yes, sir, ha ha.' *Jerk.*

'Mr Blight?'

'Holding our own, I'd say, Mr Jacobs.'

'That's what I like to hear, Blight. Don't let me catch you
holding anyone else's. Ha ha ha.'

'No, Mr Jacobs, yes, sir, ha ha.' *Jerk.*

When he had gone they would sit still for a moment in
exhaustion. Then quickly they would start work again, lest
someone say something that would enmesh them all, even
for an instant, in conspiracy, and he sense it and come back
and destroy them.

*

33

Detective Koberg was young, fit and thought himself both good-looking and endowed with charm. Most of his experiences tended to reinforce this impression, and few contradicted it. That this might be at least partly due to his status as a police officer should have occurred to him, since he had become a policeman in order to obtain a respect which he thought was due to him but which he did not seem able to command otherwise. However, it did not occur to him. Particularly when he was, as now, sprawled on Mrs Raptor's sofa with Jacinth caressing his thighs.

Jacinth was supposed to be at school, but was being educated only in the broadest sense. She was frequently being educated only in the broadest sense, but this was unknown to Mrs Raptor, who liked to get out of the house during the day and was at this moment at a sale of soft furnishings.

'Why don't you . . . ?' suggested Detective Koberg, but Jacinth already was. Koberg stared up at the ceiling which, after many visits, had a pleasantly familiar aspect though not in itself an attractive sight. It was yellowish and veined with cracks. Mice scurried behind the skirting. The house was falling apart. There was no point in repairing it because it would have to come down soon in any case: the district was going to be cleared for another scheme. Not that the old bat knew that. She let the building rot because she could get as much money letting it in its present state as she would if it was done up. The tenants had no choice. They were all dead-enders, they had nowhere else to go. He knew them all, and their reasons for being in that house, although they did not know him. If he chose he could make life impossible for any one of them, by a word typed into the computer or casual remark on the telephone. He smiled, enjoying the cool flirtation of Jacinth's tongue over the tip of his prick. He loved power, he felt he had been born for it.

'Who else are you screwing?' he asked absently.

34

She disengaged herself enough to answer, 'The old guy on the second floor,' and returned to her task.

Koberg stared down at her, for a moment speechless. Then, '*Here?*' he demanded.

'Yes,' she said, as if it were the most natural thing in the world.

He supposed he should have expected it, but he hadn't, and he felt he had been made a fool of. He pushed her away, saying with disgust, 'God, you're a little bitch.'

Her face went sullen in the way that infuriated him.

'Fuck who you like, you said. Said you didn't care.'

'But not *here*. Not on your own doorstep.'

'You're here, aren't you?'

'That's different, stupid. I don't *live* here.'

'What difference does it make?' she said, and he didn't know. Her gaze travelled up from the floor and stopped at his open fly. She giggled.

Scowling, he got to his feet. He had not intended to do this: he was here on business. However, the business required the presence on the premises of Mrs Raptor, who was out. He had half an hour in hand. He started to unbuckle his belt.

This was the signal for one of their rituals. She would run to the wall and stand with her back against it, and he would seize her and swing her round roughly so that she faced the wall, and slap the belt across her buttocks. She would cry out: obviously it was really painful. He was interested in pain, but at the moment he was more interested in its infliction than its reception. He lashed her, and felt the familiar thrill start at the base of his spine. She screamed, but she did not want him to stop. He lashed her again. This time she yelled obscene names at him. He laughed, and buried his mouth in the side of her neck. Then he pulled her down to the floor. He liked doing it with his clothes on: he pretended that this was a sophisticated preference, and it

35

was true that fucking in uniform, and particularly fucking a minor, gave him a peculiar pleasure, but the real reason was that he felt too vulnerable naked to be able to carry the act through to its conclusion.

'A white rat came in here today,' said Solomon.

Solomon always adopted an oblique manner of speech in relation to things he disliked. A white rat was a policeman.

'What did he want?' asked Hare. 'Surely he didn't want to buy a book?'

'He looked at a few.' Solomon's grimy face cracked into a grin, exposing cratered teeth. 'If he'd known enough to look properly at what he had in his paws, I might now be in the rat cellar instead of here talking to you. But he didn't know. Praise God for the ignorance of the vicious.'

'What was he looking at?'

Solomon knocked aside with a contemptuous elbow a pile of Government-funded youth magazines, and took from a shelf a fat, pocket-sized book in faded blue covers. Hare turned the pages. It was a guidebook to the city, published ninety years ago. The print was small and the pages spotted; persevering with it, he found himself perplexed by its unfamiliarity. Names not only of streets but of whole districts had been changed; he was able to identify them only by the rather charming illustrations.

'Why should the police be interested in this?' he said.

Solomon took the book from him, opened it at another place and unfolded a sheet of thin paper sewn between the pages. Hare studied it. Sets of parallel lines, some in a grid pattern, some radiating from a central point; shaded areas; a broad snake winding from one side to the other across the lower half of the sheet.

'It's a street map,' said Solomon. 'Haven't you seen one before?'

36

'No.' Hare had not known they existed. Presumably they were no longer produced because everything was signposted.

'Is it illegal?' he asked.

'It doesn't need to be,' said Solomon. 'Particularly if it's found in my shop.'

Hare continued his perusal. He made out the place where the Council headquarters was situated, on a bend of the river that was known, from its graceful curve, as the Swan, but it was not quite where he had expected it to be. Then in the neighbouring part of the map he recognised another district which he had thought to be about four miles north of the Swan.

And surely there was the Shuttle, with its maze of cobbled alleys, but much too far to the east? If it was the Shuttle, then his own district was not where he had visualised it at all in relation to the centre of the city. But then, what was the centre of the city? He had always imagined it to be the Swan, but that was near the lower edge of the map, part of a river whose sinuous course was again not what he had visualised; and the centre of the map appeared to be occupied by a park.

Solomon was watching him with some satisfaction.

'I can't work this out,' said Hare.

'You aren't supposed to.'

'What d'you mean?'

'Those who look after us,' said Solomon, 'do nothing without a reason. There is a reason why there are no maps, you may depend on it. The reason will be as mad as Hamlet and they will have forgotten what it is themselves, but reason there will be, my friend.'

'Who is Hamlet?'

'I don't know. It used to be a saying when I was young.'

'It doesn't show the Zone,' Hare remarked.

'No. It must be just off the edge, there. Or there.'

Hare frowned at this irritating map. Were all maps like

this? But one thing was undeniable. 'It was a fine city in those days,' he said.

'Beautiful,' agreed Solomon. He turned the pages. Together they looked at engravings of statues, fountains, churches. 'Where did it all go?' murmured Hare, and knew where it had gone. Under the concrete on which stood the factories and warehouses of the Company.

'It's a barbaric age,' sighed Solomon, 'in which it is not the destroyers of art who are reviled as public enemies, but the artists.'

'Hare often thought that his wife would have liked Solomon. But then, if she hadn't left him, he would not have taken to rummaging in junk shops and bookshops and he would not have met Solomon. It was odd to think that Solomon had, as it were, replaced Maria in his life.

He glanced across at the old man. He was tired today, Hare realised. Probably the visit from the policeman had upset him, and Hare had given him no chance to talk about it.

'You didn't tell me what the white rat wanted,' he said.

Solomon shrugged with a hopeless air, which meant that in a moment or two he would start talking about his persecutors. Hare sat him down in a chair and put a saucepan of water on the stove for coffee.

'He wanted nothing,' said Solomon. 'He wanted to have a look at me. A young policeman with a face like a girl and eyes like a snake.'

'But did he say why he'd come?'

'He gave no reason. They are arrogant, that kind. They don't think they have to explain themselves. Of course whatever he said it would not have meant anything.'

'No.'

'Do you know what I hate most about them?' Solomon continued. 'That they wear white uniforms. That I find an obscenity.'

'It's certainly very impractical,' said Hare.

'I remember when they did not wear white,' said Solomon.

Hare jerked his head round in surprise. 'Not wear white? I thought they always had.'

'No. There was a time when they didn't. They wore some dark colour. I forget what.'

'When did they start wearing white? And why?'

'I forget.' Solomon stared in front of him, lost in his own past. 'So much to forget,' he said.

'I have something very serious to say to you,' said Jacobs.

He looked very serious: his eyes were large and dark-ringed with worry. He stood, as was customary, in the centre of the floor, and Hare, Bolt and Blight were ranged before him like an undistinguished triptych.

Jacobs said, 'Some documents are missing.'

At least, Hare assumed that was what he had said. It had sounded like, 'Some dockets are missing,' but in view of the fact that the dockets, when they left the office, went to Blight's storeroom and were no longer any use to anyone (even supposing they ever had been), he dismissed this as not making sense.

'Never in all my years with this firm,' Jacobs said softly, 'has a docket been missed. The implications are of the utmost gravity for us all. It means we have a disloyal worker among us.'

Expressions of shock appeared on the faces of Bolt and Blight. Not of Hare. Try as he might, aware that it could prove his undoing, Hare could not register shock.

'A disloyal worker,' Jacobs repeated. His nose twitched, as if detecting the smell of disloyalty that was surely emanating from Hare. His nose had a bluish tinge, and the bluish bit was covered, Hare saw with interest, with a dusting of powder. Then he noticed with a start that the whole of

39

Jacobs's face had been made-up, very carefully, the eyes in particular so that they looked larger.

Jacobs noticed the start and misinterpreted it. 'I see the importance of the situation has only just dawned on Mr Hare. Keep awake, Hare. You never know, we may need you one day.' He paused. 'Or is it possible that you are wide awake all the time but prefer us to think otherwise?'

The faces of Bolt and Blight turned towards Hare like moons.

'Dockets may not seem to you three to be very important,' suggested Jacobs. 'Dockets by the hundred pass through this office every day. It would not be surprising if in time you developed, shall we say, a rather casual attitude towards them.'

Hare studied the floor, so that he would not have to see Bolt and Blight shaking their heads.

'But let me assure you that nothing that passes through this office is unimportant,' said Jacobs. 'Anything, every-thing, is of value, and is of interest to those who work against us.' His eyes took them in one by one. 'Disloyalty, treachery . . . the greatest crime. Divulging information that would be of use to our enemies.' His voice dropped dra-matically. 'In that place,' he whispered.

He turned on his heel, walked to the door, and turned back. His gaze rested squarely on Hare.

'There will be an Inquiry,' he said.

On his way home Hare saw the dwarf in the tail coat again. The grotesque figure followed him across the street, giving clear signs of wishing to speak to him. Hare quickened his step and by the time he reached his front door he was confident that the creature had stopped following him.

3

The Inquiry began the following Monday.

Hare, arriving for work, was stopped by the janitor, who sprang at him from his cubbyhole by the door and barred his way. Hare stared at him in astonishment.

'Come with me, please, Mr Hare,' ordered the janitor, and led him in silence to a cavernous basement room in a distant annexe. A pile of fencing masks occupied one corner of the room, and against a wall stood a big coloured target, mounted on a wooden easel. A dozen or so uncomfortable-looking chairs were arranged in a straggling row. Hare, after some hesitation, sat on one.

Because the table was set directly below the line of windows and the light was in his eyes, Hare did not at first see it or the men who sat at it. A movement from one of them – it was Jacobs, shuffling papers – drew his attention there. He saw then that four men whom he did not know sat facing him under the line of light, with Jacobs, standing at one end, making a fifth. The man in the centre was tall and silver-haired. He seemed to give Hare the ghost of a smile as the others adjusted their chairs and arranged their pens on the polished table. His name was displayed on a small wooden block in front of him. After a while Hare made it out: Mr J J Lucy. A curious faint feeling overcame Hare. Mr J J Lucy was the chairman of Universal Goods. He was seen so rarely that in the lower reaches of the Company he was believed not to exist.

Mr Lucy tapped quietly on the table, and the other four men drew themselves up.

'The Inquiry is in session,' said Mr Lucy, and glanced at Jacobs. Jacobs adopted a posture that contrived to be subservient towards Mr Lucy, on his right, and bullying towards Hare, in front of him.

'You are John Hare, employed in the warehouse transfers department of this company?'

'Yes,' said Hare.

'Stand up, if you please,' snapped Jacobs.

Blushing, Hare stood up.

'Where were you on Tuesday the nineteenth of January?'

It took a moment for Hare to realise that the question was much simpler than it sounded.

'Here,' he said with a surprised laugh.

'Here?' Jacobs swept a disdainful hand towards the fencing masks. 'Do you mean in this room?'

Hare bit back his anger. 'I was on these premises, working in my office.'

'I see. It would have been more helpful if you had said so. Please answer the questions properly.'

He glanced down at some notes. Hare, gazing at the crown of his head, hated him, and knew himself to be hated by Jacobs in return. There was something in it that transcended the circumstances and, in a flash of insight, he saw a series of himself and Jacobs in different times and places, locked in the same antagonism. But he still did not understand it.

'You were in your office on the nineteenth of January,' resumed Jacobs. 'You were there all day?'

'Yes.'

'Did anything unusual occur that day, to your recollection?'

Hare frowned. He could not remember anything about the day in question at all. The only reason he knew he had been at the office was that there was nowhere else, on a working day, he could have been.

'I don't recall anything unusual,' he said.

'You don't recall Mr Bolt drawing your attention to a consignment of AS 24s?'

'What on earth are they?' said Hare.

'I think you know quite well what they are,' said Jacobs. 'However, for the purposes of this Inquiry it is immaterial what they are. They are a Company product.'

Mr Lucy leaned forward.

'I think we might be informed what they are,' he said easily.

Jacobs was taken aback. 'AS 24s are sealed containers of a chemical used in the dye industry,' he said. He shuffled his papers as if expecting praise, or a rebuke, or a thunderbolt, none of which came.

Hare, puzzled, waited.

'It is our contention,' Jacobs resumed, 'that on the nineteenth of January your colleague Mr Bolt remarked, in your hearing, on a series of dockets relating to a consignment of As 24s and that you, knowing what they were and that for a consignment of them to be docketed through your office was an unusual occurrence, made a mental note of this information.'

'No,' said Hare, blankly.

'He did not mention them? You are sure?'

'No. I mean he may have mentioned them. He was always talking about what was on the dockets. I never took any notice.'

'Why not?'

'It was boring,' said Hare.

Jacobs's face became a mask of contempt. 'Boring? I suppose you would think so. That the documents you were

43

handling recorded the circulating lifeblood of the Company, that would not interest you, would it? You have no interest in our work, have you, Mr Hare? You have no affection for this company? No loyalty?'

A silence developed. Into it, Hare protested, 'That isn't true,' but the silence closed over his statement as soon as he had uttered it, and he knew, and knew that they knew, that he lied. Jacobs had made the most damaging allegation possible, and it was well founded. That it had not the slightest bearing on the subject of the Inquiry, which was a missing batch of dockets, was probably unimportant; but then, as the silence deepened around him and inside him, and as the faces of the men at the table showed no sign of relaxing their seriousness, he began to realise what should have been apparent all along, that this was not an Inquiry but a trial, and he was the accused.

'Have you at any time during your employment with this company made contact with the people known commonly as "marginals"?' asked Jacobs at the start of the afternoon session.

'No,' said Hare instantly.

'Am I right in saying that you no longer . . . ah . . . cohabit with your wife?'

'Yes.'

'She left you?'

'Yes.'

'How long ago was that?'

'Ten years.'

'Ten years ago. Where is your wife now?'

'I don't know,' said Hare.

'Do you know if she is alive?'

'No,' said Hare, whose heart was beginning to beat distressingly fast.

'Do you *care*?' sneered Jacobs.

'Of course I care. She is my wife.'

'And have you looked for her?'

'No, I haven't.'

'Never?'

'No.'

'But why not?' Jacobs's bushy eyebrows rose halfway to his scalp. 'Why not? You care about her. She is your wife.'

Hare said nothing. Jacobs waited, posed in half-profile with one hand extended theatrically on the table. After a while he repeated, 'Why did you not look for her?'

'I think that is my business,' said Hare with anger.

'Answer the question.'

'I am not satisfied,' murmured Mr Lucy, 'that it is the tribunal's business.'

Jacobs fluttered. 'I had hoped, sir, to demonstrate that it is unlikely that Mr Hare would not have made at least some effort to find his wife.'

'He has said twice that he did not. You will have to be content with that,' said the chairman.

Jacobs turned viciously to Hare. 'If your wife is still alive, there is nowhere she can be living except among the marginals, is that not so?'

Hare nodded.

'Answer the question, please.'

'Yes,' said Hare wretchedly.

'Is that,' jeered Jacobs, 'why you never tried to find her?'

The faintest of smiles crossed the faces of the men at the table.

'If you wanted to find some marginals, would you know where to look?' asked Jacobs.

'No, I wouldn't,' said Hare.

'Do you think your wife knew where to look?'

'I don't know,' said Hare.

'Did she manifest any uncertainty about going? Did she leave and then come back, for instance?'

'No,' said Hare. 'She just put some things into a bag and went.'

'And that was the last you saw of her?'

'Yes.'

'It does look, doesn't it,' purred Jacobs, 'as if she knew where to go? Almost as if she had been in touch with them herself. Or as if she felt a kinship with them.'

All that afternoon, and for most of the following day, Jacobs went over and over the same ground: Hare's deplorable, disastrous, should-never-have-been-made marriage. That it should never have been made was, apparently, his point: that Hare must have known Maria was a born marginal, that knowing this he should have left her to one of her own kind, and that by declining to do so he had brought his troubles upon himself and manifested a weakness in his character, if not an incipient marginality of his own.

Hare followed the building up of this indictment with the sort of fearful fascination with which a sick man studies his X-ray plate. Jacobs's observations echoed many of his own thoughts about his relationship with his wife. He had known she was profoundly unlike him, that the core of her was made, as it were, of a different substance from the core of him and was subject to laws that did not touch him. Her difference from him had been the reason why he needed her. Left to himself, he would have planned his spirit out of existence. He would risk nothing, she everything. He had, though, just a large enough speck in him of that restless, ignitable material for it to recognise its sustenance and compel him towards it. He had always known that. Jacobs knew it too.

'Your wife was an art student when you met her?'

'She was, yes.'

'Did that not shock you?'

'It was not thought to be a shocking thing at the time.'

46

Jacobs's eyebrows rose. 'Not by you, perhaps.'

'Not by anybody,' snapped Hare before he could stop himself. 'You are attributing attitudes to that period which didn't exist until years later. At the time when I met my wife, art was regarded as a profession in which there was perhaps a certain amount of loose living, because of the temperament of artists and the peculiar strain of the work – but a shocking profession, no, certainly not. On the contrary, one that was necessary to . . .'

He stopped; too late, much too late.

'Necessary to what?' enquired Jacobs.

'To . . . I was going to say that it was regarded as necessary to society.'

'*Necessary*? To *society*?'

'It was regarded so at the time.'

'Was it indeed? You interest me greatly, Mr Hare. And did *you* regard it as necessary to society, at the time?'

'I . . . er . . . yes.'

'Necessary in what way?'

'Oh, something to do with the health of society. Balance.'

'So that a society which lacked art would not be healthy. Is that what you thought?'

'I suppose so.'

'Did you or did you not think so?'

'Yes.'

'Do you think this is an unhealthy society, Mr Hare?'

'No.' (What choice did he have?)

'Why not?'

'I have changed my views.'

'You no longer think this is an unhealthy society?'

'I don't remember saying that I ever did think so.'

'You said that you did not now think this was an unhealthy society, but that you had changed your views. The implication is that you thought it was an unhealthy society at an earlier stage in your life.'

'What I meant was that my views on the nature of art had changed. I no longer regard it as necessary to the health of society.'

'I see. And have your views on morality in general changed?'

'I don't understand.'

'Do you still approve of loose living?'

'I never approved of it,' said Hare.

'You have made it quite clear that you did not *dis*approve of it.'

Hare was tired. He shrugged hopelessly. 'I was young. One grows up.'

'I put it to you that some people never outgrow their adolescent infatuation with decadence, and that you are one of them,' said Jacobs. 'I suggest that it was while that infatuation was at its height that you met and married your wife, who shared it, that you have never abandoned the ideas you held then, and that your recent actions are proof that, whatever you say to the contrary, you are not a loyal member of this society.'

That evening Hare went to visit Solomon. The trees were leafing, and birds sang at him from boughs and telephone wires as he walked. Down the alleyway, across the square – once pretty, now a concrete parking lot – past the wineshop. He walked quickly, treading underfoot the face of Jacobs. Down into the subway to cross the trunk road, up again into the roar of six-lane traffic, and away from it into the sidestreets of Morristown, which he knew so well that he did not bother to look around him but just walked, eyes fixed on the pavement a few yards ahead, absorbed in his thoughts.

So it was not until he had almost reached the spot where the front door had been that he saw that Solomon's shop did not exist any more. The ramshackle building had been gutted by fire. The suggestion of a horrible smell still hung about the blackened bricks.

On the third morning Jacobs appeared to have lost interest in Hare's marriage, and returned to the dockets.

'You persist in saying that Mr Bolt did not in your hearing say that there was a batch of dockets relating to AS 24s?'

'I'm saying that if he did I don't recall it,' said Hare. He was wondering dully what they would do to him. It seemed inevitable that he would lose his job; but if that was all they wanted, why not just sack him and have done with it?

'You do not recall asking him to repeat the information and to tell you at which warehouse they were being stored?'

'Why on earth should I want to know that?' Something belatedly occurred to Hare. 'As the dockets passed through my hands before they went to Mr Bolt's desk, it's rather odd I didn't myself notice what they referred to if I found the information so remarkable, isn't it?'

Jacobs surveyed him in silence. In Jacobs's eyes Hare saw contempt and loathing. A gust of fear caught him, then it passed, leaving him standing there empty, a waste bin into which Jacobs would toss his next question.

But Jacobs did not. Instead, he turned towards the men at the table and said, 'We are dealing with a curious nature, gentlemen. A nature so inert, so slothful, that one might well expect it never to awake at all. But there is a cleverness in this nature. It is clever enough to use its own laziness as a disguise when there is an infamy it wishes to perpetrate. For it is capable of action, oh yes, but action only of a destructive kind. That is the impulse which stirs it out of its torpor; that is the pull it cannot resist. Infamy. For nearly all the time of his employment at Universal Goods Mr Hare has been mentally and morally asleep; but when at last there wafted past his nostrils the delicious scent of an infamy waiting to be perpetrated, it awoke him from his slumbers like a magic summons. And he turned to his colleague, whose industry and integrity he had for years despised, the fruits of whose experience he had thought it not worth listening to, and he said, "That's interesting; tell me more about it."'

In the pause that followed this, the other four men at the table looked at Hare keenly; an instant later, as if the same embarrassment had struck them all, they all looked down at their notes.

Hare felt as if he had been struck a blow in some soft and secret place. How could Jacobs know such things about him? It hardly mattered that they were contorted beyond anyone else's recognition; he, Hare, recognised them.

'And so,' resumed Jacobs, addressing Hare once more, 'you picked out of the unsuspecting brain of Mr Bolt the one piece of information which had interested you in twenty years, and conceived the idea of betraying it to our enemies.'

With the allegation of treachery, Jacobs seemed to have reached the main substance of the charge against Hare. Halfway through the morning, Bolt was brought in to give evidence. He looked small and shabby in his too-bright blue suit and his eyes were frightened.

Bolt did not look at Hare; he looked straight ahead, at Jacobs. Jacobs looked over the top of Bolt's head. If Bolt had had his back to Jacobs instead of facing him their relationship would have been quite clear: puppeteer and puppet.

'You are Henry Albert Bolt, an employee of this company?'

'Yes, sir.'

Sir. Bolt would, of course.

'You work in the same office as Mr Hare?'

'Yes, sir.'

'How long have you worked in that office with him?'

'Two years.'

50

'In that time has he ever expressed interest in any of the material which is docketed through your office?'

'Only once,' said Bolt.

'And when was that?'

'It was in January. The dockets in question referred to a consignment of AS 24s.'

'Do you know what those are?'

'Yes, sir.'

'What are they?'

'Chemicals for the dye industry, sir.'

'Did Mr Hare,' pursued Jacobs, 'give the impression that he knew what they were?'

'Yes, sir. He became very excited and said, "That's most unusual; are you sure?"'

'And what happened then?'

'I said yes, I was sure, and then he said, "Where are they being stored?" So I told him, because it was on the dockets anyway; all he had to do was walk over and look at them.'

'And what did he say then, Mr Bolt?'

'Nothing. Just nodded. He didn't mention it after that.'

'What happened to the dockets?'

'I dealt with them in the usual way and gave them to Mr Blight, sir.'

'So they were clear of your desk by the end of the day?'

'They were, sir, yes.'

'Thank you, Mr Bolt, that will be all.'

As Bolt, visibly relieved, turned to go, Hare objected, 'I want a chance to cross-examine.'

'Cross-examine?' repeated Jacobs in amazement. 'Mr Hare, there is no question of your cross-examining. This is an investigation, not a trial.'

Bolt was followed by Blight. He gave Hare a condescending nod as he walked to his place.

'You are James Alphonsus Blight? On the nineteenth of January of this year where were you?'

The fabricated evidence droned on.

Blight had heard Bolt and Hare talking about the dockets, and remembered it because Hare did not normally take any interest in his work. 'Apathetic regarding the Company's interests,' Blight called him. After the conversation, Bolt had dealt with the dockets and then gone to lunch. In the afternoon, Bolt had transferred a large pile of dockets, including the material ones, to Blight's desk. Blight had dealt with them. He had not left the office until he took the box of dockets out. It was safe to assume that the dockets had not been tampered with while they were in the office. They had been removed from the records room itself.

This appeared to exonerate Hare, who had no clearance to go to the records room and should not even have known where it was. 'But I shall present evidence,' said Jacobs, 'that he did know.'

The next witness was the deaf mute who operated the computer. He gave evidence through an interpreter. It appeared that the computer room contained a bank of television monitor screens. On one of these screens, one afternoon, he had seen Mr Blight taking the box of dockets, as he always did, to the records room, and Mr Hare stealing along behind him. He had followed them on the screens until he saw Mr Blight opening the records room door, with Mr Hare watching from 'a place of concealment'.

'Thank you,' said Jacobs thoughtfully, as if he had never heard this evidence before. 'Thank you very much.'

He drew himself up. 'It is obvious that Hare knew where to get hold of the dockets before he went home that night. It is my contention that he went to the records room, found and removed the dockets and took them off the premises, concealed in his jacket. Then at some time during the next few days he made contact with those to whom he passed them.' His nose wrinkled with disdain. 'We assume the motive was money. But perhaps it was not. Would the act be any the less sordid for not being done for money? If the man before us betrayed for betrayal's sake, I think we should not on that account regard him as actuated by principle; for what principle can be involved except the deliberate inversion of everything that is decent?'

The deaf mute, who had been lip-reading, clapped enthusiastically, and was hustled out.

Jacobs now turned to the way in which Hare had disposed of the dockets.

'In spite of his assertion that he has never had contact with marginals, his contacts with them have been many and frequent. The fact these contacts have usually not been initiated by him does not make them innocent. We all know that evil is attracted by evil. A man whose path is crossed many times by marginality, who constantly sees things, hears things, finds things which emanate from that filthy half-world between our civilisation and what threatens it – such a man is either a saint being subjected to a degree of temptation which testifies to his moral stature, or he is already corrupt. Look at the face of the man before you, gentlemen, and ask yourselves whether it is the face of a tormented saint.'

The men at the table glanced furtively at Hare and looked away again.

'Before I produce proof of Hare's contact with marginals,' continued Jacobs, 'it may be as well to state something plainly. We live in a free society and part of the price we pay for that freedom is that we have living in our midst people who are hostile to our society and who in a less free society would not be tolerated. I do not refer only to the creatures who walk the streets by night because they are afraid to be seen by day; I speak also of the ones who appear like us although their minds are different, and who live and work undetected among us until chance or their own arrogance unmasks them. Probably each of us, without knowing it, is acquainted with one' (here his eye rested heavily on Hare), 'and they are very dangerous. And this fact, this dangerous-ness of the marginal, is to my mind not sufficiently stressed. We think of marginals as parasites, we regard them with disgust, we fear lest their numbers grow and their influence spreads and the state be not strong enough to fight off the torpor and dissolution they bring; but we do not fear *them*. Gentlemen, we should. For they are not victims, sick with a disease which we must quarantine lest it over-run the State, people whom we must dread like lepers but for whom, like lepers, it is possible to feel some pity. No. They are the spies and soldiers of the Enemy; they are the disease itself.'

There was a ripple along the table.

'I am sorry if my words give offence,' said Jacobs, 'but it is necessary to make absolutely clear the relationship that exists between the marginals and the threat we face, so that when I talk about the defendant's contacts with marginals there is no doubt about what I am saying. Contact with marginals is contact with the Zone; it always has been and it always will be.'

He paused for some moments to let the weight of his words sink in.

Hare was distracted by a patch of sunlight on the floor, broken into moving patterns by the branches of a tree. He became so interested in the branch pattern (after all, what else could happen that he had not foreseen?) that he did not look up as the next witness was brought in, but only as the man took his place where Bolt and Blight had stood. Then his heart missed a beat, because the witness was a policeman.

He was small and neat in his white uniform, which fitted him so well that it might have been tailored. His face was pale and had a certain delicacy of feature, which it seemed he tried to compensate for by the masculinity of his haircut, close to the scalp. He was very smart: there was not a mark or crease on his uniform, his tie was perfectly knotted, and his boots shone like glass. He stood with his legs slightly apart, hands clasped behind his back, rocking almost imperceptibly on the balls of his feet and with a faint smile that contained something of a sneer on his face. On the little finger of his left hand, against regulations, was a ring.

'You are Detective Christopher Koberg?'

'I am, sir.'

'In the course of your duties you had occasion recently to visit the house in which Mr Hare lives, number ten Warren Street?'

'That is correct.'

'Will you tell the Inquiry what you found on the premises?'

The policeman did something odd. Before replying, he turned his head and surveyed Hare with a derisory and at the same time curious look, as if he had heard something about him and wanted to match it against his impressions.

Then he said, 'I was instructed to go to the house to look for evidence concerning a robbery. It was a tip-off. I didn't know which flat might contain the evidence, so I had to search all of them. In flat three I found two bits of paper hidden under the clothes in the wardrobe.'

'Are these the pieces of paper?' Jacobs passed them to Detective Koberg for identification. Hare recognised the scrap of paper bag with its doggerel verse which had attached itself to his trouser leg in the street. The other piece of paper was pale yellow and unmistakably a Company docket.

Detective Koberg identified them. Jacobs passed them down the table. The docket was recognised with grunts of contempt, the paper bag examined with horrified fascination.

55

When both pieces of evidence had been thoroughly inspected, Jacobs dismissed the smirking policeman and addressed Hare.

'Which flat in the building do you occupy?'

'Flat three,' said Hare, and passed his tongue over dry lips.

Mounting the steps towards the fresh air, Hare felt the chill that was said always to hang over the place. There was a ticket collector at the top, which surprised him; at most stations they had been replaced by machines. The ticket collector was a sallow, sunken-faced man in a peaked cap and a black overcoat; his appearance was outdated, as if time had frozen in that spot for forty years.

No-one else had got off the train with Hare, and the stairwell and long passageway resounded alarmingly to his solitary footsteps, as if to say, Here he is, here he is. The ticket collector extended a rheumaticky hand with yellowed fingers and took his ticket. Then he looked at Hare sharply, as though the ticket had something not quite right about it, and his eyes followed Hare out onto the street.

The street was deserted. The Zone was half a mile away, but even at this distance its influence could be felt. The area had been torn and gutted and the wounds filled with concrete. The houses had fallen into ruin. Gardens had sunk, and drainage pipes, tree roots and the foundations of destroyed greenhouses lay exposed to view.

Further on, the houses had been bulldozed and whole streets levelled. The demolition was not quite complete: here and there was a signboard hanging from one hinge, or a boarded-up factory with a pile of rotting metal in its yard, or a spiderwork of catwalks connecting air with air. It was like a battlefield, but there had never been a battle here, only the shadow of one. The signboard and the catwalks stirred in the rising wind.

56

There was always a wind around the Zone, it was said. And often it would rain there, an icy, sleety rain, when it rained nowhere else. No-one knew what caused these peculiar atmospheric effects, but there was a general belief that during the past ten years they had become more pronounced and that this reflected increased activity inside the Zone. Sometimes a coloured, luminous glow was seen over the area; and sometimes people claimed to have seen a tracery of sparks, like brighter stars, moving against the sky, as if fireworks were being let off. There were also said to be days when the Zone produced long ribbons of yellowish smoke. It was not, of course, possible to see into the Zone. Many years ago the Council had demolished or bricked up all the buildings from which one might have been able to see over the wall. It was much, much too dangerous to trust to people's commonsense. Even the wall itself, owing to a confusing re-routing of streets and the retention of the vast warehouses that screened it, could not be seen until you were virtually under the shadow of it.

It was about thirty feet high, of unknown thickness, and built of a dark brick which seemed to absorb whatever light there was. So oppressive was its presence that the observer invariably felt the wall was moving towards him – not toppling, but advancing steadily until first it would fill his field of vision and then it would engulf him. Hare stood his ground, although his hands had clenched inside the pockets of his coat, and tried to study it as if it were just like any other wall and might in certain circumstances be climbed or have a rope thrown over the top of it. In fact neither would be feasible, because of the evenness of the brickwork and a projecting parapet at the top, and also because a high fence of barbed wire, recently constructed, prevented anyone from getting nearer to the wall than ten yards from its base. But in any case his mind revolted from the idea of touching those bricks. They were poisoned, he had been told in childhood;

they gave off death rays, they would blind you if you looked at them in a particular way. If you touched them your skin would peel off like a banana skin. No-one knew anyone to whom this had happened, but plenty of people knew some-one who knew someone to whom it had happened.

Hare, standing at the wire fence, extended his hand in the direction of the wall. Was it imagination, or did his hand tingle as if in a weak electrical field? He wiggled his fingers. The tips of them were growing numb with an unnatural coldness. Alarmed, he put his hand back in his pocket.

It was then he caught the sound. It was so faint that he could only hear it with his head in one position, and even then the wind kept tossing it away. A high, chill pulsing. It was inhuman and tireless, and there was a frightening intelligence in it.

Hare glanced around and behind him, at the boarded-up warehouses, the waste ground stretching back to the rubble of streets, and at the sterile strip of mud, along which the wind blew scraps of paper, that bordered the wall.

Everywhere was deserted. The noise was coming from the other side of the wall.

His mouth filled with a sour taste and his knees shook. Of course things were done in the Zone, everybody knew it; but to *hear* them done made him nauseous. He stood there for perhaps a minute longer, rooted to the spot, before he found the will to walk away. An icy rain lashed down before he had gone far, and he turned up his collar and ran.

When Hare entered the room of the hearing on the fourth morning he found it packed with people he had never seen before. They all wore lapel badges bearing the entwined UG of the Company, and without exception they looked well dressed and serious. They turned and surveyed Hare as he came through the door. He had to stop for a moment to brace himself, as if stepping into cold water.

58

He heard their murmuring behind him as he took his seat. It sounded as if they had come to see a show. But they should have come yesterday if they wanted entertainment, for surely there could be no more witnesses.

Jacobs rose, beaming at his audience, and lifted his arms in a conductor's gesture. No baton, however, appeared in his extended right hand, the middle finger of which pointed at the door through which Hare had just entered. The door opened again, and through it came Jacinth.

She was wearing school uniform and she looked about twelve. A ripple of outrage ran through the rows of seats as she walked to the witness stand.

'Tell us your name, my dear,' coaxed Jacobs.

She did.

'And where do you live?'

'Ten Warren Street, Dossdown, mister . . . sir.'

She lisped. Hare had never heard her lisp before.

'That is the house in which Mr Hare lives? He is one of your mother's tenants?'

'Yes.'

'We want you to tell us, in your own words, what you know about Mr Hare, my dear. Has he ever invited you up to his flat, for instance?'

No-one stirred as Jacinth began her story. She was word-perfect.

'At first I thought he was very nice. He was always friendly, and sometimes he used to help me with my homework.'

Behind him Hare heard breath expelled from a hundred nostrils.

'The first time he helped me it was in our flat, in the sitting room, but the next time he said that if I wanted him to help me with it I had better come up to his flat, because the television was on downstairs. So I went to his flat, and we did the homework, it was algebra, and he gave me a cup of coffee and was very nice. I went there several times after that, when I had algebra to do, and my mother didn't like it, she told me not to go there. But I persuaded her that it was all right and there was nothing to worry about. So really – ' her voice faltered, producing an immediate surge of sympathy from the audience ' – it was my fault what happened next.'

She fished a handkerchief from her pocket and blew her nose. The sound seemed to clear Hare's head as well, and a number of things became plain. The first was that the court, tribunal or whatever it cared to call itself, would stop at nothing to secure his condemnation, although why it should go to such trouble he could not understand. The second was that although it would resort to outrageous lies it was concerned that somewhere in them should be a grain of truth. The third was that he would be lucky to escape a lynching. The fourth was that somewhere in this room was Mrs Raptor. And the fifth was that he could not therefore go home.

'One day I went up with some homework,' continued Jacinth with a dab at her eyes, 'and he seemed to be in a funny mood. Sort of playful, and nervous at the same time.'

I wonder who helped her with *this* piece of homework, thought Hare viciously.

'I didn't know what to make of it and it was a bit embarrassing, and then suddenly he said we'd do the algebra later but first there were some pictures he wanted to show me. And he got this old magazine out of a drawer.'

Air again hissed between teeth. Not only a child-molester, but a pornographer too. Pornographic magazines had not been published since the licensing of printing presses had been introduced, but it was still possible to buy, for huge prices and at enormous risk, old issues printed before the Decent Read campaign. If, that is, you knew where to go.

Hare had a good idea where to go, but had never bought such magazines even when it was possible to do so legally.

'He showed me these photographs,' said unblushingly the schoolgirl a few feet away from him. 'Some of them I didn't understand, you couldn't see what they were meant to be. And some of them . . . well, I thought they were horrible. There were men and women doing things, naked.' She stopped, and Hare could hear the anger seething in the room.

'And what happened then?' asked Jacobs gently.

'He asked me if the pictures didn't make me feel funny – excited and as if I wanted to do something. I didn't say anything because I was too embarrassed, and also I felt rather sorry for him. Then he said that they made him feel like that, and he took my hand and made me touch . . .'

'No,' said Hare vehemently. Jacobs glared.

'No interruptions,' said Mr Lucy.

'He made me touch in his trousers – I'm sorry I can't say that word . . .'

She appeared to break down. The room filled with whispers and murmurs, in which Hare's shrinking skin felt the salaciousness and the hate.

'Take as long as you like to compose yourself, my dear,' Jacobs soothed. 'We all appreciate that this is very painful for you.'

She took several minutes to compose herself. Then in a faltering voice she began again.

'I'm sorry . . . it's been so . . .'

'I know how this is distressing you,' coaxed Jacobs, 'but I must ask you to try to finish your story.'

She made a last, brave effort.

'He made me do it with him – have sex,' she said. 'Afterwards he made me promise not to tell and said that if I did he would say that *I* seduced *him*. I was afraid to tell my mother, especially after the fuss she'd made, so I didn't.

I didn't tell anyone. And then a few weeks later he tricked me into going to his flat again, and when I was inside he locked the door and said if I didn't let him do it again he'd tell people at my school, and so I let him, and then after that we did it lots of times . . .'

Hare was on his feet, shouting, 'Little liar, bloody little liar,' but many hands descended on his shoulders or grabbed his collar, and pushed or pulled him back into his seat.

'Loyalty is not a rational thing,' declared Jacobs. 'Its roots lie deeper than thought, just as the need it fulfils lies deeper. If it were subject to reason, how vulnerable would be those institutions on which the human community and human happiness are founded: country, workplace, family.'

He was summing up. The rows of pink faces surmounting grey suits with blue lapel badges were turned to him attentively. An intermittent hammering had started outside the window, making Hare think of scaffolds.

'I am not a patriot because I believe my country is particularly moral, particularly cultured or' (he seemed to pause fractionally) 'particularly just. I am a patriot because, right or wrong, this is my country. Similarly, I will keep faith with the firm that employs me, not because it is a better firm than others or because I happen to agree with its commercial philosophy, but because it gives me my daily bread and the men and women with whom I work are my colleagues, whom also I will not betray.'

Jacobs paused, and let his gaze rove over the room. He was wearing make-up again. It was rather thicker than before, perhaps because he had a larger audience. Hare, by unfocusing his eyes, found he could turn Jacobs's face into the face of a clown. But this did not help because the speech, which had obviously been well rehearsed, was that of a politician. He is serious, thought Hare with a feeling of vertigo. He believes this. Or was it that he believed something else for which the things he was saying were a sort of code?

'There was a fashion in intellectual circles many years ago,' continued Jacobs, 'for denigrating patriotism because it was not "reasonable". We are now wiser. We know that that way of thinking is a slope, at first barely perceptible, which then becomes a steep and slippery incline down which the bold free-thinker plunges to disaffection, rootlessness and the assertion of individual judgement over collective wisdom, which is the root of criminality. But we are still not quite rid of it. For we are reasonable creatures. It is in our nature to judge and compare. If we judge our country, it may happen that we do not like what we see. It has happened to some people that they did not like a great deal they saw, and the feeling to which this gives rise is incompatible with the feeling of patriotism. And yet what is one to do?

'And so I return to what I said at the beginning: loyalty is not based on reason because if it were it would not survive. Very well, says our sceptical intellectual, let it not survive: why do we need it? We need it, ladies and gentlemen, because without it we would perish.

'Man is a social animal. Without company he goes mad and dies. But strong divisive forces work to sunder the family, the tribe, the social group. What holds these vital groups together? Only the tie of loyalty, woven in many cases into an intricate web of rights and obligations, a tie which in all cultures is regarded as sacred, because in all cultures it is understood that loyalty is connected with life. And that betrayal is connected with death.'

He is right, thought Hare suddenly, I have no loyalties. But what was there to be loyal to?

'This truth is not new, ladies and gentlemen,' Jacobs was saying. 'It has been known for thousands of years. It was certainly well known forty-two years ago, when the series of events with which we are all too familiar began in the Zone.'

63

People straightened themselves in their seats.

'It was clear from the outset,' said Jacobs, 'that the forces at work in that place were intrinsically hostile to our society. That was not a surprise, since even then we knew the Zone to be the negation of everything that our society is – the crystallisation of an opposite. What shocked us was that some of our citizens declared a sympathy with it. Then we saw that these citizens, intellectuals all of them, had fallen victims to their own cleverness, for they had asserted reason over loyalty and toppled down the slope that leads to trust only in one's own judgement; and having reached that miry spot they had realised that the only way they could assert the supremacy of their judgement was by saying "No" where all their fellows had said "Yes". And we saw, too, that this process is part of the very nature of the Zone, which is perverse; so that these defectors were spiritual natives of that place of reversals even before they began the process that led them there.

'The defection of some of our prominent intellectuals in that first period of crisis caused a severe wound,' Jacobs said. 'What was worse, the damage seemed likely to spread. There was a contagion abroad, and its symptoms were subversiveness, mockery and nihilism.'

He stopped with some abruptness, and fixed his eyes on Hare before continuing.

'No-one in this room is old enough to have understood fully the events of that time when they happened, but memories some of us do have, and our memories are of a great struggle. Our parents' generation, when the danger was past, vowed never again to tolerate "rational" ideas on the subject of loyalty. From that time dates the moral restructuring of our community, since it was quickly seen that the enemy fed on decadence of every kind, not merely decadence of thought. From that time, too, dates the emphasis on faith as the core of our way of life and the national shield.'

64

He paused. Then he said, 'This is the context, then, in which a man called Hare begins to feel a disaffection from his community. It seems to him, in so far as he thinks about it, to be a gradual process and one of no great importance. We know that it is of the utmost importance, and that far from being gradual it was present in him from the beginning. He thinks he is alone and insignificant. We know that he is potentially one of millions.

'He is charged with giving to an enemy confidential documents which that enemy could find useful. The evidence that he did this includes evidence which relates to his character. That character has been portrayed in vivid detail. It is the character of a marginal. Lest there be any remaining doubt about that, I am prepared to call a witness who will state that last night John Hare, for reasons no doubt well known to himself, visited the area of the wall around the Zone.'

There was whispering along the table. All looked at Hare. No witness was deemed necessary.

'This man's betrayal of his trust,' went on Jacobs, 'in the specific manner laid before us, is in a sense less important than, or is merely a symptom of, a greater evil. We already know the only thing about John Hare which really matters, the thing from which everything else arises. This man threatens the fabric of our society by denying the bond which holds it together. He and his kind would drag us through the wall to that nightmarish distortion of a society where everything is a mockery and black is called white.'

Jacobs laid down his papers and said, 'Gentlemen, we have reached the end of a long and unsavoury matter. It is time to ask for your judgement, and I know that you will make it in full understanding of the issues involved.'

The men at the table stood up and filed out of the room. Hare felt the weight of fifty pairs of eyes on him. He sat, unable to move a muscle.

Eventually he became aware of the janitor standing at his side saying something.

'You've permission to go outside the building for an hour, Mr Hare.'

Uncomprehending but grateful, Hare hurried out. He walked greedily, drinking in the spicy, fume-laden city air. After a while he stopped and bought a cup of coffee at a roadside stall. It tasted strong and fresh, and he gulped it. He realised that he was very excited, as if some extraordinary event were about to take place, some liberation. At the same time, his stomach was full of ice.

He walked on and on – how stupid of them to let him go: didn't they know he would escape? – until he had lost his bearings. Then, glancing at his watch, he saw it was over an hour since he had left the hall, and at once was seized by anxiety to get back. He *must* get back; he had to know the verdict. He stood at a street corner, wondering which was the quickest way, and at that moment saw the dwarf in the tail coat again. The dwarf pushed towards him through the eddies of pedestrians. He seemed to be trying to say something to Hare.

There was a bus going past, picking up speed. Without stopping to think, Hare flung himself on to it just as the doors started to close. He saw the dwarf's disappointed face disappear in the crowds.

The bus took him in the opposite direction from the one he needed. By the time he had made his way back to the Company offices everyone had gone home and the doors were locked. He rang the bell.

The janitor had been expecting him. He opened the door and handed Hare a long envelope. Hare tore it open. Inside was a slip of paper on which was typed the single word 'Guilty'.

The door shut in his face. Hare began walking slowly down this road and that.

4

Limbo had been all about him all the time.

In the days following his expulsion from the Company, Hare sat on park benches, on walls and in subways. He walked aimlessly, until he began to worry about what he would do when his shoes wore out. Often as he sat he wished he had something to read, but he could not go back to his flat and he dared not buy anything: the money he had on him was (a thought so terrifying he could hardly grasp it) all the money he would ever have.

The money must be spent on food and nothing else. But this in itself became a problem because he now begrudged everything he spent on food, however little it cost, and tormented himself with hesitations about what to buy until in the end he was so hungry and so exhausted that he would go to the nearest snack counter and buy the first thing he saw, and then make himself miserable over this rashness. Lack of money, Hare realised, could fill your life.

At first the money in his pockets obsessed him. It was a suffocating burden, and the necessity of measuring it out very carefully until it was all gone seemed intolerable. Sometimes he would be seized by a fierce and exultant desire to spend it all at once, or even throw it away, and be free of it. These moments frightened him, and when they came upon him he clenched his fists in the pockets of his overcoat –

whether to hold the money there by force, or to hold on to something in himself, he did not know.

He realised one day that he was at its mercy. This seemed to him so ridiculous, such an inversion of what was proper, that he was amazed he could have made such a mistake. He began walking through the streets, full of a sense of release at his discovery, and saw that everyone else had made the same mistake as he had. What would happen, he wondered, if they stopped making it? Could you refuse the hold of money and still have room for it in your life, or did it demand everything? If you could, and everyone did it, could the system continue? Or did the system require for its very functioning that some people did not have control, were at money's mercy?

Hare had changed. Perhaps he was becoming the person he had always half-been. That was what Jacobs had said. What was a person, anyway? A shifting, inconstant thing, whose attributes changed in importance and were sometimes exchanged for quite different ones, like the electrons in an atom. People were never what they were thought to be. Perhaps they were unknowable. This seemed to him true. He had never got to know anyone really well: there was always a barrier, like thick glass, through which the other person could be glimpsed but not grasped. Sometimes you were allowed through the glass, but then there would be another layer further on. There was no end to it, because the thing you were seeking was not really there; it lived somewhere else and you were chasing a reflection of it. He had lived ten years with his wife, and never known her at all.

How stupid was a society, then, which allotted people to categories and thought it had defined them in the process. And how it reduced people! It reduced them, in one sense, all in the same way; in another sense it reduced them with a shocking inequality, and the only reason they tolerated it was that other people had been reduced even more than they had. At the very bottom – not even on the lowest layer, but flung out into the ditch – were the marginals. That was what he was. Naturally he did not feel like one. You never accepted the limitations of your own category, although you expected other people to be bound by theirs.

He sat by the river and watched two ducks fighting over a crumb of bread. There *was* something that limited you: hunger. Presumably in time his stomach would shrink and he would want to eat less. He wished it would hurry up with the shrinking.

Sleeping out was difficult at first: it was not the cold that bothered him so much as embarrassment. Sleep was such a personal thing, and you were so vulnerable doing it. He did not mind what people thought of him during the day, but he did not want their scorn or pity when he could not face them. Huddled in some wretched and prohibited corner, he spent whole nights jerking awake at every passing car headlight and every sound of approaching feet. It took him at least a week to pick up the knack of sleeping. He then discovered that he had a talent for finding places to sleep in. His weekends of wandering in forgotten corners of the city proved to have been an investment. His feet knew paths which his brain, disoriented by hunger and weariness, could not have found, and they would take him faithfully to an empty house with an easily-forced window, glimpsed six months ago, or a bit of waste ground on which was an abandoned car still intact enough for him to sleep on the back seat.

But it was cold, there was no denying it was cold. Until he started to become hardened to it, and also remembered things he had read about the usefulness of newspaper and cardboard boxes, he suffered badly. He longed for a blanket. It became a vivid, exact and curiously personal longing. He imagined the blanket he wanted, imagined it so intensely that at moments he could almost feel it on his skin, and he could certainly see it when he closed his eyes. It was of wool, thick but soft in texture and not at all scratchy, and it was dark grey with a thin blue stripe. He supposed he must have had a blanket like that in his childhood.

He thought of all the things you could do with a blanket besides put it over you at night. You could fold it up and sit on it, you could use it to dry yourself, you could (although he could not imagine the circumstances in which this might happen) wear it. A blanket was a marvellous thing, he realised, and he thought of people who had cupboards full of them and knew that they did not know this. It was only possible to know it if you had only one blanket. Or none.

He saw a blanket hanging on a clothes line one morning. It was not as good as his blanket, but it would do. He had covered half the distance towards it when he heard shouts behind him and had to run. What interested him afterwards was that he had felt he had a right to the blanket. Hare had never in his life stolen anything, however small: he found it repugnant. A further realisation came to him: morality is a function of security; or, as he remarked to himself (there being no-one else to say it to), 'If you have nothing, you can't steal'.

He wandered, assuaged his hunger in increasingly bizarre ways, slept in abandoned vehicles and grew a beard. His body, he noticed, was coping well and knew what to get on with; it was his mind that did not know what to do. There seemed to be an enormous space inside it. Actually it was not space but time. There was all this time. Dawn till dusk, and then the same all over again tomorrow. At first it was almost intolerable. He felt as though the day were a chasm across which he must stretch himself like a violin string. But as the days passed he grew used to this desert of time and it became, not a desert, but a sea, in which he floated and was open to the movement of currents and watched the shipping, never doubting its own importance, rush by.

70

Several times he thought he saw Solomon, but the thin, huddled figure would always turn out to have a face he did not recognise. In his heart, Hare knew that Solomon was dead. If he had not been, disaster would have sent him straight to Hare's flat.

'I congratulate you,' said the man sitting on the other side of the wide desk from Jacobs. 'A most satisfactory outcome. You must be very pleased.'

Jacobs nodded. In the past few months he had averted a crisis, dealt with numerous tricky problems and disposed of more than one minor irritant, all without disturbing the smooth surface of internal politics. The outcome of the tribunal, to which his visitor was referring, was merely one stone in the edifice. Satisfactory? He would say so. But it would not do to trumpet it.

'Thank you, Mr Terry. Yes, it's gratifying,' he said.

'You acquitted yourself remarkably as an advocate,' said his visitor. 'Have you experience of public speaking?'

The enquiry was innocent enough, and natural, too: why should a manager in Universal Goods, who had worked his way up from the floor and presumably had little time to acquire skills outside his own speciality, be a good speaker?

But the voice which asked the question had the hint of an upper-class drawl, and belonged to an expensively educated member of the Council, whereas Jacobs had had to grab his education where he saw it. And the voice was moreover very slightly patronising and seemed to be taking into account the gulf that existed between members of the Council and employees of the Company, of whom the former would naturally be public speakers since that was part of their function, whereas of the latter it should not be expected, and furthermore the voice seemed to be laying just a little more emphasis on this distinction than was necessary to establish that it was a difference of profession – seemed to be

71

emphasising it in a way that suggested that it might also be a difference of class. Which of course it was.

Jacobs swallowed his resentment. The man on the other side of the desk – youngish-looking (that was breeding for you: Jacobs was roughly the same age but looked ten years older, with his pendulous cheeks and coarse skin), wearing a soft grey suit the fine tailoring of which was only now becoming apparent to Jacobs's eye – this paragon of the Council elite was an important man. He was also, Jacobs considered, like most of them, rather stupid. The stupidity of the Council galled Jacobs: he took it personally.

'Experience?' he said as lightly as he could. 'A little. In my job I need quite a range of talents.'

It was intended as a snub, but to his surprise his visitor met his eyes, smiled into them, and said blandly, 'I'm sure you do,' as if he knew as well as Jacobs the nature of Jacobs's job, and that not all of it was to be talked about.

Jacobs had been having a good morning before this white hope of the Government dropped in to congratulate him. He tried to restore the perspective which half an hour ago had been so pleasing.

'Anyway,' he said, 'the wretched man was found guilty, and that was all that mattered. So the business of the dockets has been cleared up, to your people's satisfaction, I hope?'

'No doubt. I haven't spoken to them, but I have no doubt they will accept the verdict.'

Until that moment Jacobs had not doubted it either. Now, he passed in a second from uncertainty to a horrible conviction that they would not.

'Naturally,' he said. 'Not to do so would be to call into question the competence of the tribunal, on which you yourself were sitting.' He gave a little laugh, which sounded false in his own ears, and cursed himself for his lack of finesse.

Mr Terry said impassively, 'My presence on the tribunal

72

is neither here nor there, I'm sure, but the presence of Mr Lucy is itself a guarantee of correct procedure.'

Containing his grin was one of the most difficult things Jacobs had to do in the course of that conversation. He would have liked to thump the arm of his chair and crow, 'Lucy is one of *ours*, laddie!' and see the confidence leak from the face opposite him like water out of a rusty pail. Instead he said, 'Quite so,' and rang his secretary to tell her to bring coffee.

As they sipped it, Mr Terry asked casually, 'What progress on the Drawbridge site?'

'Drawbridge' was the Company codename for the new factory in Morristown. Jacobs had been involved in several aspects of the project, and had brought it successfully to its present stage.

'I think we can guarantee completion by the late autumn,' he said. He smiled, since it would be expected.

'Really? But that's excellent. You seem to be forging ahead now that that little problem has been solved.'

'Oh yes,' said Jacobs.

'Unfortunate for the poor chap involved, of course. Did he come forward to claim insurance?'

'No,' said Jacobs. 'I doubt if he had any insurance.'

'Oh, surely. Books, you know. Periodicals. A high fire risk. And it was his business, after all, whatever one may think of it. He must have been insured.'

Jacobs said nothing.

'It isn't possible, is it, that he *died* in the fire?'

Jacobs shook his head vigorously. 'Quite impossible. The police carried out a thorough search.'

'Mmm. So you think he just disappeared? Seems rather odd.'

'He was an odd man. Not quite right in the head. Delusions. Sailed pretty close to the wind altogether. He had no interest in selling any decent literature, you know. And the place was filthy. If he hadn't had a shop, you'd have said he was a marginal.'

'I see,' said Mr Terry thoughtfully. 'What caused the fire?'

'He cooked his meals on an antiquated paraffin stove. Apparently it just blew up.'

Mr Terry gazed before him, as if seeing the blazing stove, the toppling inferno of books, the terrified old man.

'The place was barely habitable,' said Jacobs angrily. 'He lived in complete squalor. People like that . . .'

A fleeting expression of distaste crossed the councillor's face. 'Quite,' he said, placing his coffee cup on the edge of Jacobs's desk and getting to his feet. 'I mustn't take up any more of your time. Many thanks for the coffee. Just thought I'd drop in.'

'A pleasure. Much appreciated,' said Jacobs. He felt like a peasant. Clumsily he opened the door and just prevented himself from bowing his visitor out.

Going back to his chair, he recalled the flicker of distaste on Mr Terry's face when he said, 'People like that,' and began to sweat as it occurred to him that perhaps the distaste had been for him, not the book dealer.

He sat down heavily. The phone rang, jarring his nerves. He picked it up.

'This is Koberg,' said a voice.

One day when Hare was sitting on a bench, the dwarf came and sat next to him.

Hare did not immediately turn and look at the dwarf: that would have been a crude response. Instead, he tried to think about it. It meant the end of his solitary wandering, and he was relieved because he had realised that he was not strong enough to be alone without being mad. But it also meant the end of his freedom. Once he had accepted the company of marginals he would have accepted definition as a marginal. It would be impossible, then, ever to become anything else.

He was still thinking about this when the dwarf said, 'Is your name Hare?'

'Yes,' said Hare, shaken.

'There is a message for a man named Hare, if he ever comes out,' said the dwarf.

'A message for *me*?' Hare was appalled. Going over to the other society was one thing, finding it waiting for you with a message was quite another. 'From whom?' he demanded.

'Your wife,' said the dwarf.

He felt something had kicked him violently. His heart began to pound like a steam hammer. He could not marshal his thoughts at all. Excitement, dread, love, anger (what was he angry about?) stormed through him in seconds, and departed, leaving him battered and empty. The vacuum was filled by impatience.

'What's the message?' he asked hoarsely.

'She would like to see you, when you are ready.'

'Where is she?'

'That is not part of the message,' said the dwarf.

'What? Do you mean she doesn't say where she is? Then how am I supposed to find her? Do you know where she is?'

'No,' said the dwarf.

'Then how – someone must know where she is.'

'Probably.'

'When did you last see her?' demanded Hare.

'To my knowledge I have never seen her.'

'Then who gave you this message?'

'It came down the line. It wouldn't help you to know. Believe me, now that I've delivered the message I know no more than you do.'

'It seems a pretty pointless message,' said Hare bitterly. 'How can I see her when I don't know where she is?'

'Perhaps she will come to you.'

'Then why send the message? The message implies that I have to find her.'

'But when you are ready.'

'What does that mean?'

'Are you ready?'

'Of course I am,' almost shouted Hare, but he wasn't, and this thought comforted him a little. He sat in silence for a while, and the conversation began to replay itself in his mind. 'I'm sorry,' he said, 'I've been very rude. It was rather a shock.'

'I suppose so,' said the dwarf. 'I've never had a wife.'

This was delivered in the tone of voice in which a man might say he had never had a motorbike, but its pathos struck Hare forcefully. He turned to look at the dwarf properly for the first time. As they sat side by side on the bench, the top of the dwarf's head came to just below Hare's shoulder, and the dwarf's feet dangled above the ground. His head was large for his body, and this was particularly noticeable in the case of the forehead, which was broad, deep and furrowed. He had serious brown eyes. His hair, black and grey in about equal parts, he wore in a sort of basin cut, high in the front but falling to his collar at the back: the effect was vaguely medieval, and the ancient spectacles perched on his nose enhanced rather than detracted from it. He wore full evening dress, down to the patent leather shoes, which however were held together with string. He looked clean; at least, cleaner than Hare. But, unwashed or not, Hare had once had a wife.

'Don't feel sorry for me,' said the dwarf. 'You'd be wasting your time. Of the two of us, you're the one I feel sorry for. When did you last have a meal?'

Hare could not remember.

'I thought so,' said the dwarf. 'You'd better come with me. You haven't learnt how to look after yourself, have you?' He slid to the ground and half-turned, proffering a small hand. 'My name is Ezra.'

*

The house stood on its own in a half-acre of weeds at the end of a deserted street. Two eroded stone griffins overlooked an imposing gateway from which the gates had long since been removed for scrap. At first glance the house looked as derelict as the district: half-smothered by ivy, the windows boarded up, a bird's nest built on top of chimney. A second glance showed, however, wisps of smoke issuing from another chimney and a well-trodden path through the weeds leading from the gateway round the side of the house. Hare followed Ezra along the path, negotiating obstacles – a wheelbarrow without a wheel, an old duplicating machine, a porcelain sink, a rusting gas cooker.

It was dusk. As they stepped inside the back door Hare's impression was of a warm, slightly rotten-smelling gloom. Ezra steered him by the elbow down a passageway and through a door.

'Here he is,' said Ezra.

Faces, redly illuminated by candles, looked up at him from around a table. On the table were dominoes, beer cans, a bunch of wild flowers stuck in a bottle, and a pile of flattened spherical things arranged on newspaper.

'Hello,' said the faces. They looked friendly.

'Hello,' said Hare.

'Our friend is hungry,' Ezra said.

The newspaper was pushed towards him, and four voices chorused, 'Have a doughnut.'

A chair was found for him, and someone opened a can of beer and put it at his elbow. He sat, thankful and dazed, and warmer than he had been for weeks, and to his embarrassment felt tears coming to his eyes. He bit into the doughnut, and with difficulty prevented himself from weeping into it.

Ezra made introductions. The girl with the black hair and imperious eyes was called Alleluya, the man with the pot belly and neckerchief was Brag, the fat woman swathed in cardigans was Big Gwen, and the white-haired old gentleman with a green bow tie was Mr Beechcroft.

The fifth member of the household sitting at the table was a young man with a childlike, radiant face. He did not speak, he only smiled at Hare as if he had been waiting for him all his life. He was introduced as Filthy.

'I'm sorry?' said Hare.

'Filthy', said Ezra. 'That is his name. He chose it.' And when Hare still looked bewildered, 'You'll see. He has bad days.'

Filthy followed this conversation with an approving smile, saying nothing.

Ezra pulled up a chair and helped himself to a doughnut. 'Where did these come from?'

'Gwen found them an hour ago,' said Mr Beechcroft. 'Left behind on a wall.'

'Really? They're delicious.' Then he paused, doubtfully. 'You tested them?'

'Of course we tested them,' grunted Brag. 'Broke two apart'.

'We found needles in a loaf of bread the other day,' Alleluya told Hare with a nod.

'Needles?' Hare didn't understand.

'Put there on purpose,' said Ezra. 'It's not the first time. There are people who really hate us.'

Hare was horrified. 'You mean people set traps for you? Like . . . ?'

'Like putting down rat poison, yes.' Ezra was unemotional. 'You must know how we are regarded.'

It was true: marginals were thought of as vermin. Hare had often been within an ace of thinking of them in the same way himself. It is difficult to make yourself impermeable to the values of the society you live in, even when you loathe them. Contact contaminates. Who had said that? Jacobs.

'Where's Angel?' asked Ezra.

78

'Out.' Brag studied his broken fingernails, and everyone else looked at Ezra. There was an uncomfortable silence. Hare broke it by saying, 'Do you find much of your food on walls?'

'Quite a lot,' said Brag. He was plump-faced and looked as if he did fairly well out of other people's forgotten shopping. 'On walls and under benches, and in various places where its owners have failed to take care of it. But a lot gets thrown away that's perfectly edible. We could pick up a sackful of vegetables from the market every day: bruised apples, cauliflowers gone a bit brown in the middle, that sort of stuff.'

The smell that had greeted Hare on his entrance was thus explained.

'Dustbins?' Hare enquired brightly, remembering that the first time he had seen Ezra the dwarf had been rooting about in one.

There was an affronted silence. 'Good gracious, we don't get our food from *dustbins*,' said Ezra.

'It wouldn't be hygienic,' Alleluya explained.

'We do get *other* things from dustbins,' Big Gwen said kindly. 'Practically everything in this house came out of a dustbin or off a tip. Clean it up, it's as good as new, often as not. I get all my clothes from a very nice district over by Folly Bridge.'

'It's quite amazing what people throw out,' said Ezra. 'Chairs, tables, floorboards . . . We break the floorboards up for firewood.' He indicated the corner of the room where a fire flickered in the grate of an old kitchen range.

'We go gathering from dusk onwards,' Mr Beechcroft explained.

'In pairs, usually,' added Alleluya. 'Solitary gatherers have been attacked.'

'We stick to certain areas.'

'So as not to poach on the territory of other groups.'

'We work each area about once a fortnight. If we visit an area more often than that, it seems to arouse hostility.' Mr Beechcroft pursed his lips. 'I think we may attribute the needles in the loaf of bread to over-exposure.'

'Nah,' said Brag. 'They just don't like us. Can't say I blame 'em. I wouldn't like us if I was them.'

There were smiles. Hare, confused by the voices and the welter of information, and sleepy from the warmth, yawned hugely. He would sleep under a roof tonight, and there might even be a blanket.

There was a movement over his shoulder and vegetables thudded on to the table. Ezra's hand then appeared, putting down knives. Alleluya, Big Gwen, Filthy and Mr Beechcroft each picked up a knife and a vegetable and started peeling. Brag got up with a preoccupied look and wandered away.

'Brag!' said Alleluya.

'Oh, let him go,' said Ezra, climbing on to a box to lift a large saucepan down from a shelf. 'It isn't worth it.'

Brag went out, banging the door behind him.

'He should be made to contribute,' pronounced Mr Beechcroft. 'He does nothing but talk.'

'He put up a shelf once,' said Big Gwen.

'It fell down the next day,' said Ezra.

'It fell down the same day,' said Alleluya.

They all laughed quietly. Hare said, 'It's kind of you to take me in like this.'

They stopped peeling and darted him embarrassed smiles.

'It's not a question of kindness,' said Ezra. 'We don't go in for kindness, in the sense you mean. We just look after each other. There are only two societies, and if you don't belong to them you belong to us.'

'What about the Zone?' said Hare, after a moment's thought. It was a question he had always wanted to ask of marginals.

Ezra looked surprised. 'The Zone?' He gave a short laugh.

'That's the greatest confidence trick of all time. There's nothing in the Zone. It's empty.'

In the days following his conversation with Mr Terry, Jacobs's thoughts returned to it several times. Every aspect of it caused him unease: Mr Terry's motive in coming to see him, the effortless way in which his visitor had dominated the conversation, its tone and its subject-matter.

Mr Terry had wished to discuss two subjects – the Inquiry and the new factory at Drawbridge – and Jacobs had sensed a lack of candour in his visitor on the first point and had himself been reluctant to talk about the second. However, while the Inquiry and the events out of which it arose could presumably be regarded as a closed chapter, there were elements of Drawbridge which could not.

Drawbridge was important and there was something funny about it: something anomalous even in a system full of anomalies. It had been on the books for years – a major site to accommodate a huge engineering factory. The specifications were unusual and included a reinforced concrete floor capable of taking extraordinary stresses. When Jacobs saw the drawings for some of the plant to be installed, he understood why. The machines were massive. He could not imagine what they would be used to produce, and did not ask. Since he had not been told, he presumed he was not supposed to know. To exhibit curiosity would have been an elementary error and never crossed his mind.

The site for Drawbridge had been chosen years ago: he had helped select it himself. It was in Morristown, one of those areas of creeping blight which the Company encouraged by buying up houses and doing nothing with them, on the principle that the land would sooner or later be useful. In respect of size, location and geology, it was by far the best site available. There was only one problem: a recalcitrant shopkeeper who manifested a deep attachment to this deserted slum.

For a long time the Company seemed to have lost interest in the project. The drawings stayed in the safe; the houses in Morristown continued their slow decay; from time to time Jacobs exerted pressure on the shopkeeper lest he become complacent. Then one day a memo arrived on Jacobs's desk couched in urgent terms. He was to expedite Drawbridge. No further delay could be tolerated.

Jacobs did not ask what had suddenly made Drawbridge a priority, any more than he had asked what Drawbridge was. He knew his duty, and that it would do his career no harm to perform it with particular efficiency in this case. The shopkeeper was a marginal, or as near as made no difference. Jacobs had been told to expedite the matter. He expedited it, in the only way it could be expedited.

'People like that . . .' he had said to the fastidious Mr Terry.

Recalling that conversation, he wondered what, really, was the value of one human being compared with another and whether he, Jacobs, had the valuation right. Other scales of measurement were possible – his education had not been so scanty as to prevent him from discovering that – but he regarded their hypothetical existence as an interesting but useless curiosity, like the possibility of alternative systems of mathematics. There existed in Jacobs's mind the concept that all human lives are equally sacred, without any related notion that this concept might be practically applied, let alone that it should be. Now, from nowhere, a maverick thought rode into his brain: suppose that concept were *true*? If one had to treat everyone equally, without regard for who they were and what they had, then . . . well, he saw at a glance that everything would have to change. The day-to-day business of the Company would be made impossible, since the Company functioned on the principle of taking as much as possible from those who could least afford to give it, and rewarding those who were doing nicely already. The imbalance was the dynamo that kept everything running, and attempts to upset it – or, rather, rectify it – were treated quite properly as threats to social stability; but it could not be denied that it was, if you took a purist view of things, unjust. And as for government, not the pussyfooting and orating that were all the Council did, but real government, such as was needed to deal with crises and keep things tidy – that sort of stuff would be out of the question. It was a monstrous idea, equality of treatment. How could anyone have taken it seriously even as a principle? Then, just for a moment, he saw what it held: a quality which did not exist in his own life. Simplicity. You would not have to spend half your time plotting strategies, either to get what you wanted out of somebody else or to prevent someone else getting what he wanted out of you. It would be like having a great wind blowing through your life.

For an intoxicating, terrifying second it blew through his.

He shuddered. It would blow everything away.

The window of the room Hare slept in, being at the back of the house, was not boarded up, and faced east. The sky was a dull silver, gleaming gold at the horizon, when he awoke on the first morning. As he watched, it lightened, and there came a volley of chirping from the eaves.

Hare was used to waking at dawn. He slipped off his mattress and walked to the window. He looked down at the garden, and caught his breath.

The garden's perimeter was a riot of weeds and brambles, like most of the garden at the front, a head-high jungle which obviously had been left to grow wild for years. But enclosed by this tumultuous border, and completely screened from passing view by it, was a secret garden. In a tidy plot were rows of onions, potatoes, beetroot, cabbage and other

83

vegetables. A path ran down the middle, and at the end was a low wooden hut for tools.

Hare tiptoed down the stairs. He opened the kitchen door as quietly as he could, and got his second surprise of the morning. Sprawled at the table was a thin, pale young man with a cadaverous face. Lank black hair fell over his brow and he was dressed in a black sweater, tight black trousers and black gym shoes. There was an expensive watch on his wrist.

'Hello,' said the apparition. 'Coffee?'

He poured something out of a jug, added milk, and pushed the cup towards Hare. It was quite pleasant, but it was not coffee. It had a nutty, slightly burnt flavour.

'We make it ourselves from dandelion roots,' said the young man. 'You dig up the roots, clean them, roast them in the oven until they're rock-hard, and then grind them up. It takes *weeks*. And all over town are perfectly good coffee beans just asking to be brought home.' He sighed deeply, and lowered long eyelashes to his cheek. 'Dear Ezra, he reads books you know. It can't be a good thing. Do you read books?'

'I'm afraid so,' said Hare.

'Oh, Lor',' said the young man, and they exchanged a cautious grin.

'You're Hare, aren't you?'

'I am. And you must be Angel. You were out when I arrived.'

'Ezra's cocoa parties leave me rather cold,' said Angel, and tossed back the hair from his brow with a studied movement. 'Besides, I work at night.'

'You work?' Hare was startled.

'I do.'

'What sort of work?'

'I'm a burglar,' said Angel.

Hare stared at the table and tried to collect himself. It was

84

six in the morning. Here he was talking to, not merely a professional criminal, but – he guessed – that rare and dangerous thing, a homosexual. The mininum sentence for the latter was five years. He didn't know what burglars got. He glanced at Angel sideways. Angel lowered his lashes again, demurely; Hare realised he was enjoying the joke.

'You're the first I've met,' said Hare, with conscious ambiguity.

Angel's eyes widened. 'Really? But how do you know? We don't advertise ourselves, dear. You might have met lots.'

Hare laughed. He said, 'How long have you been a burglar?'

'Oh, years.' Angel was casual. 'As a kid I was the best in the business. You slow down a bit as you get older.'

'You can't be very old now.'

'Old enough to think twice about running along rooftops. The milkmen get younger all the time.' He waved his hand towards the other side of the kitchen. 'All that's my work.'

In the sharp morning light the kitchen had lost its comfortable obscurity. It was badly in need of tidying. The sink, a magisterial porcelain affair as big as a cabin trunk, was entirely occupied by dirty crockery and saucepans. A brass tap dripped on to the plate at the top of the pile. Next to the sink stood a wooden chair on which was an orange crate filled with vegetables and fruit in various stages of decomposition. There were several cardboard boxes, most of them empty, one of them containing a cat. What Angel's wave had presumably been indicating, however, was a dresser on the opposite wall, the shelves of which were crammed to overflowing with tins, packets and jars. Hare's eyes travelled over it. Soup, cocoa, sugar, oatmeal, peaches, sardines, lentils, jelly, currants, flour ... it seemed very unlikely that it could all have been left on walls and under benches.

'Surely you don't run along rooftops with tins of peaches?' Hare said.

85

Angel laughed. 'No, I just put them under my arm and walk out of the shop with them. But don't *you* try it. Actually, I usually buy the stuff: it's easier.'

'But where do you get the money?' Then he realised that Angel had already explained where he got the money. It seemed disproportionate to burgle houses and spend the money on soup. At the same time, he approved. 'I hope they appreciate it,' he said, with a feeling they might not.

Angel shrugged. 'Ezra thinks we shouldn't steal. He thinks it makes us no better than they are.'

Hare was puzzled. 'No better than they are?'

'Well, dear, there wasn't any private property when we were all leaping about in the trees, was there? At some point somebody nicked what was everybody's and said it was his. And they've been doing it ever since.'

'I suppose so,' said Hare. He had never thought of it like that. 'Is Ezra the leader here?'

'We don't have leaders,' said Angel. 'We're against hierarchies, centralised organisation, authority and rules. In *theory*. Well, we don't have rules and we don't have punishments, but we have public opinion instead, and I'm not sure that's any improvement, myself. And although we don't have leaders, Ezra runs the place all the same. And *I* think it's just as well, because somebody has to know what's supposed to happen next, and everybody else here is either too lazy or too barmy or just plain bent.'

He yawned, and stretched himself like a cat. 'I'm going to bed,' he said. 'Good thing about working nights is it gets you out of the gardening.'

He strolled over to the sink, picked up a piece of wood from the floor and hit the tap with it. The tap gushed water, the pipes wailed and drummed like a war-party of savages, and there came an angry shout from upstairs. Angel, with a little smile, rinsed his mug under the jet of water.

Hare said, 'How did you know my name?'

'We've been expecting you. Ezra said he was trying to make contact with you, but you didn't want to be contacted.'

Hare reddened. 'How did he know who I was?'

'Oh, it came down the line,' said Angel vaguely.

Hare bit back his frustration.

'I don't suppose *you* know where my wife is, do you?'

'Sorry,' said Angel. He did look genuinely sorry. 'But I'm sure you'll find her. People find all sorts of things, once they get out.'

Later, Ezra gave Hare a guided tour.

The house had little in the way of furniture, but efforts had been made to make it homely. Sacks on the floor substituted for carpet. Other sacks hung at the windows, precariously tacked into the plaster with drawing pins. Everyone had a mattress. 'People just throw them away,' said Ezra in a tone of amazement.

The sitting room was known as the Stable because it had a picture of a horse over the mantelpiece. This room contained several decaying armchairs and a sofa. Brag was asleep on the sofa.

'Get up,' said Ezra, and shoved the recumbent body with his foot.

Brag opened an eye and regarded him malignly. 'Why should I?' he said, and closed it again.

Next to the Stable was the bathroom. This was Roman in its dimensions and medieval in its standards of comfort. Ventilation was provided by a broken window pane. 'Must mend that,' frowned Ezra. 'Are you any good at repairs?'

'I'll try,' said Hare. 'Have you got some glass?'

'Don't be silly,' said Ezra. 'Where would we find glass? I'm talking about cardboard.'

Hare gazed about him. The pipes ran round the walls as if uncertain of their destination, and released drips at intervals upon the floor. A large cast-iron bath stood on clawed feet against one wall, and on a ledge above it, also on clawed feet, stood a gas boiler of great ornateness and dignity. A scorched patch of ceiling above the boiler testified to an eventful history.

'It doesn't work,' said Ezra unnecessarily. 'The gas is cut off. There's cold water.'

Hare turned one of the brass taps at the head of the bath. The plumbing system was immediately convulsed by a huge coughing fit. Pipes throbbed and thumped around the walls as if in an attempt to shake themselves free. After several seconds, cold water spat violently from the tap. Hare turned the tap off again.

'I don't know why the water wasn't cut off,' said Ezra. 'Perhaps they want us to live here. It is impossible to fathom their minds.'

The house contained eleven rooms. Hare was shown all of them, and then the garden, in which Big Gwen, Alleluya and Mr Beechcroft were already working.

'We grow a lot of our own vegetables,' said Ezra. 'But there's the winter, of course. The trouble is' — he smiled — 'the produce is so delicious it puts you off eating half-rotten cauliflowers from the market.'

'Don't you . . . um.' This was difficult. 'I met a self-proclaimed burglar in the kitchen this morning,' said Hare, taking the bull by the horns. 'I gather that you do sometimes have money to buy food.'

Ezra stiffened slightly. 'Not all of us are happy about Angel's activities. It's one of the issues on which we have a difference of opinion.'

'I suppose,' said Hare, 'it would be surprising if you didn't have differences.'

'Perhaps. Nevertheless it's a pity. Theoretically we should agree on a much wider range of issues than we do.'

'What do the other marginal groups do?'

'Some of the communities virtually live by theft: they call

88

it redistribution. Other have decided against it. And some, like us, tolerate both views and do a bit of one and a bit of the other, and never quite thrash it out. It's unsatisfactory.'

'But couldn't you take a vote on it?'

'A vote?' Ezra appeared surprised. Then he gave a little laugh. 'No, no we couldn't do that. We never vote on anything. We don't believe in majority decisions.'

Hare was baffled.

'Then how *do* you reach decisions?'

'We discuss until agreement is reached. *Everyone* agrees. If you take a majority decision, there's always someone who disagrees with it and will be unhappy implementing it. We believe that people must do what they think is right, not what a majority has decided for them is right.'

High-minded and unworkable, thought Hare. But a moment's reflection told him that it must work, because they did it.

'How on earth do you get everyone to agree, people being what they are?'

'You'd be surprised how often they will all agree,' said Ezra. 'In the end. You have to be patient.'

'Don't you get the odd difficult customer who won't co-operate?'

Brag appeared at the sitting room window, and proceeded to urinate in a glistening arc into the garden below.

'We get the odd difficult customer,' said Ezra.

5

Jacobs read the last page of the typed report for the second time. He read it with his mouth clamped shut, breathing slowly through his nostrils, the way he had trained himself to do in moments of stress. There was nevertheless a film of sweat on his forehead. This was bad. How bad it turned out to be would depend on his skill in handling it, but nothing could mitigate the fact that it had happened, and that in itself was bad enough.

He flicked the report away from him across the polished desk, and it came to rest against the furthest of the line of telephones, the white one. He used that telephone only in emergency. In ten years he had used it not more than half a dozen times. He was not thinking of using it now: the problem that had arisen was in the category of 'trouble', not of 'disaster'. Only in the latter case would he pick up the white telephone. The penalty for picking it up without sufficient cause was not something he cared to speculate about.

More than once the white telephone had saved his skin, together with more valuable ones. Why then was there resentment in the glance he cast at it? The truth was that Jacobs, through many years of service to the Company, some of it service of a strange and devious kind, had come to know a great deal about the Company and the Council it pretended to but did not obey, and had come also to have a high opinion of his own knowledge and competence and a rather low opinion of the knowledge and competence of others. Others above him, that is, since those below him in the hierarchy he did not bother to think about, and as for equals – he occupied a curious position, and had none.

Jacobs was ambitious. He wanted the rewards of intelligence, industry and silence, and it seemed to him that he had not been given his full share of them. He had a wife and three daughters at home and it seemed to him that they did not respect him enough. His energies and resourcefulness demanded a larger sphere. It was a sign of status to have a white telephone on his desk, but he was under no illusions about the role in which he picked it up. Sometimes in his daydreams he imagined he was at the other end of the line. As a young man, indeed, he had nursed hopes of reaching that dizzy summit, until he realised what sort of world he lived in and saw his coarse features, scratched-together education and the occasional crudeness which he could never quite expunge from his speech as the crippling handicaps they were. He had done well, very well, to get as far as he had.

And he could get further. For two or three rungs ahead the ladder of promotion was clear. He would make Divisional Manager with no trouble. But that was not what he wanted. He already had, on account of certain services rendered, a Divisional Manager's desk and very nearly a Divisional Manager's salary, and he did not want a Divisional Manager's work. That would be far too tedious. What he wanted was something which many of his colleagues would not have understood.

It was customary for directors of the Company (and how many there were seemed to be a secret: Jacobs had never managed to find out) to be made honorary members of the Council. In exceptional circumstances the privilege could be extended to senior managers. It was an empty privilege – the right to drink in the members' bar and use the Council crest on one's stationery was all it amounted to – for the Company members, although permitted to listen to debates, were not allowed to vote. The custom dated from the time when the Company had been a young and vigorous organisation whose importance in the community the Council declared a wish to acknowledge, meaning that it wanted to muzzle it. Since then the position had been reversed: the Council was now the compliant (usually) creature of the Company, which made it all the more important from the Council's point of view that Company members should still be debarred from voting, so that the myth of the Council's sovereignty should be preserved. What reduced the solemn procedures in the Council to the level of farce was that no issue was raised, no subject debated and no decision taken that had not already been raised, debated and decided in the rooms on the top floor of the Company headquarters, those rooms which with one exception had windows of opaque glass that did not open, and into which Jacobs had been three times in thirty years.

It was in the Company, therefore, that the power lay. For a man who enjoyed work, didn't mind getting his hands dirty either literally or metaphorically, and exulted in making his mark on the world, the Company was the place. The Council was for nancy-boys who preferred the appearances of power to the reality of it. Everyone in the Company above the level of junior manager knew that. Jacobs had always known it, but it did not diminish in the slightest his desire to be one of those exceptional senior managers co-opted to the Council. It was not that he invested with great importance the pleasures of drinking in the members' bar or using the Council crest on his writing paper. What he wanted was to be accepted in the very citadel of the class system which had told him he was not good enough.

His gaze fell on the report again. He had been on the way to achieving it, until this.

The Company manufactured, in its numerous factories and workshops, mills and sheds, a range of goods so enormous that it could not be grasped by a single mind and had long ago been entrusted to a computer. There was room, in the labyrinths of the Company, for many mysteries. Goods disappeared, or turned out not to be what they were thought to be, or where they were thought to be. Warehouses turned out, if you inspected them, not to contain what they should, and sometimes not to contain anything at all. Several of them, to Jacobs's knowledge, were stuffed with perishable goods which had deliberately been left to rot. Employees themselves might turn out not to exist, except as names on a payroll. Jacobs had been told long ago not to attempt the penetration of these mysteries, but he believed that he understood them and the part they played in the Company's business, for a great deal of the Company's business was not what it seemed.

Among the Company's products were some that were illegal. It was constantly grumbled, in the higher reaches of the Company, that the Council told the Company what results it wanted and then objected to the methods necessary to achieve them. An example typical of this muddled thinking, to the Company's mind, had occurred about eight years previously when the Council passed an Act prohibiting the further testing of a crowd control agent being developed for the police. The Council feared public disquiet if the existence of the substance became known. The Company, knowing that the police wanted the product and would in the end force the Council to lift the ban, had argued against the Act. The Council, for once, had ignored the Company's advice, whereupon the Company had ignored the Act. The substance in question – a mixture of chemicals producing a highly toxic gas – had continued to be tested, improved and

93

stockpiled ever since. The police, at senior level, were aware of the situation. There was a natural understanding between the Company and the police force, founded partly on the fact that they were supplier and customer and partly on the fact that both of them felt they suffered from too much interference.

In the Company's case, interference manifested itself most clearly over the dockets kept in the document storage room. The dockets recorded every movement of goods on the warehousing and retail side of the Company's business: a vast amount of information, most of it trivial, not worth transferring to computer but requiring nevertheless to be stored somewhere accessible for a limited period. The storage period at the moment was four months; a few years ago it had been six months, and the time had been reduced as business expanded and the number of dockets doubled, then trebled, while the amount of storage space remained the same because the Company had better things to do with its space than expand the document retrieval section.

Left to itself, the Company would probably not have kept written records beyond a month, if at all. The essential data were on the computer. However, the Company was not left to itself. It had, constantly peering over its shoulder like an anxious nanny, the Council. The Council was powerless to do anything except make a fuss, but it was able to make a very loud fuss, such as would largely paralyse the Company's operations in certain areas if the fuss were clearly heard by the public. It was therefore necessary to prevent nanny from seeing what, at times, one was doing. Nanny, as was to be expected, insisted on an unobstructed view, in pursuance of which members of the Council would appear from time to time, theoretically without warning, in the Company offices and warehouses 'for a chat'. 'Theoretically' because, in practice, it was difficult for members of one organisation to make surprise visits to another organisation when the men

94

at the top of both organisations were the same. Nevertheless the fiction was carefully preserved, and nowhere more carefully than in the case of the periodic checks the Council insisted on making of the stored dockets. These checks were the only reason for keeping the dockets, and the Council was adamant on the necessity of keeping them because, it said, they contained information which was lost when the data were transferred to computer. This was true, and was one of the conveniences of the computer.

Dockets which might suggest to the alert investigator that the Company was engaging in activities which, legally, it should not (the crowd control agent was only one of many cases) were routinely intercepted by Jacobs. He would simply remove them at some stage of their passage through the system, tamper with them in such a way that they appeared to relate to some harmless type of manufacture, and put them back in circulation. He took a sly pleasure in channelling the altered dockets through Blight's office in the basement and watching the expressions of bewilderment on the face of the only man in the office – possibly the only man in the Company – who ever thought about what these pieces of paper really meant. The forgeries had never been noticed: Jacobs was clever, and the inspectors were looking for reassurance, not its opposite.

Then a few months ago the unthinkable had happened. Two Council inspectors had made a surprise check which was a genuine surprise. Jacobs had removed a batch of dockets for doctoring and had not had time to replace them. Whether by chance or because they had inside information, the inspectors discovered the gap in the records. The missing dockets related to the outlawed gas.

Jacobs had had to act like lightning, while doing everything possible to confuse and delay the inspectors. The factory which produced the chemicals had to be cleaned up and made to look as if its legitimate products – a range of

95

dyestuffs – were its only ones, and the containers had to be moved to a safe hiding place. The latter had caused Jacobs grave anxiety until in a moment of inspiration he remembered seeing a set of old government plans among some Company papers. The Company's secrets were safe for a hundred years where he had put them.

To account for the missing dockets, a scapegoat was required. A man in Blight's office was accused. Jacobs was glad to get rid of him: he was too intelligent to be doing the job he was doing and too unreliable to be promoted. An inquiry was held and guilt publicly attributed. The exercise had served more than one purpose: it was always useful to reaffirm loyalties and strengthen ties. Jacobs had reaped much credit from it.

He had been pleased with his handling of the crisis; taken together with his decisive action over Drawbridge, he thought it merited recognition. And now . . . .

Now some jumped-up ninny of a Councillor just out of college, some wet-behind-the-ears little nitpicker of a mother's darling who'd never wheeled a barrow of bricks in his life, had declared his dissatisfaction with the Company, with the Inquiry and with the way the whole business had been conducted. 'We cannot escape the impression,' he wrote in his report, in that cool, prissy, never-say-quite-what-you-mean way they taught them to write at those expensive schools, 'of a certain lack of frankness on the part of Universal Goods in the way facts have been presented to us and questions answered. While unable to say categorically that we disbelieve the Company's version of what happened to the missing dockets, we take this opportunity to express our disquiet that information of such importance is apparently so little safeguarded, and that assertions about it are so uncritically received. We recommend the setting up of an independent inspectorate with wider powers than are possessed by existing inspectors of the Company's business . . .'

Jacobs hissed. It was dangerous, it was an insult and — worse — it was a sign that something was afoot in the Council. His antennae had told him so months ago. The donkey was getting tired of being led while being complimented on its leadership. It had decided that lead it really would.

It couldn't, of course. When the time came, it would find it did not have the power. But there was going to be a struggle. There was a new race of young would-be rulers over at Council Hall, and they wanted to see blood.

Jacobs fretted at his lower lip. Some of the blood was likely to be his.

His eyes rested again on the white telephone. But it was the black one at his elbow that rang.

He knew exactly whose voice he would hear as he picked it up.

Things had not been going very well lately for Detective Koberg. Part of it he put down to the jealousy of colleagues and superiors (people always seemed anxious to do him a bad turn if they could; he was constantly amazed by the baseness of the human race), but some of it could be attributed only to fate. He attracted bad luck, he thought sometimes. He reacted to it by becoming viciously moody, which made him feel worse and attracted more kicks from an unsympathetic world, and the spiral would continue, becoming blacker at every turn, while the pressure in his chest increased, until he found a way of relieving it somewhere in the ill-lit alleys of the slums.

Circumstances had not yet reached that pitch, but he could feel the pressure starting to build.

On the same morning, he had had an unpleasant scene with Jacinth and had received a stinging reprimand from his sergeant. The scene with Jacinth had taken him by surprise: she was six years younger than he and still a schoolgirl, and he expected from her unquestioning obedience. Usually she gave it, but on this particular morning when he dropped round for a half-hour's diversion, being in the area, she had said something which revealed to him appalling prospects of what she had all along been secretly thinking. She did not, it seemed, revere his knowledge of the world, his grasp of what made people tick and his ability to bend them to his will: she thought he was conceited, cold-hearted and a bastard, and she told him so. He had hit her, as was only to be expected, and to his consternation she had hit him back, quite painfully, making his eyes water.

He had not had time to sort it out – either to vent his rage properly or to make her see why he was the way he was and that most people were even worse. What he did manage to say she didn't listen to. She had become very self-possessed recently; he didn't like it. She was too young to be like that, and it was the thing he hated in older women. He had flung back at her that she had behaved pretty badly herself about the tenant on the second floor, to which she replied, in a tone he'd never heard her use before, 'What else could I do? You told me to do it. You're all the same, you bastards, and you own the fucking world.'

It was not particularly important. But it was upsetting, like stepping on a stone and feeling it move under your foot. Jacinth would have to be taught a lesson, but it could wait. What had happened a couple of hours later at the station was more serious.

The sergeant had called him in over a piece of routine investigation: the theft of valuables from a house in a high-class neighbourhood. Koberg had had a list of people to interview, compiled from statements and the sometimes ridiculous suggestions of the police computer. He had interviewed the first five people on the list and then stopped. He knew he was not going to get anywhere, for the good reason that the victim of the robbery did not want him to. There had been a banknote under the saucer when he was given a cup of coffee. Insurance, Koberg presumed, although it might not be so simple. In any case, people of that class did not like having dealings with the police. Koberg knew what was good for him. He had fudged a report saying that all avenues of enquiry had led to a dead end.

The sergeant at the station was new, keen and no fool. He could not prove that Koberg had been bought off, but he told him shortly what he thought of him. Koberg had listened with his face burning, incredulous. He was a policeman of proven ability. His conviction record was the best in the district. It strengthened his determination to obtain a transfer at any cost.

Koberg was not happy at the station: he had not been happy there since the new sergeant came. It was not simply that he felt picked on; the atmosphere had changed. He had got on well with the previous sergeant. They had had an understanding. The previous sergeant would not have made a fuss about Koberg's report on the robbery; the whole matter would have been handled differently from start to finish. The previous sergeant had been transferred, abruptly and without explanation, about four months ago. Shortly after his departure, Koberg had also applied to transfer to another station. So far his request had not been granted.

He had reason to hope that it soon would be. Koberg had a friend in high places – well, high enough. Suffice to say, a friend who could pull strings and had a motive for pulling them. Koberg did not believe you got anything for nothing, and in this case he had earned a favour. What the friend did not know (Koberg did not believe in showing all your hand) was how badly he needed the favour.

Koberg lived above his income. For a young policeman with a taste for style, it was almost impossible not to. He knew several others in the force in the same position. He had an expensive flat, he bought new clothes whenever he fancied them, which was often, and he had a sports car. Even secondhand, it had cost him getting on for a year's salary. He had borrowed the money from a firm specialising in such transactions, which required no security and no references and exacted a rate of interest so high that it made him sweat to think about it. These days he was obliged to think about it rather often, because he had fallen behind with the repayments of the debt. As a rule he financed these repayments out of a variety of sources, some of which were very obscure and connected in a delicate way with his work. There was another source, unconnected with his job, which might have cost him his job nonetheless if it had become known. He gambled. Twice a week he visited an illegal casino in the backstreets, where naturally no-one knew he was a policeman and where he took care not to dress like one. He was a very successful gambler. He knew when to stop and when his luck wasn't running. He had nerve and self-discipline and despised gamblers who didn't. He never drank when he gambled, because drink interferes with your judgement. He was discreet.

And recently he had been losing. It had never happened before, not like this. He knew why it was. He had allowed the threats of the firm which had lent him the money for the car to upset him. Nasty threats they had been, not confined to repossession of the car. Now, if you really needed money, you didn't win. Your need set up a sort of electrical field around you, and repulsed the luck which you would other-wise attract. It sounded fanciful, but he had many times proved it true. The trouble was, there was nothing you could do about it. If you needed money you needed money, there was no way of making yourself not need it as you approached the gaming table.

The question of the transfer therefore took on another aspect. The new sergeant, a busybody forever poking his nose into things that didn't concern him, had shown an unhealthy interest in some of Koberg's more delicate professional relationships, and as a result the sources were becoming increasingly reluctant to part with money. If everything went wrong, and it looked as if it might, it would add up to Koberg's worst nightmare, in which he lost everything and had to go back to where he had started from, a rattrap childhood among the hopeless poor, whom now he persecuted because of the loathing and fear they aroused in him.

He needed a new field in which he could cultivate sources without interference. He knew of several promising ones. But it had to be done soon. It was necessary to put some pressure on the highly-placed friend, and remind him of the origin of the friendship.

6

Hare found a piece of cardboard and plugged up the gap in the bathroom window. The action released something in him long dormant.

Mrs Raptor had not allowed the tenants to do minor repairs, lest in doing them they uncover the need for major repairs. Unable to express itself, Hare's instinct to do something about ill-fitting doors, loose floorboards and dripping taps had atrophied until he no longer noticed these things. Now, in new surroundings, it began to reawaken.

The tap in the kitchen first engaged his attention. This dripped steadily, and in order to minimise the dripping was usually turned on and off with the piece of wood Hare had observed Angel using on the first morning. As a result of repeated banging the handle had developed curved ends as if it was trying to turn into a swastika, which destiny however it would not attain because one of the ends had already snapped off and the other three would presumably not be long in following.

Hare gazed at the mangled tap and a memory stirred within him. After a moment he said, with a feeling of discovery, 'All it needs is a new washer.'

'Oh, is that all?' said Brag, with his feet on the table. 'I'll keep my eyes open. You never know when a new washer will turn up, carelessly abandoned on a rubbish heap.'

Hare got up early and had a word with Angel on the

subject of washers, spanners and lubricating oil. Two days later he found a package wrapped in newspaper next to his mattress when he woke up – burglary in reverse, as it were. The package contained the items he had asked for together with a hammer, a hacksaw, two screwdrivers and a file.

Hare set to work. It took him most of the day because of the difficulty of getting the tap apart without breaking it, and he was delayed by having to mop up the flood which resulted from forgetting to turn the water off. But in the end, to his own surprise, he succeeded. When the tap was reassembled, it worked. People went on hitting it for another week.

Encouraged, Hare embarked on other jobs. It was as well that he only gradually became aware of how much needed doing, because if he had seen from the outset the broken slates, rotten guttering, bulging stonework and leaning chimney pot that his sharpened eyes saw a month later, he would not have started. As it was, he made discoveries at a pace that did not destroy his optimism. In time the fifth stair ceased to squeak, the kitchen door was made to shut, and the window in the bathroom was repaired with real glass.

'Anyone would think this was a proper house,' said Brag.

'I hope you're not doing it because you feel you ought to, dearie,' said Big Gwen. 'You can live here whether you do a hand's turn or not. *He* does.'

'I'm doing it because I want to,' said Hare. It was the first time for years he had done anything that made sense. His work for the Company had been something between a penance and a riddle. But what could be more useful than making a tap turn, a door close, a window open?

Windows turned out to be contentious, however.

'We don't want to make it obvious that we live here,' Alleluya explained. 'That's why the windows in the front are boarded up. We're illegal, you know.'

103

'Load of rubbish. The milkmen know we're here,' said Brag.

'How do you know they do?'

'Because that's what they're for,' said Brag irrefutably.

'I must say, I should think in all this time they've noticed the smoke coming out of the chimney,' said Big Gwen.

'Then why do they let us stay here?'

'Because if they drove us out, we'd just go off somewhere else and be a nuisance.' Brag subsided heavily on to his favourite kitchen chair and untied the string that held his boots on. 'Going to need a new pair of these soon, with all this walking.'

Hare had not given up his wandering of the city.

For the first few weeks after he had joined the marginals, he hoped to find his wife. The message had seemed to contain a promise that he would see her soon. He scanned the evening crowds for a face that might be hers; then, realising that he was looking in the wrong place, he ventured to the ghettos, and was met by glares of hostility. He enquired of other marginal communities, although Ezra had told him she was not with any of them. In the end he accepted that he would not see her yet, and resigned himself to waiting.

He was shunned on these outings, as marginals were. People crossed to the other side of the road, or slipped into doorways until he had passed. After he had gone by, they turned and stared: he could feel their stares on the back of his head. On the underground (he still had a bit of money left, and he liked riding on the little automatic trains) a space would appear around him and widen until he had the carriage to himself.

None of this bothered him particularly: he did not expect anything else. What did, at first, disturb him was how much the city had changed in a few weeks. Then he realised that what had changed was the point from which he viewed it.

He had always thought of the city as an arrangement of buildings, streets and parks. Sometimes now as he walked through it it seemed to be a single thing, alien, consuming the people who lived and worked in it. Some of them, he sensed, were in league with it, but he could not understand the point of the conspiracy. He noticed, too, that nearly everything he looked at belonged to the Company. Shops, factories, offices. Warehouses, naturally. Almost every other building seemed to be a warehouse. But what exactly was a warehouse? Walking past one of them he heard something that sounded like gunfire.

One day, thinking of Maria, he went back to the district where they had lived. He turned down a road which used to lead to allotments. The road became a lane, swerved unexpectedly, and he found himself looking down a steep slope at the largest greenhouse he had ever seen. It was surrounded by a wire mesh fence, and a thick stream of yellow vapour issued from a chimney at the side of it. The door at the end of the greenhouse was open. Just outside it lay the corpses of six dogs.

A broken wooden sign stood at the top of the slope. The piece of wood carrying the first letter had dropped off and it said 'ANGER'.

It was supposed to be a horticultural station specialising in houseplants, Hare later remembered.

Hare liked Angel. The provocative manner was a defence; a caricature of a caricature, behind which Angel thought thoughts which Hare found at first surprising. Angel was serious about his politics in a way in which no-one else in that house was. He had grown up in the Glen, one of the most notorious ghettos, and had a passionate hatred of the system which produced such poverty.

Hare asked him one day how many marginals there were in the city.

'Goodness knows,' said Angel, 'nobody's counted. A few thousand? Maybe more. I mean, it's possible' – his eyes widened mischievously – 'it's *possible* that everybody's marginal except the Council, isn't it?'

They contemplated this possibility in rapt silence.

'But I don't think so,' said Angel.

'No.'

'Think of it, though. If there are more of *us* than there are of *them* – many more, not just a few more, but enough to make up for the milkmen – then that puts a different complexion on the revolution, doesn't it?'

Hare gazed at him. 'The what?'

'Oh dear, you're not much good, are you?' said Angel. 'We are supposed to be *revolutionaries*. I thought you knew.'

'I don't see any guns,' said Hare, 'unless you keep them under the cauliflowers.'

'Oh, not that kind! Really, for a man who reads books you do say silly things sometimes.' Hare grinned. 'We are revolutionaries by *implication*,' instructed Angel. 'Look at the way we live. No power structures, no laws except rotas for cooking which Brag is free not to observe. Liberty. Individual responsibility. Voluntary co-operation.' His voice became serious. 'But no violence. We're against power, and power rests on violence. They turn into one another. So it's pretty stupid to use violence to attack power, isn't it, if it's because it's power that you're attacking it?'

He poured himself some more dandelion coffee.

'So our resistance has to be passive. We don't support the system: we withdraw from it and create a counter-system, that's all we can do. We have to wait for their system to collapse. In the end it will. In the end it will be too huge, too unwieldy and too insane to be controllable, and there will be an almighty crash. And then, as the dust settles, we will begin to reconstruct. Without power and without policemen. Relying solely on the instinct for co-operation, and the natural feeling for justice, and the desire of every human being for self-fulfilment.' He had taken refuge in mockery again. 'Beautiful, isn't it?'

'Yes,' said Hare sincerely.

'The trouble is it's taking so long to happen. It isn't half tempting to help the crash along a bit. But that's against the logic of it, you see.'

'Yes.'

'However, if there were *really* millions of us, it would be a different matter, because the trouble with passive resistance is that it only works if you can do it on a huge scale. And even then there's the police.'

'Yes.'

'But if there were really *millions* of us' – despite himself, Angel's eyes were glowing – 'even the milkmen couldn't stop us. We would just go on walking towards them until they had no bullets left, and then we'd take their guns away and go on walking, and we'd walk into the offices of the Council and tear up their laws and set fire to their filing cabinets and mahogany desks, and we'd walk into the Company's ware-houses and throw them open to all the people who'd never had anything but shit all their lives, and we'd walk into the prisons and set free all the kinks – '

' – and all the burglars – '

' – and all those unjustly imprisoned by a tyrannical regime, and it would be . . . it would be . . .'

'The millenium,' supplied Hare.

'What?'

'They used to call it the millenium,' said Hare, and thought of Solomon.

It was a few days after this conversation that Hare noticed the doors.

He was sitting one evening in a subway that was the entrance to an underground station. He was never able to sit longer than ten minutes in a place because a policeman would appear. Nevertheless, in ten minutes he could see quite a lot that interested him. He was sitting in a huge, tiled, echoing space through which at intervals knots of people rushed feverishly. The walls of the subway were covered with posters advertising clothes, jewellery and furnishings. The people in the advertisements were young, attractive and healthy-looking. The people who rushed past Hare were haggard, weighed down with suitcases, briefcases, carrier bags and children.

Standing up to stroll to the further end of the subway, he experienced a moment's disorientation. It was something which happened to him quite often when he was out walking: it was not that he didn't know where he was but that he saw where he was as if for the first time, and found it astonishing. It was then that he saw the doors.

The subway, the corridors and platforms – for he pursued his discovery – were full of them. It seemed to him there must be dozens of them, many of them looking as if they were never opened, being covered in a layer of grime which made them indistinguishable from the wall. Some even had seats, weighing machines and other immovable objects fixed to the ground right in front of them. Perhaps they were not doors at all, he thought, but something different, although he could not think what that might be.

After that he saw doors everywhere. One night he stood by the river watching the ripples from a passing police launch disturb the reflections of streetlamps and floodlit buildings, turning them into a drifting anarchy of little lights. Deep in the floating patch of shadow under the bridge something gleamed and disappeared, and Hare could have sworn that for a fraction of a second a door had opened at the base of one of the stone piers.

*

'A lot of tools seem to have found their way here in the past few weeks,' said Ezra.

Angel, who was sitting at the table, began to whistle under his breath. Brag joined him, an excruciating semitone lower.

'I've been doing repairs,' said Hare. 'I can't do them without tools.'

'I realise that.' Ezra looked strained.

'Do you object to the work I'm doing?' asked Hare.

'No. It's very welcome.' Ezra sighed. 'But do you really need three saws?'

Well, yes, he did. There were for different jobs. He was about to launch into an explanation, but didn't. Perhaps Ezra was right.

'I think it's degrading to steal from *them*,' announced Alleluya.

Brag snorted. 'They steal. Whole society's based on it.'

'That's no reason why we should,' Alleluya retorted. 'I think the most important thing we have is our moral superiority over them.'

Brag yawned.

Big Gwen stuck her feet out in front of her. They were encased in a pair of muddy slippers. 'Angel got me this nice comfy pair of slippers to do the garden in,' she said. 'I could never stand for long in anything else, and you can never get a decent pair of slippers out of a dustbin, whatever Ezra says.'

'There are doors all over the city,' remarked Hare to Angel.

'Doors?' repeated Angel vaguely. It was seven in the morning and he looked as if he had had a hard night. 'Well of course there are.'

'No, there are doors where there shouldn't be. In subways and stations and under bridges and half way up walls. I keep seeing them,' said Hare. 'Have you seen them?'

There was a slight pause before Angel said, 'Can't say I have,' and went off to bed.

It was a few days after that that Hare saw half a dozen grey-painted vehicles with large wheels and no windows, only a visor-like slit at the front, come out of the warehouse known as the Palace.

They were rather larger than the average car, built of heavy sheet metal riveted together, and were high-slung with a peculiar beaked appearance at the front. On top of each was mounted a swivelling object like a cannon but with a wide, fluted barrel.

Filthy was sitting on the stairs as Hare came in one evening, looking like flotsam left by the tide. He had something in his arms, and was crooning to it.

'Hello,' said Hare.

'Poppy,' Filthy appeared to say.

Hare stopped. It was the first thing Filthy had ever said to him, and it seemed a pity not to understand it.

'Sorry, what did you say?'

'Poppy,' said Filthy.

Hare decided not to pursue it. He went on up the stairs to the sitting room. The chimney of this room had not been swept for years and had a tendency to smoke. It was smoking as Hare entered. The room was horizontally divided, at roughly shoulder height, into a sector in which it was possible to see and breathe and a sector in which it was not. The window was open but the smoke showed no interest in going out of it. Those around the fire had solved the problem by sitting down, in which position their heads were below the smoke zone. Hare sat down too.

'Perhaps we should sweep the chimney,' he suggested.

Alleluya turned on him. 'Why have you come here, upsetting everything?' she demanded. 'We were happy before you came. We didn't want our taps mended.'

Hare was shaken. He had thought this might happen, but he was not prepared for it this evening.

Big Gwen laid a hand on his knee. 'Don't you worry, dearie. She gets like it sometimes, it just comes out.'

'I get like *what* sometimes?' spat Alleluya.

Angel, coiled languidly in the worm-eaten velvet armchair with broken springs, said, 'Well, I think it's lovely, having doors that shut.'

'Then why don't you go back and live in a comfortable house that *has* doors that shut, since that seems to be all you care about?' snapped Alleluya.

'There's nothing admirable in having doors that don't shut,' observed Ezra, scrupulously fair as always. 'It's just draughty.'

'It is making us,' said Alleluya through her teeth, 'like *them*.'

Despite the perverseness of it, Hare could see what she meant. You started by making a place habitable and ended by choosing matching furnishings, and somewhere on the way you had crossed an invisible line between what was necessary and supported life and what was superfluous and supported something you might even hate. The trouble was that you could never tell where the line was, only that you had crossed it, and once you had started on the process it was very difficult to stop.

'If you like, I won't do any more,' he offered.

There was an uncomfortable silence. Brag said, 'Now look what you've done,' to Alleluya, who glared at him and began to pick at the skin on her hands.

After a while she said, 'I don't care what you think; I don't think we should have anything to do with them.'

'We *can't* not have anything to do with them,' said Angel. 'It's a ridiculous pretence that we can. We're parasites. We have to be, because there's no room for us in their world and they *own* the world. The only choice we have is between being parasites on their terms and parasites on our terms.'

'Oh yes, there *is* somewhere else we can go,' said Alleluya.

There was a sudden silence.

'Sometimes I wish *you'd* go there,' said Angel.

The silence resumed.

Hare glanced round, puzzled. It seemed there was something they would not talk about in front of him.

Except Brag, of course. Stretching himself with a yawn, Brag said, 'Load of rubbish. The Diggers are parasites the same as us. They just like to make things uncomfortable for themselves so they can feel pure.'

Everyone looked at him. He was occupying the only comfortable piece of furniture in the room, the battered horsehair sofa which was held up at one end by a pile of bricks. On this he sprawled, with tomato soup in his beard and his trousers gaping open from the waistband to disclose an area of grey underclothing. The recent remains of an apple added to the detritus on his shirt.

'You're a pig,' said Alleluya.

Brag smiled.

'Yes, you are,' said Angel. 'Why can't you keep your mouth shut?'

Ezra said, 'It's not only Brag, is it?'

'Will someone please tell me what you're talking about?' requested Hare.

Ezra sighed. 'The Diggers are marginals who live underground,' he said. 'No-one knows about them except other marginals. They're anxious that the police shouldn't find out about them, and so no-one who joins a marginal house is told about them until they've lived there for three months. That's why we didn't tell you.'

'Damn silly rule,' growled Brag.

'It isn't a rule. It's their request, and we respect it. Or some of us do.'

'When you say they live underground,' said Hare, 'you mean they live in hiding?'

'No,' said Angel. 'They live *underground.*'

'Underground where?' said Hare, bewildered.

Brag pointed to the floor.

'They live in the tunnels, dearie,' said Big Gwen, 'and I don't know how they can stand it myself, but I'm sure it's very admirable.'

'What tunnels?' said Hare.

'I think it's stupid,' said Brag.

'Well, you would,' said Alleluya. 'You don't understand that some people might have principles, and might want to live by them.'

'But they don't live by them,' said Brag. 'If they really cut themselves off from the world they'd be dead. What would they eat?'

Mr Beechcroft lowered the three-month-old gardening magazine in which he had been immersed since the start of the conversation, and said, 'The fact that something can't be done perfectly isn't a reason for not trying to do it at all.'

'Wonderful,' said Brag. 'Should we knock the glass out of the windows again?'

'I think this is a very silly conversation,' said Big Gwen.

'It is, but we might as well finish it,' said Angel. 'I don't see the point of making yourself miserable for the sake of a principle, particularly when the principle can only be half-aplied. And what's more, I won't be told that because I like a window to have glass in it that makes me a materialist. I grew up in a place – '

'Here we go,' said Brag.

'Listen, you dirty old windbag, I know what poverty is,' said Angel. 'And I can tell you, being able to *choose* to do without things is a luxury. You don't realise how lucky we are. It's sheer hypocrisy, what goes on in this house.'

His scorn had a chilling effect. They sat in silence for

several minutes under their canopy of smoke. Eventually Ezra said, 'Well, as we're all here, or at least all here except Filthy, who can't be persuaded to get off the stairs, perhaps we can talk about something we might agree on instead of something we have never been able to agree on. Gwen has suggested that we have a rota for gathering as well as a rota for cooking, the reason being – '

'I'm against it,' said Brag.

Everyone sighed.

'You haven't heard the reason,' said Ezra.

'I don't need to hear the reason. I'm against it on principle.'

'You're against everything that makes it easier for people to know what they're doing,' said Big Gwen. 'It took us two months to get you to agree to the cooking rota.'

'Which he never keeps to anyway,' said Alleluya. She narrowed her eyes at Brag. 'When did you last cook a meal?'

'No-one would eat it if he did,' said Angel.

'Rotas,' pronounced Brag, 'are a form of compulsion. If my name is down on a rota, somebody is telling me what to do. I reject that.'

'We know you do,' murmured Mr Beechcroft.

'It's a violation of first principles as far as I'm concerned. Voluntary co-operation, that's what we live by, isn't it? *Voluntary.*' He struck the edge of the sofa with his hand. 'That is a sacred word. *Voluntary.*'

'What about "co-operation"?' suggested Hare.

Ezra said, 'The only principle you understand is that Brag should never have to do any work. If you had your way no meeting would ever reach any decision and no decision if it was reached would be adhered to, and as a result no community you belonged to would survive longer than a week. Now, will you please shut up and let us get on with something.'

Mr Beechcroft suggested that a sheet of paper be put up

in the kitchen each week so that people could put their names down against the day they preferred to go gathering. Brag said that that was a rota. Alleluya said it wasn't, because people would be bound only by their own word, which they ought to be anyway.

'Why don't we take a vote on it?' asked Hare, before he remembered. A pained look passed across the faces of the others.

'What is the general feeling?' asked Ezra.

At that moment the door opened and a dreadful smell came in.

'Oh my God,' said everyone in unison. 'Filthy!'

His eyes in a grimed face were beseeching. His hands hung at his sides with a helpless air and the fingers flexed involuntarily. There was excrement at the bottom of his trouser leg and over his shoe.

'Poppy,' said Filthy. 'Poppy, poppy.'

Big Gwen got up, took him by the hand and led him from the room. A few moments later there came from along the landing the sound of gurgling pipes and splashing water.

They sat and waited, not talking. After a while the door opened and Big Gwen came back with Filthy. His face was radiant. He was holding the object he had been crooning to on the stairs. It was a child's doll. 'Poppy,' he exclaimed, and waved it for them.

In the vehicle shed of the Company paper mills, Hare saw something so huge that at first he thought it was part of the structure of the building. Then it started to move and, astonished, he saw the wheels. The man in the driving cab sat twenty feet above the ground.

It pulled out of the shed, moving like Leviathan. The signs covered it like red flies. ANGER, ANGER, ANGER.

7

'I hope you don't mind my renewing the acquaintance,' said Mr Terry. He stirred his coffee and replaced the spoon in the saucer with a discreet chink. 'I like to keep in touch, and I'm sure there aren't many people more informed about the workings of the Company than yourself.'

What does he want, thought Jacobs.

'It isn't really information I'm after at the moment,' mused Mr Terry. 'More an exchange of views. I doubt if there's much you can tell me that's specific. These things are intangible, more often than not. An understanding, a sympathy. I'm sure you know what I mean.' He paused, smiling vaguely, and Jacobs watched him. 'You must be aware,' he pursued, 'that there has been at times a closeness between elements of the Company and the police force which could best be described as improper.'

Jacobs kept his gaze steady and allowed a faint surprise to cross his face.

'I can't say that I was aware of it, no.'

'No? Direct communications between Company wholesale departments and police supplies departments, for instance? That practice is utterly unfamiliar to you?'

Jacobs writhed under the sarcasm. The sort of contact to which Mr Terry was referring was almost routine. It was also completely illegal. All communications between the Company and the police departments it supplied were supposed to be

116

channelled through the Council, down to the most minor telephone call. The process was exceedingly cumbersome but there were good reasons for it. Jacobs was not prepared for this line of enquiry, and was not sure how to handle it. In a more confident mood he might have denied the allegation outright. But there was something about Mr Terry which sapped his confidence; indeed there was something about Mr Terry which made his blood run cold.

He decided on modified frankness. It seldom let him down.

'I can't pretend I've never heard of it,' he admitted. 'This is a very large organisation, Mr Terry, and large organisations can be unwieldy, and as a result an employee occasionally tries to cut corners. Frankly, I can't always condemn that. There are times when it's good commercial practice. Just once in a while someone cuts a corner which must not be cut. That I deplore. But in the circumstances it's not altogether unpredictable. We deal with it very severely.'

'I'm sure you do,' agreed Mr Terry, 'when you find the offender. What sort of cases have you come across?'

Jacobs swore inwardly at having been so simply trapped.

'Mostly misguided zeal. An order comes through for certain equipment, the equipment is not available in the quantity required, or the specifications have been changed so that the order can't be fulfilled exactly, and some clerk will pick up the phone and speak to the police department for which the order is destined instead of to the ministry department which ordered it, simply because it's more efficient.'

'More efficient?' enquired Mr Terry coldly.

'The ministry will have to consult the police anyway. Often the police are the only people who can answer our chap's query. It can save . . .' Jacobs bit his lip, having been about to say 'months'. 'It can save a lot of time.'

'And that is thought more important than legality?'

The scorn in Mr Terry's voice angered Jacobs more than

117

anything that had been said so far, but he kept his face expressionless. 'As I say, I deplore it.'

'You deplore it,' repeated the immaculate representative of the ruling caste opposite him. 'I will be open with you, Mr Jacobs. Misguided zealots in the cause of efficiency are neither here nor there as far as I'm concerned: I'm after bigger fry.' His eyes, which had been fixed on a point on the wall just above Jacobs's shoulder, now came to rest on Jacobs's own, and Jacobs had the frightful sensation of his brain being burrowed into. 'Deliberate and systematic evasion of the Council's supervision, that is what I'm talking about.'

'From what motive?' frowned Jacobs.

'Let's say a combination of things. Cutting corners can become a habit, can't it? After a while it is unthinkable to take the proper, cumbersome route. But the main motive, I would say, was a criminal one. The Council's supervision was evaded because the law was already being broken. Have you any knowledge of chemical agents being manufactured for the police after the Act was passed specifically prohibiting it?'

Jacobs looked shocked. 'No. Nor can I believe it.'

'It's difficult to believe, I grant you. But evidence exists. Not very much, as yet, but I think we shall find more of it. If we do find more, Mr Jacobs . . .' he stared for a moment out of the window before returning his amiable, intelligent gaze to Jacobs's face ' – it is obviously very serious. It will be a conspiracy we're talking about. You understand me? A conspiracy between elements of the Company and elements of the police force.'

Jacobs understood him perfectly.

'I don't see . . .' he began, shaking his head.

'The point of such a conspiracy? It could be just opportunism. The police want the equipment – we know that, they lobbied very hard against the Act – and the Company wants the sale, and perhaps to keep a production line open, or something of the sort. And both of them know that the amount involved can be hidden quite easily in the annual security estimates. But I don't think the motive is quite as simple as that. I referred earlier to a mutual sympathy. Frankly, Mr Jacobs, I think the police and the Company have been getting friendlier with each other than is healthy, and friendship in itself can be a motive in some circumstances.'

'I'm sorry, I still don't understand,' said Jacobs, and this time it was the truth.

'The function of the police force is primarily to uphold the law and protect the lawful government,' said Mr Terry sweetly. 'It is only secondarily, if at all, to protect a *style* of government or a commercial enterprise, whatever that enterprise may be.'

'But surely,' Jacobs protested, 'the government normally instructs the police to protect the said commercial enterprise as part of its duties?'

'That is precisely my point,' said Mr Terry. 'You are assuming an identity of interest. I am not so sanguine. Believe me, Mr Jacobs, governments trust no-one. They cannot. Moreover, it is not their function to.'

Jacobs stared at his desk. He had been right in thinking there was more to this soft-talking councillor than met the eye. Mr Terry appeared to know something that Jacobs himself had not caught wind of. He seemed to be hinting, not merely at a conspiracy to deceive the Council, but at a political conspiracy against it. Could the Company be involved in that? He remembered Drawbridge and its sudden urgency, and with an unpleasant sensation he recognised that behind such Company secrets as he knew lurked others which might dwarf or even nullify them. What was it Mr Terry knew? This might be bluff, or some elaborate ploy. But, whatever it was, it spelt danger, because the mere fact that Mr Terry was playing his hand in this way meant that events were moving fast in the Council, and that Mr Terry was on top of them.

'You are afraid,' said Jacobs, 'that in certain circumstances the police might decide their loyalty was to the Company, not the Council?'

Mr Terry spread his hands in a deprecating movement. As usual, Jacobs had been too crude.

'I find that astonishing,' said Jacobs.

'I could astonish you further. The corruption in the police force is widespread. We're taking what steps we can: internal enquiries, transfers; in some cases dismissal. Discreetly, of course.'

A purge, thought Jacobs wildly. He needed a drink, but it was only eleven o'clock in the morning.

'Corruption in the police force,' he repeated, trying to gain time to think.

'I'm afraid so,' said Mr Terry. 'So now you see, I'm sure, why I am so concerned about this casual liaison between the police and Company employees. However trifling the level on which it occurs, we simply cannot overlook it any longer.'

'Forget it,' said Jacobs. 'I can't do it. Things have changed.'

'They'd better not have,' said Koberg.

They were sitting in a riverside bar frequented by ruperts. The walls were white and silver, the counter was stainless steel, and behind it was a long mirror surrounded by little white lights which flicked on and off. There was loud and continuous music. Young people came and went, talking shrilly, knocking against Jacobs's chair and not apologising. Koberg had insisted on this meeting place. Jacobs, after ten minutes in it, had a bad headache.

'It's out of my hands,' said Jacobs, trying a smile and an I-can't-help-it shrug. 'Notice has been taken in high places of certain irregularities. More to the point, action is being

taken. If you've seen any policemen disappear rather suddenly into civilian life that might have something to do with
it.'

Koberg darted him a sharp look.

'At the moment,' clarified Jacobs, 'the police force is under
scrutiny for corruption. Contacts between the police and the
Company are also under scrutiny.'

'Whose scrutiny?' demanded Koberg.

'The Council's.'

Koberg gave an incredulous laugh. Blond, fashionably-
coiffed heads turned in their direction. Jacobs began to
sweat.

'Don't tell me you're frightened of *them*!' jeered Koberg.
'Since when have they been able to do anything?'

'I told you things had changed.'

'You can't tell me they've changed that much. The Council
couldn't wipe its own arse.'

'There are new men at the top. I've just been talking to
one of them. They'll be wiping a lot more than arses before
they've finished. Meanwhile I'm looking after mine, and if
you're wise you'll do the same. They mean business, Koberg.'

'Listen,' said Koberg, 'I don't give a fuck about your
problems. You agreed to do something for me, in return for
something I did for you, and I want delivery.'

'I *can't* deliver,' said Jacobs, exasperated. 'It could cost me
my job.'

'Tough,' said Koberg.

'It could also cost you yours.'

Koberg had not thought of that. Jacobs saw the expression
on the young, girlishly good-looking face – surprised and
hurt, as if a friend had let him down. Then the face assumed
a calculating look. Koberg thought rapidly and said, 'No, it
wouldn't. All I've done is apply for a transfer, which I'm
entitled to do. We met because I was involved in that Inquiry
you were doing: nothing wrong with that. And you were

impressed by my work and decided to put in a good word for me with certain people you know when you heard I was looking for a transfer.' He considered it, with a look of satisfaction. 'Nothing in that to lose me my job.'

'What you don't seem to grasp,' said Jacobs, 'is that it doesn't matter how we happened to meet or even who we are. The only thing that matters is that an employee of the Company would be seen trying to obtain a favour for a member of the police force, and in the circumstances that is out of the question.'

'Have you tried?'

'For heaven's sake,' snapped Jacobs, 'there is a *plot*. The Company and the police are both involved. The Council are running about like terriers looking for evidence. A request from me wouldn't even be considered, don't you understand that?'

There was a moment of silence. Koberg's face was stiff with anger. He said, 'I don't like being talked to like that. I don't like being taken for a fool, either.' Nearly half a minute passed in even heavier silence, and then he burst out bitterly, 'You haven't even tried, and you won't try. How do I know what you're saying is true? I can't check it, can I? Who can I ask? Ring up Lady Lucy and say, "Excuse me, Mr Lucy, you won't remember me but I had the honour to be in the same room with you recently; is it all right if your Mr Jacobs puts in a word for me at HQ?" I'd get a long way like that, wouldn't I?'

His voice had risen and they were attracting openly curious glances from the other customers. 'Shh,' said Jacobs, seriously alarmed by the uttering of Mr Lucy's name in a place like this.

'You think you can put one over on me because of who you are,' went on Koberg vehemently, and to Jacobs's surprise. 'Well, let me remind you of something, *Mister* Jacobs. *I've* got something on *you*.' He lowered his voice

122

and leant forward, stabbing the table with his finger. 'I could finish you.'

His head came up and Jacobs, shocked, stared into his cold seawater eyes.

'Don't think I wouldn't,' whispered Koberg.

Jacobs's brain went numb. Not all of it: a small bit stayed on alert and prompted him to mutter, 'You'd finish yourself as well.'

'Not if I confess,' said Koberg. 'Not if I say you threatened me if I didn't do it, and I haven't had a good night's sleep since, and I've resolved to make a clean breast of everything. I think those new men you're talking about might rather like the sound of it.'

They would, too, thought Jacobs, cold with fear. The boy had no idea what he was saying, but his instinct was diabolically sure. What a stupid, ugly and horrible thing blackmail was.

But it was bluff! Relief flooded him. Of course it was bluff. Koberg would have to be crazy to . . .

And that was the trouble. The relief ebbed away. For Koberg was not crazy, but he was not entirely sane either. Something was making him desperate. He could be tipped quite easily.

'And think about this,' continued Koberg. 'I'm just a humble policeman, I've just been doing my job, and perhaps I took it a bit too far. But *you* . . .'

'I've just been doing my job, too,' cut in Jacobs angrily.

There was a momentary silence, caused by Koberg's surprise at being interrupted, and in the lull it afforded Jacobs thought about what had just been said. He had indeed considered at the time that he was doing his job in the only way it could be done. He had not realised until this moment that Koberg would naturally apply the same description to what *he* had done. He had thought that in Koberg's case the criminal element would be so apparent that not even Koberg could overlook it. But now here was Koberg, flushed, of all things, with self-righteousness . . .

Jacobs's gorge rose. He turned away to hide his distaste.

'You think I'm shit, don't you?' Koberg had noticed and his bitterness was intense. 'You're all like it. You sit in cosy offices and get other people to do your dirty work, and then you wrinkle up your noses, ever so fussy, when you see us, because we smell. It was *your* instructions.'

'You made a mess of it,' growled Jacobs. 'I told you just to burn the building down.'

'He never fucking left it, did he? I didn't have any choice.'

'You could have got him out of there on some pretext.'

'What pretext? I tell you he never left it. He had friends who did all his shopping. You mean I should've arrested him and then burned the place down? Don't be stupid. You don't know what you're talking about.' His face had darkened with anger. 'He could have got out, you know,' he said. 'He was just too frightened.'

Jacobs stood up, went to the bar, and got two more drinks. The beer was very expensive here, which was probably why Koberg had specified the place. While he was waiting for the beer he ordered a brandy as well, and drank it at a gulp. He returned to the table, his head slightly clearer.

Koberg greeted him with a friendly smile. 'Tell you what,' said Koberg. 'I'll take it on trust, what you say about not being able to oblige me. But one favour deserves another, and it happens that I'm short of money. A couple of thousand in cash, and I'll never bother you again.'

'Go to hell,' said Jacobs, 'you disgusting little rat.'

Koberg got up, walked past him and out of the bar.

In a room high above the city traffic Mr J J Lucy sat late. The room was a large and pleasant one, decorated in pastel shades and with the angularity of its furniture relieved by a

124

number of well-grown foliage plants. Against one wall was a tall bookcase whose contents bore very little relation to the Company's business. Thick rugs covered the floor. Mr Lucy did not believe that the room in which one spends most of one's working life should be merely functional.

There were charts on his desk, intricate and coloured, drawn by a lowly clerk in Records who should have been an artist. Mr Lucy appreciated art and regretted its banishment. He had hopes of its reinstatement within a few years when the current upheaval in the Council had faded from memory. There had been a dearth of culture for too long, Mr Lucy considered; life had taken on a coarseness of fibre which he found depressing.

His eyes skimmed over the charts. They showed the trading figures for past two months of the Company's various departments. Some of them would have puzzled middle-tier managers who knew what their departments had done in the past two months and would have expected to see this performance reflected in the zigzagging coloured lines. Mr Lucy scanned the charts for other information, and was content with what he saw.

He got up from his chair and walked to the window. It was a fine evening; in the bluish dusk, over the tops of the buildings in which lights were beginning to glimmer, he could see for a long way. He stood for a while looking. He saw banks, offices, factories, streets of houses and shops, the few miles of track where the underground railway ran above ground, the patches of dereliction where new building had not yet started, and the snaking river. Moving upward, his gaze met a dark band which ran the whole breadth of the window. This was the wall of the Zone. Briefly Mr Lucy raised his eyes and looked at what lay beyond the wall, then he turned away from the window and went back to his desk.

From a drawer he took a pair of binoculars. If one had an eagle's-eye view, one might as well make the most of it, and

Mr Lucy amused himself from time to time in observing the activities of people who did not know they were being observed. It relaxed him, and it was always useful to learn about the oddities of human nature.

Some of them really were odd; and now, just as people were switching on the lights in their houses but had in some cases forgotten to draw the curtains, was a good time to observe.

He took a wide sweep with the glasses, returned to a particular window and, with an incredulous smile, corrected the focus.

8

Hare was out gathering with Ezra when a woman in a ragged red dress walked past him.

He and Ezra were investigating a mound of rubble on a building site. They were working by matchlight, since Ezra disapproved of the torches provided by Angel and the street lamp was not near enough.

As the woman walked past, Hare glanced up and burnt his fingers for the third time. It was the woman he had seen on his walks in the Shuttle.

'What's the matter?' said Ezra, deep in rubble. 'Milkmen?'

He straightened up and saw her. 'Ah,' he said.

'Who is she?' asked Hare.

'She's one of the Diggers.'

Hare supposed he had known this when he asked the question.

'Do you know her?' he said.

'Slightly. Her name is Danny. She is . . . well respected.'

'You mean she's one of their leaders?'

'They don't have leaders,' said Ezra primly.

'I'm going after her,' said Hare.

Ezra hesitated, then said, 'May I ask why?'

'I want to find out more about the Diggers.'

'I could tell you a lot about them,' said Ezra, 'but no doubt you would prefer to get the information at first hand.'

The woman had reached the street corner. Hare became impatient: if he didn't hurry he would lose sight of her again.

'I'm sorry,' he said, and on impulse grasped Ezra's hand. 'I'm very grateful to you. I'll come back.'

'Do you hope to find your wife among the Diggers?' asked Ezra.

'I suppose I do.'

'The message from your wife came through the Diggers,' said Ezra, 'but she is not with them. A written message was left with them. They don't know where she is.' He grasped Hare's hand in a shy gesture. 'Good luck.'

Hare was angry that this information had been kept from him for so long, but Ezra's face in the lamplight looked so sad that he could not reproach him. He turned away and set off after Danny.

He followed her for several minutes, gradually gaining on her, not wanting to run, and then half way down a long street she vanished. He did run then, and at the spot where he had last seen her found a narrow alleyway obstructed by overflowing dustbins. As he started walking down it a cat shot towards him and got under his feet. There was no sign of Danny. After a few yards the alley came to a dead end with a high brick wall.

Hare studied the possibilities. A fire escape, a drainpipe and a high window not in reach of either. None looked likely. Then he saw the grating in the wall, set a foot above the ground, half-obscured by the shadow of the fire escape. It was a door, he was sure of it.

With his fingers hooked in the holes, he tried for several minutes to move it. It was unyielding. He had begun to think he was wrong, when unexpectedly it shifted and swung outwards, hinged vertically as an ordinary door would be.

Standing there beside the opening, uncertain what to do next, he was struck by the fact that if a passer-by happened to see him the consequences might be disastrous for whoever lived on the other side of the grating. He had propelled himself through the gap in fear of being seen, and closed the grille behind him, before the realisation of what he was doing could stop him. For it was pitch dark and he had no torch, and his feet were on a steep and narrow spiral staircase that descended he knew not where, and behind him the grating had shut with a businesslike click.

He could not open it again.

He could only go down. He did not even know if the stairs continued: they might break off a few steps below the top, he might be inches from a sheer drop into infinity. A very faint light came through the grating; it was not enough to see by, it merely confused his eyes. Thank God he had matches.

He struck one, and the first flare showed him eight, ten iron treads spiralling down into darkness. If the top was sound, so probably was the rest. He would go cautiously, testing each step. The stairs could not go down to any great depth . . .

But they might. In his mind's eye an endless staircase unrolled, to which he was stuck as to flypaper.

Steadying himself, he began to descend. It was not too bad as long as he thought only about the bit of staircase he was on, and not what was above and below him. There was a slight elasticity in the staircase, the steps sprang a little with his weight. They clanged, too, under his leather soles. The clanging echoed round and round in the small space, becoming another element, like the darkness, through which he must descend.

The darkness grew denser.

He began counting. This was pointless because he had not started counting at the top, but it gave his brain something to do. After twenty he paused and lit a match, and broke into sweat. He was suspended in an abyss. The walls pressed towards him. The earth had been cored like an apple and he was falling down the middle of it. He dropped the match as the flame burnt his fingers, and saw it extinguished almost immediately in the draught of air as it fell.

He continued downwards. Twenty-eight, twenty-nine, thirty . . . forty . . . fifty . . . Then he was stumbling on the level, and chuckling with relief. Under his feet was earth: damp, solid. Above his head . . . he would not think about that.

Stretching his arm, he found the wall. It was rough to his fingertips, dry, and sloped inward as his hand followed it up.

Another match. He must be careful with them; but at this moment he had to see. He struck one, forgetting to position the box first near the area he wanted to see, so that in order to inspect the wall he had to carry the lighted match to it and the match blew out. Cursing, he lit another one, and brought it cautiously up the wall. It showed enough for him to risk moving sideways to the other wall, a few paces away. He scanned with the match until it burnt him.

He was in a tunnel, about twelve feet in diameter, dry and well ventilated.

He began to walk forward slowly, his fingertips keeping contact with the wall on his right. The floor was even, and he was reasonably confident of not tripping or falling down a hole; nevertheless the darkness was like a hand across his face, and from time to time he had to stop and light a match although he knew he should save them. There had been about thirty in the box when he left Ezra, and he did not know how far he would have to go in the tunnel before he found . . . what? Perhaps the woman in the red dress had not come through the grating at all.

His fingers encountered something flat, smooth and circular, slightly raised from the surface of the wall. In the centre of it was a shallow depression into which the tip of his middle finger fitted neatly. It felt like a switch of some kind. He pressed it.

There was an explosion of light. He shrank against the wall with his arm flung across his eyes, irrationally terrified not of the brightness but of what it might bring. As the moments passed and nothing happened, only the clicking and buzzing of the lights overhead, he lowered his arm and looked.

The walls were not, as he had thought, quite bare. Along each one, not far above the floor, ran three or four black-sheathed cables as thick as his wrist. They were covered with a sticky-looking layer of dust. He touched one and his finger came away black: the rubber coating had started to perish.

Hare began to walk along the tunnel between the two sets of cables. The fact that he could see, and therefore be seen, made him again conscious of the noise he was making, and varying his pace only seemed to make the noise louder. The lights were quite feeble in some places. Scarcely had he noticed this than he saw that he was in fact coming to the end of the lighted stretch.

He walked on into the growing gloom. He had been scanning the walls for another switch and now at last he saw one, but it was encrusted with greenish mould. He pressed it; nothing happened.

He slowed his pace, giving his eyes time to adjust to the diminution of light. But after a further hundred yards, when it was barely light enough for him to see the glimmer of his hand resting against the wall, the tunnel curved sharply and he was in total darkness.

Hare was frightened, and wondered at his stupidity in not being frightened earlier, or at least not frightened enough to turn back. He realised he had nothing with him to eat or drink. He had a horrifying vision of himself crawling, dying of thirst, through a labyrinth of tunnels in the dark. He must turn back now, before he was too tired and began making stupid mistakes, like forgetting the direction he was walking in.

He remembered he had been unable to open the grating from the inside. In his present situation, the problem seemed a minor one. It was not that that drew him cautiously forward when he knew he should turn back, but the thought of facing again the total darkness of the first stage of his journey, when if he edged a little further he might find another light switch. Thus edging, with his groping hand thrust out along the wall, he pitched over something at knee-height and fell headlong.

He sat up and felt around the edges of the thing he had fallen over. It was roughly cubic, with a dampish clinging feel to the fingers. He struck a match.

Coarse grey paper, moulding slightly, but not so much as to obliterate the familiar green stamp: a man in armour, holding in one hand a sword, in the other a bird's nest. The paper was soft with damp. He ripped it off.

There were lots of cardboard cartons, soft but still intact. The match burnt down to his fingers and he dropped it with a yelp. Without lighting another one, he opened the end of a carton and explored its contents. Long cylindrical objects, cold but not metallic . . . dynamite? He drew his hand back as though stung, but then made himself touch the cylinders again, because the sensation reminded him of something. Something banal, domestic, lifesaving. He dug his nail into one and with a pleasure remembered from childhood felt a soft brittle crumb flake up between nail and skin.

He struck a match, and stared bemused in its tiny light at fifty boxes of Universal Goods premium quality wax candles.

But for the candles he might have turned back; but how could he refuse a gift so munificent and bizarre? Moreover the candles had sharpened his curiosity. If he found candles, what else might he not find? He lit one, put a couple more in his pocket, and set off again.

He still had to walk quite slowly, because he was afraid of blowing out the candle flame, but he was grateful for the companionable light. On the other hand, the shadows it cast on the walls of the tunnel were horrifying. He began, for the first time, to feel trapped. He was trapped with himself in a tunnel. He stopped and raised his left hand, outspread, between the candle flame and the wall, and saw a monstrous shape delineated. That was his hand. Useless to call it a trick of the light when it was as true a representation of his hand as any other.

It was then he came to the wall. The tunnel seemed to brighten fractionally, and his heart lifted, until he saw that the light was being thrown back by some obstruction. He went over it carefully with the candle. The tunnel had been blocked off. A blank, unbroken brick wall: nothing written on it, nothing stacked against it, just the wall at the end of the tunnel.

But this could not be all? People didn't sink a shaft to connect with a tunnel that went nowhere? Or had he missed something? Moving the candle from side to side, he saw that the cables had disappeared.

Hare was now very tired and wanted to sit down, but knew that he must not. He started to retrace his steps.

He had made a note of the time when he started off after finding the candles. From then until the time when he came to the brick wall it had been roughly forty minutes. Being tired, he was probably walking more slowly now, but it still seemed to be taking a very long time to get back to the corner where he had stumbled over the boxes, and from where he would see, further down the tunnel, light. When he looked at his watch, he saw that he had been walking back for more than an hour.

Either he had not passed the corner where the boxes were,

133

or he had walked straight past it and into an unsuspected passage which was a continuation of the one which ended with the wall. In either case, he was now in a different part of the tunnel. To put it another way, he was lost.

He fought down his panic, and walked on.

Without warning he came to a break in the wall to his right, and explored it with the candle. There was a door. Fixed to the door was a rectangle of card, soft with mould, on which lettering was faintly discernible. He cleaned it with his sleeve and peered at it. It said, 'MUSEUM STAFF ONLY'.

A horizontal metal bar was fixed at hand-height. Hare lifted it: the door creaked open and inward, and as he stepped forward all the lights went on.

He stood still in astonishment. He was in a natural cavern whose walls rose to a shadowy ceiling from which hung clusters of lights on chains. The light was all directed downwards, brilliantly illuminating the walls, and on the walls hung row upon row of oil paintings culled from three centuries of art.

Hare snuffed out his candle and looked.

They were beautiful, the paintings, very beautiful; they were more beautiful in this hard, harsh place beneath the earth than they could ever have been in a properly lit gallery with polished floors underfoot. But it was their humanity rather than their beauty that touched him: the alert, inquiring gaze of a fish-seller; a child, pensive over his lesson; a young woman, intent, writing a letter; a man laughing; a man in a rapture of prayer; a man touching, very gently, the hand of his wife. This is what it is to be human, thought Hare: the richness, the pain, the at times intolerable difficulty.

He began to walk round the walls. Everything was here: the mixed inheritance of the race. Faith, cruelty, tenderness, fear. Lust. Grace. This is what we are, thought Hare, and

134

pity filled him. He had never thought about it before, the great company of which he was a part, to which he was bound in every cell, by every scrap of bone.

He sat down on a packing case, for he was exhausted, and closed his eyes. The paintings swarmed round him.

He slept for two hours. It was warm in the cavern: there must be a mechanism for keeping the paintings at the right temperature and humidity. He left them with reluctance.

The tunnel was damper now. Once his foot slipped on slime. There were once again cables running along the sides, but always they were covered in a sticky greenish mould, and when he touched one its protective coating flaked away, revealing some webbed material. Six hours by his watch after he entered the tunnels, Hare came to a place where he sensed the passage widening. He followed the wall on his right, lost the other wall, and felt the roof lift above his head. He raised the candle: nothing, a black sky. The air here was damper than he had yet felt it, and as he stopped to rest he heard the rustle and plop of water, and once or twice a tinny reverberation which his fatigued brain could not account for and dismissed.

Tentatively he moved forward, keeping to the wall. Now that he was not pressed in on both sides by the walls of a tunnel he realised how comforting had been that confinement. Now there was space all round him, and his imagination began to fill it.

Looming shapes. A blackness deeper than the blackness he walked in, a blackness superimposed on blackness. An impression of rectangles, something blocky . . . a building? No, no. He pushed himself on.

He stopped, shuddering, at a huge skeletal arm flung across his path. If he walked on he would walk into it, if it was there. However, to walk round or duck beneath it meant acknowledging that it *was* there. And if it was there, that

135

broken, bony nightmare, what other phantoms were lurking in the greater pool of darkness beyond?

Afraid more of his fear than its cause, he went towards the bony thing; but at the last moment his courage failed and he flinched away. He half-ducked, half-turned in an awkward movement. Something caught his foot and he pitched forward, falling painfully among a lot of hard, sharp-edged objects which bruised his shins and lacerated his wrist. Winded, he grasped the flaring candle but could then do no more than stare about him, and as he stared the most terrifying shape of all defined itself in the flickering light, the inevitable conformation which for hour upon hour he had striven in the dark tunnels not to see. A face. The pale glimmering eyes were a full arm's reach apart, the fanged mouth was monstrous.

He yelled, but the sound was tiny, and before he could yell again he felt his strength slipping away, and then the darkness closed in like a bag drawn tight.

There was an arm round his shoulders. He became conscious simultaneously of the pressure, of a rocking motion, and of a smell. The smell was pungent and sour, and contained a peculiar mustiness. Hare opened his eyes. He was in the embrace of a rancid bundle of rags, which now attempted to pour something down his throat. He shook his head and struggled to his knees. His knees hurt.

'Are you all right?' asked the ragged man. He had a thin face, wispily bearded, and looked worried. Hare saw this by the light of a powerful torch set on the ground.

'Yes, thank you,' he said.

'I heard you shout,' said the ragged man. 'What happened?'

'I fell,' said Hare. He felt stupid and wished to say as little as possible. He picked up the torch and directed it upwards.

There, still, were the pale watchful orbs, and below them the leering mouth.

In the torchlight, however . . .

He flicked the beam back and forth until he was sure. A metal face pocked and pitted with decay, a face on which glistened in the torchlight a dew of rust, while the chrome of the great headlamps was blistered and green. On their upper surface, on the engine covering and inside the cab, was a thick, black, soft-looking layer of something veined with furry whitish mould.

'Bats,' said the ragged man. 'There's a chimney high up in the rock, it goes to the surface. That's why the air's so fresh. Stupid of them, they should have thought of bats.'

'What is that thing?' asked Hare.

'A tractor,' said his rescuer. 'What did you think it was, a dragon?' He giggled, a sound like a squeaky violin. 'I'm surprised you came in without a torch. Which way did you come?'

'I came down a metal staircase and got lost,' said Hare.

'As good a way as any,' said the ragged man. 'We've counted forty-nine entrances so far. Sure you won't have some water?'

He proffered again the flask which Hare had refused. This time Hare accepted. The water was delicious.

'My name's Tapper,' said the ragged man. 'Shall we go?' He began to walk away, pursuing a winding path across the floor of the cavern, turning the beam of his torch in this direction and that. Hare followed as best he could. Tapper, as he walked, muttered to himself — or perhaps he was muttering to the other occupants of the cavern, who sprang into ghostly life in the torchbeam as if summoned by it.

Axles, pumps, coach-springs. Fuel tanks. Wheels as big as a small car. Cabs like museum cases, cabs like garden sheds, cabs like sedan chairs. A coiled chain, each iron link the circumference of a child's waist, rusted into a pyramid.

Round-nosed radiators, lorries that looked like boats. Batteries deliquescing in ancient puddles. Something shadowy crouching above caterpillar tracks. A steel hook the size of his head, dangling inches from his head. On every vertical surface, the sad orange dew of rust. On every horizontal surface, and springing softly underfoot, the black, white-veined crust of droppings.

Then – 'That's impossible!' cried Hare.

Or should be. He had not seen a steam locomotive since he was a small boy. If this iron mountain should ever clank its way back into the light, half the population would have to be told what it was. Not that it ever would move again. The bolts had rusted through, allowing the metal engine-covering to slip forward and rust to pit the casing; the funnel was badly corroded and the footplate encrusted with filth. The great piston-driven wheels looked as if they had the will to turn again, but the rails had warped and rusted to the wheel-rims, and, most ridiculous, the front of the train had stuck to the buffers against which it rested while the lower part of the buffers had rotted away, so that it looked like a giant with a pair of toy spectacles stuck to his moustache.

'How the devil was that brought in here?' wondered Hare.

'Some of the tunnels have track running through them. There are links with the deeper levels of the underground system.'

Hare remembered the doors on the station platforms. His bewilderment deepened. 'When was it brought here? It must have been years ago. All this stuff must be thirty years old or more.'

'That's right.'

'But why is it here? Why has it just been left to rot? What is it all *for*?'

'It was forgotten about,' said Tapper. 'Nobody could see it, it was underground. It wasn't supposed to exist at all. It existed only on a piece of paper, and the piece of paper was mislaid. It happens all the time in offices.'

He set off again, with Hare stumbling behind him.

The cavern of the engines was only the first of a series of caverns linked by passageways. Picking his way along behind the Digger, Hare tried to make sense of the shapes half-defined by the torchbeam. One of the caverns was almost filled with wooden crates or tea-chests; there was just a lane down the middle through which they walked. One appeared to be empty until he collided at the end of it with a collection of birdcages. Another was piled high with office desks, a fourth was devoted to rolls of wire netting and rotary lawnmowers. Sometimes the labels on crates could be deciphered. Thus at the end of an hour Hare knew that the caves contained paper clips, rulers, zip fasteners, primus stoves, candles, saucepans, typewriter ribbons, rat poison, enamel mugs, bicycle pumps, lead pencils, nylon string, saw blades, plastic spoons, garden shovels and paint, all beneath a thick layer of bat droppings. But after an hour he was too tired to care.

'I have to sit down,' he said. 'And I'm hungry.'

'We're nearly there,' said Tapper.

Ahead – or was it exhaustion playing tricks with his eyes? – the darkness seemed less dense. Hare walked mechanically, placing his feet along the safe level path shown by the torch. The brightness was not illusory: it increased, and at last his companion stopped and switched off his torch, and Hare saw that they were in another cavern, as large as the one where the machines had been, lit by long fluorescent tubes which hung ticking and crackling from a rock ceiling some distance above.

Rows of sacks covered the floor of the cavern. Tapper began to walk between them.

The sacks had once been neatly piled to a height of about eight feet. But everywhere the rows had bulged and crumbled like the walls of a ruined castle, so that some of the corridors were blocked with tumbled sacks and some were overhung with an arching wall that threatened to collapse on whoever walked beneath it. In places the walls had windows: sacks had been pulled loose from a bulging section, leaving a gap which for some reason had not yet caved in, as if the sacks were stuck together.

And some of them were, he saw. They were covered in a glistening sticky exudation which had hardened like glue. He prodded a fallen sack – it was stiff and resistant. He sniffed the stickiness on his finger, then tested it cautiously with his tongue. Sugar.

At once he set off in pursuit of the Digger, who now was not to be seen. Hare tripped over fallen sacks of sugar, hurried down blind alleys of sugar and had to retrace his steps, banged his head on overhanging slabs of sugar, and found, at last, his guide sitting on a small platform of bags of sugar stabbing a penknife into a sack and scooping the sugar into his palm. He licked it and grinned. 'Hungry?'

'I can't live on sugar,' objected Hare.

'Pity. It's what we've got most of.'

Tapper got up and shook himself, scattering sugar, and set off down another corridor. Hare followed. As corridor succeeded corridor, Hare was surprised to find how much could be inferred from the appearance of a sack. The sacks further on were much larger than the sugar sacks and contained, it might be assumed, a lighter substance. The hessian was a paler colour and a coarser weave, and was covered in a fine white powdery deposit. Flour, decided Hare, and then saw that he was right and that others had thought so, too, for jagged holes had been gnawed up the side of one hessian rampart, and on the floor below was a tumulus of spilt flour scarred with rodent tracks and plump black droppings.

From this point on, it was clear that the stores had been

systematically plundered by rats, humans or both. Sacks had been up-ended and ripped open, or simply slashed across, a handful of the contents grabbed and then flung on the floor. The reason was apparent: the food had been here for years, it had decayed in some cases to the point of unrecognisability. Hare, nerving himself, took a handful of something black, furry and vaguely cylindrical and, by careful picking-apart, discovered it to be dried apple rings. An adjacent purple pulp, spotted with white, he left alone. From a sack of walnuts came a stifling, sour odour which moved him on; the next passageway was built of macaroni, and he was surprised to hear a white mound of it crunch healthily underfoot, but when he thrust his hand into an opened sack the contents convulsed and something darted squeaking past his feet.

'Mind what you're doing,' reproved Tapper. 'We don't have vaccines down here.'

'Isn't there anything fit to eat?'

'Dried milk?' Tapper indicated a tower of rusting tins, off which the labels had peeled and stood in coils upon the floor. 'Cocoa?' Depredations had been made on this tower, a tin roughly opened and several, to judge from the state of the stack, removed. 'Gelatine crystals?'

Hare growled.

Perhaps the Digger was moved by Hare's misery; at any rate he beckoned, and skipped away through the corridors of dried peas, maize oil, yeast extract and dehydrated onions, Hare following. He rounded a corner too fast and collided with Tapper, who was standing before a wall of big cylindrical tins.

'Lift me up,' commanded Tapper.

Hare did so, with some difficulty. Tapper selected a tin, retired with it to a pile of sacks and pulled off a key soldered to the side. He began to open the tin with this key. Particles of rust fell through the widening gap on to the food inside. Which was a rather odd colour, Hare noticed: mauve.

'Should be all right,' said the Digger when he had finished. 'We had some last week and no-one died. Well, only Silas, and that was corned beef.'

He dug into the tin with his knife and cut out a piece of something which, if it had not been for the colour, Hare would have said was ham. He raised it with deliberation to his mouth. He chewed, nodded, passed the tin and the knife to Hare.

It was ham. Indeed, it was the best ham Hare had eaten for years. He decided to ignore the fact that it was mauve. He cut and ate piece after piece, occasionally remembering to push the tin towards the Digger, who said he was not hungry. Eventually he sat back with a contented sigh. 'How long has it been here?' he asked.

'About thirty years,' said Tapper, after some thought. Hare's stomach stirred with alarm; but he was too tired, and too full, to worry. A pleasant heaviness had fallen upon him; he tried to force his eyes to keep open, but they closed despite his will. He rested his head against a crate that smelt of fermenting pears, and dozed.

He dreamed that all the bats in the city had flocked into the cavern and were fluttering around him with little high-pitched cries. They were white, not black, as he had always imagined bats to be, and this was the result of their being underground so long.

He woke reluctantly, because the crate held his head at an uncomfortable angle which it was painful to adjust, and the light was glaring. Nevertheless something was insistently pulling him awake – pulling quite literally, for, opening an eye, he glimpsed a ragged ghostly figure tugging at the hem of his trouser leg. Instinctively Hare kicked, and the figure fell backwards with a howl.

Similar ghostly ragged figures were all round him. They muttered to themselves as they foraged among the sacks and tins or crouched in an attitude of possession over heaps of mouldering raisins. The cavern echoed with their murmuring and the soft rip of hessian. Hare climbed on to a crate, then from it to the top of an unsteady pile of sacks, where he lay prone, holding the slipping sacks in place with his outstretched hands.

The cavern was huge. The lanes of macaroni, the forts of sugar, the ziggurats of tinned milk seemed to stretch for as far as he could see under the ticking lights.

A few lanes to his left, a sort of squad was operating: sacks were opened, the contents inspected, and the sacks were then either dumped to one side or carried away in the direction of what Hare presumed to be the exit.

In the act of settling a sack on his shoulder, one of the squad looked up and saw Hare, crouching on his pile of sacks.

'What are you doing up there?' he said. 'Come down and make yourself useful.'

9

'There have been Diggers in these tunnels for about thirty years,' Tapper told Hare as they sat together for the evening meal. 'The main thing we have to worry about is vitamin deficiency. Fortunately, those who stocked the place left enough vitamin pills here to last us a century.'

'Who did stock the place?'

'I'll explain it all later,' said Tapper.

He had made the same reply to Hare's questions several times. Hare had seen enough to realise that the tunnels were far more than storage rooms. There were long dormitories, containing iron-framed beds with thin, patched mattresses and dark grey blankets oddly like the one he had dreamed about in the days before he joined Ezra's marginals. There were huge bathrooms, white-tiled sections of tunnel, from the walls of which projected crusted zinc pipes terminating in flattened nozzles like snakes' heads, while in the middle stood a row of porcelain basins fitted with heavy brass taps. The basins and the wall tiles were crazed with thousands of tiny blue veins. The water came from an underground stream, Tapper said. There were storage tanks as well, but the supply had never dried up. Near the bathrooms were the latrines, holes in the ground set over an abyss, from which rose a pungent smell. Hare had peeped into the kitchens, too. Vast cooking utensils hung from meat hooks, and on scrubbed tables stood cliffs of dinner plates. The sinks were like coffins.

In reply to his baffled and reiterated question, 'What is all this *for*?', Tapper had merely said, 'I'll explain later.'

Sitting next to Tapper at the long table, Hare looked around him. The dining hall was another natural cavern, but trouble had been taken to make it homely. Lights in cracked green lampshades hung from an artificial ceiling. The walls were whitewashed and decorated with bright abstract patterns.

In this space were set a number of wooden tables at which sat something like three hundred people. They were all dressed in the same extraordinary assemblage of rags, beside which the dress of Ezra's household appeared stylish. Scraps of shirt and scraps of sheet were sewn together without regard for colour or shape or anything except the area to be covered, and it was impossible to tell the sex of the wearer from the apparel because men were as likely to be wearing tunics as women to be wearing trousers. The commonest single item of clothing was a dark green jacket with a lot of straps and pockets and buckles on it. This, decorated to the owner's taste with stars, animal shapes and other devices, was being worn by about forty of those present. It had – strangely – the look of a uniform, and Hare saw that all those wearing it looked very young: not one of them had a beard, although several seemed to have bits of brown paper stuck to their chins.

Between the tables passed people bearing large pans of food. These were set down at intervals and the food was ladled out.

'We take it in turns to cook,' said Tapper. 'And to wash up, keep the place clean, and so on.'

'You have rotas?' enquired Hare carefully.

'Of course. It's the only way you can do it. With several hundred people living here, there's got to be some organisation.'

'Does anyone ever try to evade their share of the work?'

Hare was curious to know how the Diggers would deal with Brag.

'We've had a few cases: people who don't understand how to live in a community. We deal with it firmly.'

'How?'

'If they won't co-operate they eat alone,' said Tapper.

'And that's enough?'

'You'd be surprised how much people hate eating alone,' Tapper said.

Hare looked at the faces of the Diggers at his table — animated, intent, smiling. He saw Danny, gesticulating with her bony hands to make a point, breaking off with a laugh to pass a plate to her neighbour, who also was laughing. The hall was filled with cheerful clatter. Hare felt the affection of the Diggers for one another and how painful it would be to be cut off from it, and saw how appropriate the punishment was.

On the other hand, if you didn't *like* living in a community . . . But then there would be no point in being here.

'Some people aren't suited to life here,' said Tapper, 'and we have to persuade them to go back for everybody's sake. Someone who isn't happy here can be very destructive.'

'Suppose you got several people behaving unco-operatively, a dissident group as it were?'

Tapper gave him an odd look. 'A dissident group would be by definition a group that wanted to live somewhere else.'

Hare's food arrived: a plate apparently containing a golfball, a piece of shoe and a pile of marbles.

Tapper leaned over and examined it. 'Braised beef, mashed potato and peas,' he announced.

'Peas?'

'Yes.'

'But they're blue!'

'Well, yes, sometimes they go that colour. It's a chemical

change, nothing to worry about.' His own plateful arrived and he attacked it with gusto.

'Do many people go back up?' Hare asked a little later, having been defeated by the braised beef.

'Not many. You see, nobody comes here straight from *there*. Everyone here has come from a marginal community. And sometimes people do go back to the marginals, particularly if they want children – although in fact we do have children here and they thrive.'

'You have children here?'

'Certainly.'

And, looking around, Hare saw some, making islands with their potato and jabbing each other with their forks, in what appeared to be a healthy manner.

'Once you've lived down here . . .' Tapper's voice took on a note of pride. 'The marginals . . . well, I don't want to criticise them, I have friends up there. But they have some very confused ideas, and the way they live is a compromise. It's entirely dictated by the amount of tolerance they're shown by the police. Don't you want that piece of meat? Sure? Thanks.'

'Don't the police know about you, then?' asked Hare.

'No. We're careful how we come and go, and if the police do see us wandering about they think we're marginals.'

'They might just be allowing you to live here because you'd be more of a nuisance somewhere else.'

'They don't know that *here* exists,' said Tapper. 'They've lost the maps. And if ever they notice something a bit peculiar they assume it's to do with the sewerage or the underground telephone cables or something else which isn't their business. That's the wonderful thing about bureaucracy. If it worked properly life would be impossible, but as it is one can live quite passably in its blind spots.'

Hare's plate was whisked away and replaced by another

147

one, bearing on it a highly coloured blob. Tapper glanced at it and said, 'Orange surprise.'

It tasted of marmalade and something Hare could not identify. 'Tomato sauce, I should think,' said Tapper. 'We discovered some the other week.'

It didn't taste too bad. Hare ate it slowly, and tried not to think about the ingredients. For the fifth or sixth time, his eyes raked the rows of people sitting in the hall. Meal times would be his best chance of seeing whether his wife was here. She would have changed, of course, but he would know her. So far he had not seen anyone who looked like her at all.

'This is the generator,' said Tapper.

Hare did not hear him say it: he inferred it from Tapper's lip movements. The noise of the thing seemed to shake the rock. Hare presumed it was safe: there were no signs of the roof crumbling. Even so, he was glad when Tapper motioned him away down one of the corridors.

'Doesn't it ever break down?' Hare asked when they could hear each other speak.

'From time to time. We've got pretty good at repairing it. It isn't getting any younger, of course.'

'What will you do if it breaks down for good?'

'Live in the dark,' said Tapper.

If the generator did not break down, Hare thought, the diesel would run out. Tapper had said that the huge tanks in the neighbouring cavern were getting dangerously low. One reason why the tunnels were so erratically lit was that they were trying to save fuel. How would they replenish it? They disliked stealing from the surface: they prided themselves on being able to live on forgotten foodstocks among the decaying furniture of this demented underground housing scheme. Stealing also exposed them to much more risk than it did the marginals; and stealing thousands of gallons of diesel was

148

no small undertaking. They might just have to let the lights go out, as Tapper said. But without electricity the tunnels would be uninhabitable. It provided more than light; they would not be able to cook their food, and they would have no way of dealing with the damp.

After the generator, 'the heart of the system', Tapper was going to show him 'the brain'. This was reached by the long passageway down which they were now walking. Here the walls had been boarded and plastered, but the plaster had crumbled away in places, leaving a black hole which suggested rats.

The passageway was punctuated by swing doors. These had heavy bolts on them, and a small pane of glass at eye level so that you could see what was on the other side. Incomprehensible notices, elegantly handwritten, began to appear on the walls: 'In case of alarm, ring hand bell before proceeding to klaxon'; 'Crowbars will be found in the passage leading off the Communications Room'; 'Quiet must be observed at All Times'. Above the fourth swing door was a notice saying, 'No Unauthorised Personnel Beyond This Point'. Doors with numbers on them now appeared leading off the passage. Twenty yards further on, Hare and Tapper came to a door set on its own, with the words 'Control Room' stencilled on it in white. Tapper turned the handle and beckoned Hare in.

The control room looked very much like an old-fashioned office. There were painted walls and a false ceiling, and lino – with scarcely a scratch on it – covered the floor.

In the room were four sizeable desks and a large table. At each desk was a comfortable-looking chair with arm-rests, and on each desk was a leatherbound blotter (spotless) and a telephone which would have received respectful attention in an antique shop. An extraordinary contraption which reminded Hare of his mother's clothes-airer stood in a corner: to it the cables of the telephones were attached, and

149

then proceeded to run in complicated routes all over it, and were joined by other cables originating he could not see where, and this elaborate tangle was surmounted by a row of switches which did not appear to be connected to anything.

Other fittings included a shelf of telephone directories, a flower vase, an umbrella stand, and a small piece of carpet laid under one of the desks. This desk also had a more comfortable-looking chair than the others. On one wall was coiled a fat snake of fire hose terminating in a heavy brass nozzle. A framed drawing of something, its outline faded to unrecognisability, hung on one wall.

'This room is the key to the whole complex,' said Tapper. 'As far as we know it was never used. None of it was ever used. It was obsolete before it was finished.'

'But what *is* it?' demanded Hare. He seated himself in a chair and put his feet up on the desk. 'I refuse to be shown anything else until I know what it is I'm seeing.'

Tapper looked regretful. For a moment Hare thought he would not be able to resist continuing the mystery. Then he said, 'I'm sorry if I've overdone it. When anyone new arrives I show them round. I think it's rather an interesting place.'

'It's very interesting,' said Hare. 'What is it?'

Tapper grinned. 'This place,' he said, settling himself on a desk, 'was intended to be an underground shelter for the Government in time of war.'

He got no further.

'*War?*' protested Hare. 'There hasn't been a war for . . .' He stopped, suddenly uncertain. It was a subject on which the history teaching in schools never properly touched, and the information he had pieced together from the books in Solomon's shop had never made a coherent picture. Wars were ancient and barbaric. He had a vague impression that the country had last been involved in a war about two centuries ago.

'Seventy-nine years,' said Tapper.

'*Seventy-nine years?*'

'The past has been rewritten, and nobody reads books anyway,' said Tapper. 'We have proof.' He pointed to the desk under which the carpet had been placed. 'There was a typed document in a drawer of that desk: a report drawn up by some committee. "SECRET" stamped all over the cover. Parts of it are difficult to understand, but it seems that a crisis had arisen and the committee was asked to investigate ways of dealing with it. In doing so they kindly provided us with an explanation of what the tunnels are for, and also told us when the last war ended. Thirty years before the report was written, and it was written forty-nine years ago: it's dated. The arithmetic isn't difficult.'

Hare sat frowning.

'You mean that this warren of tunnels was just for the Council to meet in if there was a war?'

'Not to meet in, to live in. That's the reason for the bathrooms, the dormitories, the kitchens and so on. Not to mention the food.'

'An enormous shelter. From what?'

'Aerial bombardment,' said Tapper.

'What does that mean?'

'I don't know. It's the phrase the report uses.'

'What about the rest of the population?' Hare said. 'Did they have a shelter?'

Tapper shrugged. 'They were supposed to take their chance. The population level is too high anyway: it says so in the report.'

'What were all those machines for?' asked Hare.

'They stored a range of basic machinery which they thought they would need for reconstructing the country after a war. It was all kept secret because no-one was supposed to know how devastating the next war was likely to be.

Industry would have been wiped out, apparently. So would agriculture . . .'

'The tractor!' exclaimed Hare, delighted at being able to make sense of something.

'Yes. And the locomotive.'

'And the cranes and the shovels and the lawnmowers . . . *lawnmowers*?'

'The bureaucratic mind,' said Tapper.

'And what,' demanded Hare, remembering the most bizarre of his encounters, 'were the birdcages for?'

'God knows,' sighed Tapper. 'Perhaps they were going to stockpile birds.'

'But why,' said Hare, 'was everything just abandoned? What did you mean about it being obsolete before it was finished? And if they were so sure there was going to be another war that they went to all this trouble, why hasn't there been?'

Tapper never answered these questions. A bell fixed to the ceiling set up a long silvery vibration.

'I'll have to go,' said Tapper. 'I should have told you: there's a funeral today. Poor old Silas. Attendance is not compulsory, but you might like to come.'

As he went towards the door he pointed to the drawing on the wall.

'Have a look at that while you're in here.'

It was faded by time and discoloured by damp. At first Hare could not make out what it was: it seemed at the same time formless and intricate. He thought it was a diagram of some kind.

Then he saw writing, very faint, in places. On closer scrutiny, he realised that he had seen something like it in Solomon's shop.

It was a map of the city. Puzzled, he stared at it.

*

Silas lay on the bed with his arms folded across his chest and his eyes closed. Over him were scattered dozens of messages written on scraps of brown paper bag: 'Good luck, Silas,' 'We'll miss you, Silas,' 'Silas, it was me who took your penknife.'

Silas had thick wavy hair and impish features. His face in death had assumed a smile of reflective pleasure.

Around him, a small circle of Diggers was arguing.

'It was food poisoning.'

'Rubbish, he electrocuted himself. Silly old fool never took the proper precautions when he was mending the wiring.'

'It's dangerous, that wiring is.'

'Well, of course it is, it's been here sixty years. If Silas hadn't kept on mending it, it would be a lot more dangerous.'

'I tell you it was food poisoning. That corned beef was black.'

There was a chorus of, 'Oh, Dick!'

'Things do go funny colours down here,' someone said. 'Haven't you got used to it yet? It was only black in places.'

Dick extended a quivering arm and pointed to the body on the bed. 'Ask Silas,' he said, 'whether it was only black in places.'

Tapper nudged Hare forward to a seat. They were in a long, low room painted white with rows of chairs. Something about the place reminded Hare of his childhood: trying to locate the memory, he found it was of the day he had visited a church with his mother, at the time when churches still functioned and people still went to them. A moment later he realised that a church, of sorts, was what it was. A cross had been painted in primary colours high on the wall facing him, and religious texts in small wooden frames hung on the two long walls. There was a raised platform for the preacher. Where the altar should be, however, was a plain wooden box with a lever sticking out of it, and directly behind that, under the cross, was a hatch in the wall.

The Diggers took their seats, still talking. The argument about what had killed Silas was continuing. Someone muttered loudly, 'What a lot of nonsense. Why can't we just bung him through the hole and have done with it?' Hare, glancing round, saw that the remark had come from a row occupied by the young Diggers in green jackets.

A man in a tattered black overcoat darned with red thread walked forward to the platform and stepped onto it. A voice from the back rose in protest.

'Jack did it last time.'

'Do you want to do it?' Jack asked the protester. The protester said he did not, but he thought someone else ought to. Jack addressed the room: 'Does anyone else want to do it?'

There was a sort of communal sigh. Jack proceeded.

He was plain and to the point. Listening, Hare found himself moved by the sheer simplicity of the proceedings.

Jack said, 'Silas is dead. We all knew him. Some of us were fond of him, some of us were irritated by him, but all that is beside the point now. He was one of us. And because we were his companions, we are here now to say goodbye to him. We don't think it will make any difference to him, our saying goodbye, but it's what people have always done when someone dies, and we haven't found a better way of doing things. So now, before we send him through the door, let's remember him. Let's hold him with us for a few minutes longer, alive.'

There was a brief silence. Then a man in the first row stood up and said, 'I remember how he helped me back two miles through the tunnels when I fell and hurt my ankle, and he missed his dinner, and never said a word about it.' A woman said, 'I remember how he always made jokes to cheer you up, and the jokes were so dreadful that they did

154

cheer you up.' And they continued, recalling small kind-
nesses and large ones, acts of generosity and quirks of
character, until everyone who wished to remember Silas
publicly had done so.

Then Jack said, 'Are we willing to let Silas go?' and
everyone replied, 'We are willing to let him go.'

Two men and two women stood up and moved to the
corners of the bed on which Silas lay. They wheeled the bed
down the aisle between the seats, around the curious box
with its lever, and brought it to rest in front of the hatch in
the wall.

Jack walked to the box and pulled the lever with a long,
careful pull.

The panel of the hatch began to move upward. It opened
on to blackness and a whiff of something that stung Hare's
throat.

With a jerk the four bearers upended the bed, and the
body of Silas, assisted by a shove on the top of the head, slid
down the mattress and shot through the hole. After a few
moments came a soft and faintly unpleasant thud. The panel
in the wall slid down again.

With expressions of satisfaction the Diggers began to
stand up and walk away.

'There used to be music to go with it,' said Tapper, 'but
we disconnected the machine.'

The scraps of brown paper with their messages fluttered
about the floor.

Hare was allocated an iron-framed bed with two blankets
and a pillow filled with lumps, a toothbrush, a towel and an
enamel mug.

'Oh, and you look as though you could do with a new
shirt,' said Danny, and gave him a much-darned object in
faded blue which roughly fitted.

'Anything else you want,' she said, 'just ask. We've probably got it somewhere.'

Hare had got out of the habit of wanting things. He also observed that on the whole the Diggers did not have personal possessions, except for their clothes and the penknife that most of them seemed to carry. The penknives were all of the same type, utilitarian and sharp-bladed, and he presumed they had come out of one of the packing cases, but the Diggers carved patterns and initials on them so that each one was different.

As the days went by, Hare began to see what a diverse community the Diggers were. Many of them had once held good jobs; they had parted with them in a variety of ways. Joe, the engineer, had gone on a drinking bout, neglected to check a subordinate's calculations, and lost his job when a subway collapsed: Hare dimly remembered it. The community doctor, known as Bone, was a real doctor who had given up his practice because – he said – in a pathological society there was no point in trying to produce healthy citizens. Smart had been a chemist employed by the Company; he had suffered a nervous breakdown and was still, six years later, nervous in the presence of people he did not know. Hare could not get him to talk about his work.

There was a lawyer who said he had been driven out of the profession for protesting at a rigged trial although some of the other Diggers said it was for impropriety. There were several school-teachers who had incontestably been dismissed for failing to inculcate the approved moral standards in their pupils. There were joiners, welders, plumbers and electricians who did not know why they had lost their jobs unless it was because they had asked the wrong questions, or seen things they should not have done. Tapper had trained as an architect. ('I couldn't bear what was happening. All these lovely streets going under the bulldozer so they could build a new factory. Some days I used to sit in the office and cry. They sacked me.') Danny had been in banking. 'It's very

156

interesting,' she said, 'but ultimately it's about the subordination of human beings to the interests of something quite abstract, and when I realised what that often meant in terms of people's lives I couldn't do it any more.'

There were poets, painters and musicians, too. The musicians had formed an orchestra which played every Saturday evening in the dining hall; the strings section had been reduced to one cello because of the difficulty of replacing strings when they broke, but the percussion was in good shape.

Hare enquired among the painters for his wife, but they did not know her.

The Diggers worked hard. They put much effort into maintaining the tunnels; the generator and electrical system needed constant repair, there was bedding to be mended, furniture to be patched up, decorating to be done.

'There's a ton of paint here,' Tapper said to Hare. 'We might as well use it. Are you handy with a paintbrush?'

Hare said he was, and helped paint the walls of the schoolroom.

'What do you teach them?' he asked as he brushed.

'Reading, of course, though there isn't much to read down here. But then, there isn't much to read up there either, from what I remember. Maths. Poetry. We teach them what we know ourselves, which if you put it all together is quite a lot. But the main thing is to stop them from lapsing into complete barbarism, which they would doubtless be very happy to do.'

Hare recalled a whirlwind of small Diggers which had swept past him in a passageway that morning. He supposed all children were naturally barbarians: he did not know much about them. He did know, however, that they had a tendency to rebel against expectations when they got older. He wondered how the Diggers coped with this.

'What do your teenagers do?' he asked.

157

There was a pause while Tapper concentrated on a tricky corner. Then, 'Have you seen them about?' asked Tapper.

'I've seen some youngsters who must be about fifteen or so. They all seem to wear dark green jackets. And they cut their hair short.'

That had surprised him. None of the older Diggers bothered about their hair – it was the length it was, and if it got in the way they tied it up with something.

'They shave, too,' said Tapper. 'Those who are old enough to. A real mess some of them make of it: chins like ploughed fields. Still, I suppose it isn't easy with a fifty-year-old cracked mirror. You have to give them credit for perseverance.' He chuckled. 'They're getting through the brown paper bags like nobody's business.'

'The what?'

'We won't let them use sticking plaster,' said Tapper. 'We keep it for emergencies. The revenge of the old.' He stopped painting and picked at the wall with his thumbnail. 'They call themselves The Bag,' he said, 'and between ourselves they're rather a problem at the moment.'

10

They sat in a rough circle, some on the floor, some on beds. The Bag's dormitory was also their living room. Untidy, brightly painted and boasting several pieces of carpet, it was private territory on which the older Diggers did not normally intrude.

Hare was there by invitation. They were interrogating him.

'You lived in a room in this horrible house all on your own?'

'Yes,' said Hare.

'Weren't you lonely?'

Hare considered. It was difficult to explain to a community of people who, on the whole, liked each other how it felt to live in a community of people who, on the whole, didn't like each other and wanted to be left alone by each other. 'Perhaps I was lonely without realising it,' he said.

'I don't understand how they can live like that,' said Dido. She was a serious girl with frank hazel eyes and a wide, mobile face. 'All they seem to think about,' she said, 'is how much money they can get for things. Don't they care about each other at all?'

'You know they don't,' said the young man who had his arm round her. He was called Fitz, and had a criss-cross of scars on his chin. 'It's in the Report. It's all quite clear.'

'Why do they want money so much?' asked someone.

'Money can be exchanged for just about anything,' Hare said, 'so people believe it can transform their lives. It's security, it's power, it's status.'

'What's status?'

'How you stand in relation to other people,' said Hare. 'Whether you're better or worse than others.'

They stared at him.

'It's just as I said,' said Fitz. 'They're insane.'

A dark-haired girl named Leah said, 'Tell us about your job. What sort of things did you do?'

Hare tried to tell them about his years with Universal Goods, but the story, as he told it, seemed more and more unlikely and the person about whom he was talking seemed less and less connected with him. He was not surprised to see his young audience frowning.

'You mean you did all these things and you never knew what they were for?' said a boy who had his feet up on the wall.

'A lot of jobs are like that,' Hare said.

'But that's awful!' said Leah.

'It's inevitable,' said Fitz. 'The Report states that people should not be allowed to know what they're doing.'

'But surely that doesn't apply to ordinary jobs?' objected Dido.

'What is an ordinary job? It's all connected. In any case, if what they're working on is secret, but it's got to be secret that it's secret, you have to start by establishing the principle of people not knowing what they're working on, otherwise they'll immediately be suspicious and *want* to know what they're working on.'

'Mmm,' said Dido.

'And who knows,' said Fitz, 'perhaps he was working on it?'

'I wish I knew what you were talking about,' remarked Hare.

160

'Haven't you read the Report?' asked Fitz.

'The document that was left in the Control room? No. Tapper mentioned it.'

'Read it,' said Fitz. 'It explains everything.'

A boy with a round, monkeyish face asked shyly, 'Have you been on a train?'

'Yes,' said Hare, 'many times.'

'What's it like?'

'Oh, *Al*!' chorused his friends.

'They make a clickety-click noise and sway around, and they have a funny smell, sort of musty but quite pleasant, which you never smell anywhere else,' said Hare.

Al looked entranced.

His question had opened the floodgates.

'Is driving a car difficult?'

'Have you ever been drunk?'

'What's it like to swim?'

'How do you eat an egg?'

'How old do you have to be to get married?'

'If you get married and then change your mind, do you go to prison?'

'Have you ever seen a horse?'

'What does new-mown hay smell like?'

Hare's eyes stung.

'I'd like to read the report that was left behind in the desk of the control room,' Hare told Tapper.

Tapper said certainly, it was still there. He found the key ('This is a historic document in its way, so we keep it locked up') and opened the drawer.

Hare took out a fawn cardboard folder with 'SECRET' stamped on it. Inside, similarly stamped, was a document of about forty pages punched at the edges and held together by little cord tags. The title page announced that it was the Report of Working Party D 13. The pages were typed in the wide-spaced innocent fashion that those old machines had produced. Hare lingered over them for a few minutes with an antiquarian's interest. Then, skipping the introductory pages, he began to read.

1. Background to the Study

The cessation of hostilities thirty years ago was hastened by the use of a weapon whose destructive power placed it in a category far beyond that of any other weapon ever invented by man. The morality and political wisdom of its use have been much debated; this study concerns itself with the unforeseen effects which have arisen, or may be expected to arise, from the mere fact that the weapon exists.

Within twelve years of its use, the knowledge of how to make the weapon had spread to all major industrial countries, whose ability to wage war was therefore checkmated by the fact that all their likely opponents also possessed it.

This produced a totally unprecedented situation, but the fact was not immediately appreciated. A balance of power which deterred war-making was no new thing. In the past it had meant that the struggle, if it came, would be a long and bloody one and might not be worth the cost; often, therefore, it was not undertaken. But it is to be noted that such wars *were* fought; and, since they were fought, the possibility of war was always perceived as a real one.

The new balance of power was founded on weapons capable of inflicting destruction almost unimaginable in scope, and inflicting it moreover in a few minutes. Since any nation thus attacked would instantly release upon the aggressor its own similar weapons, this meant that it was not a rational option for any nation to go to war: it might as well kill its own people.

Dismay at the widespread possession of this horrifying weaponry gave way to expressions of relief that there was once again a balance of power and a 'deterrent to war'. For some years, it seems that no-one in government perceived the difference between the old deterrent – unacceptably high casualties and risk of military defeat – and the new one: annihilation. The first deterrent

162

could be, and on occasion was, ignored; when this happened, the resulting war served to validate the deterrent by preserving its context: wars went on. The second deterrent could not be ignored: it was absolute, and it *destroyed the context in which it operated.*

War became impossible. However, the *pretence* had to be kept up that war was a possibility, or the language of the deterrent would not mean anything. A long series of logical absurdities has flowed from this paradox, which the world is no nearer resolving than it was thirty years ago.

Partly out of habit, and partly because they were caught in this trap of logic, governments continued for another ten years or so to pretend that war was still possible while maintaining that they had the best possible deterrent against it. Unfortunately, assertions that war is possible must occasionally be supplemented by vivid demonstrations of its possibility, and the resultant tightrope-walking nearly did precipitate a war. Those in power had failed to take into account that events acquire their own momentum and that wars can start without either side wanting them to. The scenario of an unwanted, unstoppable war became a distinct possibility with the automation of the launch systems, which quickly reached the stage where the only role for human beings in the conflict would be as casualties.

The dire peril that hung over the world was grasped in time not only by governments but by their populations, and as a result there were widespread political upheavals. Governments of all complexions were forced to acknowledge that war was no longer a sane policy option.

This step, unprecedented in human history, went almost without comment. The public had been concerned with the immediate threat, and wished to forget the subject of war once the threat had been removed. It took some years for the import of what had happened to begin to sink into the popular consciousness.

Gradually the idea that war had become impossible took root in people's minds. At about the same time, a number of social changes took place which, occurring within a few years of each other, suggested the first stages of a major psychological shift. The focus of these changes has been a rejection of discipline: the abandoning of the work-ethic and the dismantling of sexual taboos are particularly striking. The cause of this psychological shift and its ultimate direction are the subject of the following pages.

Above him the lights ticked. The control room was spartan, but what furnishings there were breathed power. Mahogany, leather, brass.

Hare had a sensation of crushing weight. He looked up at the massive crossbeams that supported the roof, and felt for the first time where he was: somewhere deep under the city, separated by a hundred feet of earth and rock from – what? What stood above his fragile head? Some gigantic building, perhaps. Or an arterial road along which pulsed cars, buses, lorries. Perhaps tree-roots grew down towards his cranium; perhaps, even now, a grave was being dug towards him, a coffin lowered.

He turned the pages.

2. Functions of War in Peacetime
(i) Economic functions

In a democratic society, expenditure on national security is the only part of the economy which is not subject to democratic controls. All governments have exploited this fact for their own purposes. Naturally, the defence sector imposes exigencies of its own: research into new weaponry tends to generate a momentum which outruns the initial specifications, and there is equally a tendency for weapons to be produced simply because they have been invented.

Nevertheless, the fundamental unaccountability of defence expenditure, the vast sums of which it disposes and its intrinsic wastefulness furnish a tool for the manipulation of the economy without which most governments would find themselves in difficulties.

Hare stopped, bewildered. The words were familiar but the concepts were alien. How could wastefulness be useful? How could war have a function in peacetime? What upside-down world had these people inhabited?

He thought at that moment of the Company. There was another upside-down world. Presumably the same sort of people were in charge of both.

(ii) Political functions

Governments have always attempted to use war in their own interests. A population uniting against an aggressor does not strike, demand higher wages, snipe at government policy in the press or complain when the press is muzzled. It does not ask inconvenient questions or refuse to believe what it is told. It is usually docile.

The trouble for government is that these desirable effects are only brought about at the cost of actual war, a cure which may be worse than the disease. Moreover, if the war drags on, accompanied by heavy losses, the conditions for revolution are present. The ideal for government would appear to be the imminent threat of a war which never occurs. Such a situation obviously cannot be prolonged, and any government seeking to provoke it runs the risk that a war really will result, the 'adversary' not having grasped the nature of the game.

The way in which the war-threat is most commonly used by governments to contain their population is therefore a long-term, low-key strategy, perhaps even largely unconscious. People define the group to which they belong (in this case the nation) in terms of those who do not belong to it. This is the core of patriotism: the feeling that one's country is unique, precious and in some way to be venerated *because* it is one country among many, against which it is judged. An all-inclusive group cannot inspire the same loyalty. Definition is crucial here: people cannot feel loyalty to a group which is not defined, and a thing can only be defined in terms which distinguish it from other things.

People give their loyalty to a country, then, as a defined entity, and if it ceases to be a defined entity they can no longer be loyal to it. How is it most likely to lose its identity if not by military conquest, and how can it protect itself from this if not by military force? In the very identity of a nation, the idea of war is implicit. The ability to defend itself by arms is the minimum qualification for any state that claims to be sovereign. This is not a historical accident but a psychological necessity. If the idea of war were removed, a profound subterranean shifting would take place in people's attitudes to their country.

Tapper had entered the control room and was watching him with curiosity. Hare raised his head.

'This is a very strange document.'

'Yes,' said Tapper.

'I don't think I understand it. Is there any chance it's a joke?'

'A lot of people have said that,' observed Tapper. 'By the time they got to the end they'd all decided it was serious.'

'Have you read it?'

'Yes. Years ago.'

'What did you think of it?'

'I felt sorry for the man who wrote it,' said Tapper. 'Put it back in the drawer when you've finished. Here's the key.'

The unarticulated connection between the State and war which we have outlined lies at the root of the individual's obedience to the State and the State's power over him. The citizen resigns much of his autonomy to the government, while the State, as its part of the bargain, protects him from cradle to grave against enemies.

Since national cohesion is indissolubly linked with the idea of war, many governments have been exercised by the task of maintaining the population's consciousness that it may one day have to go to war without inviting either disbelief on the one hand or an actual outbreak of hostilities on the other. In practice, the past has consisted of a series of self-correcting episodes of peace and war, in which the memory of war has served to keep alive the consciousness of the State as a potentially threatened thing. Wars are fought, in short, not to end wars, but to ensure that wars go on being fought.

Note: It is not absolutely necessary, for the purposes outlined above, that the State should be under *military* threat. The military is merely – as it were – the most convenient form of threat. Other threats, provided there is a chance of combating them, may serve.

Fitz was engaged in acrimonious conversation with Danny and Joe at lunchtime. It seemed that he had refused to help clear a blocked section of tunnel.

'It's pointless!' Fitz was saying as Hare sat down. 'There are *forty-nine* entrances. We don't need to use that tunnel at all.'

'How do you know what we might need to use in the future?' asked Danny.

'It's obvious. We never have needed it – '

'In your limited experience,' said Joe.

'My age disqualifies me from being right about anything, doesn't it?' Fitz was having trouble keeping his temper. 'You've all been here so long you think this place will go on for ever, and you can't see what is staring everybody in the face, which is that before long the generator is going to break down.'

'Oh, nonsense,' said Joe easily.

'What would you know about it? Your subway collapsed, didn't it?'

Danny hid her mouth with her hand.

'It's work for the sake of it,' said Fitz. 'You're no different from them up there. Work is virtuous, we've all got to do it whether it makes sense or not.' He turned to Hare. 'Would you say that clearing a tunnel which no-one is going to use makes sense?'

Danny said, 'You may be making a valid point, but that isn't the issue. The issue is your refusal to work at a job which you say is pointless when the general opinion is that it should be done.'

'Don't I have a right to my opinion?'

'Yes. You don't have a right to act on it when the results of your action are disruptive.'

'I don't have a right to *act* on my *opinion*?'

'No, you do not,' said Joe, 'you arrogant little – '

'Joe, please,' said Danny. 'Of course he has a right to act on his opinion *within limits*.' She glanced at twenty green-jacketed Bag who were listening intently to the conversation. 'The point is, where he leads they'll follow.'

'What incredible hypocrisy,' said Fitz, and stood up.

'And another thing,' said Joe. 'If you get that girl pregnant – '

'Joe, will you shut up?' said Danny.

Fitz leant on the table, breathing hard. After a few moments he said, 'You don't like that, either, do you? You don't think we should be allowed to have sex!'

'I don't approve of promiscuity,' said Joe.

'Why don't you mind your own miserable business?' said Fitz, and walked off.

Danny said, 'Oh dear,' and pushed her plate away. Joe got up and excused himself. Hare reflected with interest that the abandoning of the work-ethic and the dismantling of sexual taboos were what had worried the author of the Report.

(iv) Psychological functions

War works as the exemplar of conflict. It expresses in extreme degree the principle of opposition which is one of the great organising principles not only of human society but of nature (as in the way animals compete, for instance, for mates, food and territory). Society employs this principle in numerous ways: in sport, in art, in sexual behaviour, in judicial procedures and debates.

Clearly, none of these phenomena will cease to exist if war ceases to exist. Yet our thinking about them will be changed, probably in ways which cannot now be envisaged. Over generations, language will change. Attitudes to sport will change. Storytellers will have to find a substitute for what in many cultures has been their major subject.

Literature has always focused on war because war is interesting. To those engaged in combat, it can offer an experience so intense that for the rest of their lives they seek to recapture it. Nor does the exhilaration come solely from the danger and from noble sentiments of patriotism. War is glamorous and public, and gives legitimate rein to the destructive impulses. It also arouses and satisfies the instinct for self-sacrifice, for which outlets are limited in normal life (for males, that is; women are able to satisfy it through their children).

War, since it is a statement that some things in human existence are more important than life itself, enhances the meaning of existence. Since existence is for most people a riddle and a disappointment, this is a valuable function.

For the purposes of this study, however, the most important psychological function of war is that indirectly it justifies authority. We have said in 2 (iii) that war justifies the citizen's obedience to the State and the State's authority over the citizen. There are, it is apparent, many other forms of authority. They include that of the parent, the teacher, the employer, the instructor, the warden. If war is the organising principle behind the State, it is the organising principle behind the social units which are microcosms of the State – family, school, workplace. If the age-old tension which has held the State together is released, the smaller units will feel the same internal dissolution. If the police, representing the State's authority, are not respected, there is no reason why the same cold and sceptical eye should not fall upon the authority of teachers, parents and anyone who wears a uniform. In these circumstances all hierarchies, since they embody authority, will be regarded with suspicion. And authority of a more intangible kind – intellectual authority – may find itself without worshippers. The idea of expertise may pass out of currency, followed by expertise itself.

We suggest that this is an alarming scenario, dealing in largely unknown factors and having virtually limitless scope.

'Interesting, that report,' said Hare. 'It seems to be saying that war was a jolly good thing.'

'Oh, that's not the important part,' said Fitz. 'It isn't relevant, all that war stuff. I mean, it was so long ago. The important bit is at the end, where it talks about controlling the population.'

Hare was surprised. He supposed it was a difference between generations. His own generation had been brought up to think of war as cruel, wasteful of life, and something of which a civilised society should be ashamed, and to believe that that was why wars were no longer fought. The Diggers disapproved of the taking of life on principle. And now here were the Diggers' children dismissing 'that war stuff' as irrelevant. He found it disturbing.

'It worked, didn't it?' said Pug. He was a tall youth who cut his pale hair very short and was always cleaning his nails with his penknife. 'The population *is* controlled, except us.'

'That's why they hate us,' said Dido.

'Are you sure they hate you?' asked Hare.

'Yes,' said a dozen voices.

All of them had visited the surface, it appeared, and their experience there had been traumatic. They had been jeered and spat at, had stones thrown at them, and had been beaten and manhandled by the police. It was clear to Hare that they did not practise the discretion of the marginals, who understood that they were not supposed to exist and therefore behaved as if they didn't. Marginals never spoke, never caught anyone's eye, never took up space that anyone else might want. Marginals, too, were used to the reactions they got, whereas The Bag weren't. They had grown up in the tunnels, protected.

'One man tried to set his dog on me,' said Al, 'but the dog

wouldn't attack, it just sniffed at me. There was a crowd standing round me, calling me names and telling me to go back where I came from. They thought I'd come from the Zone. Someone kicked me on the shin, and someone else said to him, "That was stupid, now you'll have to disinfect your shoe." All I was doing was looking in the window of a shop.'

'It's not what we do, it's who we are,' said Fitz.

'The only person who was nice to me was the dog,' said Al.

'Al likes dogs,' Leah said to Hare. 'He keeps threatening to bring one back.'

'We aren't allowed animals down here,' said Al. 'I think it's a shame.'

Several of The Bag murmured agreement.

Hare's gaze wandered round the walls, which were painted with murals in sometimes startling colours. One wall consisted of caricatures of the older Diggers, done with considerable wit. The other walls were taken up by what seemed to be a surreal cityscape shading into landscape. The eye, moving from left to right, encountered first a group of featureless modern buildings at the foot of which small human figures lurked or scurried, then a pleasanter group of tumbledown houses set on crooked cobbled streets which Hare found oddly familiar, and finally passed through a species of urban wasteland into green fields, a farm with animals, and what seemed to be a village.

The landscape was bathed in golden light, the grass was a vivid green starred with daisies; the scene was idyllic and touching. The village in particular had been painted with great care and what Hare could only call affection. He supposed it had been copied from an illustration in a book. Certainly the farm animals had been copied, for The Bag could never have seen pigs, sheep and cows. The animals were too big for their surroundings, which might or might not have been intentional. They had soulful, rather charming expressions.

Al saw Hare looking at the mural, seemed about to say something, then changed his mind.

Fitz spoke instead. 'D'you know what Joe said to me today? He said I didn't have a right to act on my opinion.'

All of them laughed uproariously.

(v). Recommendations

Since, in our view, the gravest threat posed by peace is that to the internal stability of the country, it is to this that our most urgent recommendations are addressed.

To deal first, however with the issue at the heart of the paradox we have inherited: *there can be no question of the weapons which have imposed this peace being dismantled.* They must remain *in situ.* It is on them that the peace rests, and to remove them would be to remove the paralysis which has descended on war, with results that cannot be foreseen and might be catastrophic.

It is also clear that the continued existence of the weapons must be kept as far as possible out of public consciousness. After global war had been narrowly averted, they acquired an opprobrium which has not yet faded. Even if it were to fade, the prominence which has attached to the weapons in the past is no longer suitable in an avowed era of peace. Weapons cannot be disentangled in the popular mind from the possibility of using them, which in turn relies upon a set of sentiments and a matching rhetoric for which there is no place. Bluntly, we cannot now afford an enemy, and the weapons we possess are so devastating and indiscriminate that they could only be justified by a demoniacal foe. Ordinary people cannot be expected to adopt a set of attitudes as complex and subtle as are required by the circumstances; it is therefore better to spare them knowledge of the circumstances.

The best strategy for government, we suggest, is to issue a reassurance in the most general terms and thereafter avoid mention of the issue. In time the question of what happened to the weapons will be forgotten because people do not want to think about it. In the longer term, public amnesia may set in on the subject of how war was 'abolished', and this amnesia should be encouraged.

The weapons will require periodic replacement of components. The appropriate factories must therefore be maintained. Indoctrination of employees is unlikely to present a problem since they will not know of what products the items they are manufacturing are parts. Broadly speaking, the less the employees in the peace sector understand about the work they are doing, the better.

The question of the armed forces has been dealt with by the government. Neither publicly nor in military terms is there a role for them. Now that all warning and firing systems have been automated, there is no need for a human presence, and former personnnel should be absorbed without delay into the police force.

Hare shivered. It was cold in the control room: the only slight warmth came from the fluorescent lights. The words swam in front of his eyes, each in its tiny sea of space, each an enigma.

What did it mean? He tried to think about a weapon which couldn't be used, couldn't be talked about and couldn't be taken away, and decided that in the circumstances he was not even sure what a weapon was. He wondered if they were stored in one of the Company's huge warehouses. The Company must be implicated somewhere: its interests encompassed everything. Which meant that he himself, as Fitz said, had probably been involved.

Hare attempted without success to connect his years of paper-shuffling with some great and obscure conspiracy. He had never been able to believe that his work at Universal Goods had any significance whatsoever.

But the Report had been written forty-nine years ago. It was a long time; long enough for things to have changed completely, with no-one the wiser because no-one would have known what was happening in the first place. Doubtless the weapons, whatever they were, were rotting quietly in some labyrinthine depot, along with other forgotten blunders.

We now turn to the other strategies which must be considered by government.

As remarked, we regard the removal of war as first and foremost a political danger. This danger is not to the external security of the State, since every state is confronted by the same problem, but to its internal stability. Lacking an out-group which can be identified as hostile or potentially so, the population will – we predict – experience a disorientation, a self-doubt and a loss of purpose which if it occurred in an individual would be termed an identity crisis. These effects are likely to be Protean in their manifestations and in the long term incalculable: symptoms which have already appeared include a rejection of 'work', an insistence on the right of unrestricted sexual gratification and a general and broad-ranging intolerance of authority and discipline. We suggest that it will not be long before contempt for the law becomes commonplace; the idea that there are circumstances in which it need not be obeyed is already gaining ground among traditionally law-abiding sectors of the population.

Linked with this rejection of moral and legal order, we expect to see an increasing amorphousness and classlessness in society, tending towards chaos, as the hierarchies, including gradations of social class, are eroded, and as the concepts of superiority and leadership come under attack.

Clearly, in such a society, the survival of a central governing body is gravely threatened. Disintegration of the State will occur within decades unless urgent measures are taken. The most important of these measures will be to find a substitute, or series of substitutes, for the 'enemy'.

We have considered, first, an economic threat. Such threats are not difficult to manufacture, can be manipulated at will, are readily identifiable as coming 'from outside', and frighten everyone while being properly understood by no-one. One economic threat can, with skill, be kept going for a decade or more, after which it can be succeeded by another 'caused' by the remedies applied to the first.

A certain price has to be paid for this solution: it requires the convincing appearance of severe economic straits, and the only way to simulate this may be to bring it about. The government must therefore be sure what it is doing; and at best it may find the necessity inconvenient, preferring to present itself as a government that has brought prosperity.

A related problem may be noted here. We have remarked in 2 (i) on the role played by the defence sector in the economy. This role is of crucial importance for economic stability. A substitute for the defence sector, capable of the same prodigality that character- ises arms expenditure and similarly unaccountable to the public purse, will have to be found within five years. It goes without saying that this function will have to be concealed.

'The stuff about the economy is over our heads,' said Fitz. 'We were hoping you could explain it to us.'

'You'd better ask Danny,' said Hare. It was over his head, too. The Bag felt that the Report's arguments were less important than its assumptions, and in this he agreed with them. He had never come across a set of assumptions so chilling.

The Bag took the Report to be an accurate mirror of the values of the society in which it was written. In this too he was bound to agree with them, although he flinched a little at the vehemence of their condemnation.

'It's rotten from top to bottom,' said Fitz. 'It's selfish, greedy, cruel and hypocritical. Look at the way it treats the marginals.'

'Look at the way it treats us,' said Pug, making a face.

'And not only is it rotten but it must have been rotten for a long time,' went on Fitz. 'That sort of thinking doesn't happen out of nowhere. Whoever wrote that crazy stuff — about the survival of authority, and how to make people believe lies so they'd behave themselves — knew that the people he was writing it for would agree with him.'

'Probably the people he was writing *about* would have agreed with him, too,' said Al. 'They want governments, don't they? They want to be told what to do.'

'Yes,' said Hare, 'I think you're right.'

'Then they deserve what they get,' said Fitz. He brooded for a moment, then said bitterly, 'God, they've made a mess of the world. How *could* they have made such a mess? And what makes me so angry is that it's *our* world as well.'

As Fitz said this, Hare had the feeling of a milestone having been passed. He had been waiting for one of the Diggers to say it. It flashed through his mind that The Bag could be dangerous if they set their minds to it.

His eyes drifted, for some reason, to the mural.

'Who did that?' he asked.

'We all did,' they said. 'Al did the difficult bits.'

A shared vision. As he studied it, it seemed to tell a story, for his eye travelled from the office buildings to the decaying slum houses and then into green fields, as though in a process of rejection. He saw now that the village, which was at the very end of the picture — its destination — had been carefully thought out — had indeed been planned, with almost an architect's eye.

There was a terrace of houses with gardens, all different, fronting a green, and to the side of them a row of cottages outside which people had stopped to talk. A road wound up the hill to a school house. Dogs ran about in the road, and someone had dropped a bag of apples. It was Dido. With something of a shock he saw that all the figures in the painting were portraits of The Bag.

'Let's show him the drawings,' said Al.

Someone fished under a bed and came up with a boxful of

papers. These were spread out with care on a mattress. Hare drew in his breath, and began to pick up, one by one, dozens of painstaking drawings, on squared paper, of buildings. There were sketches, elevations and ground plans, there were treatments of individual buildings, of terraces, of houses grouped in a landscape. Some of them were signed, others had a note written in the corner. 'Pug's place' said one. They were drawings of the village in the mural.

'Tapper showed us how to do them,' said Dido, seeing Hare's astonishment.

Hare looked at them in silence. Admiration would have been inappropriate: they were too important for that.

'What are they?' he asked at last.

'It's the place where we want to live,' said Dido simply. She drew her finger down Fitz's cheek, to the place where a bit of bloodstained paper adhered to his jaw, and he allowed himself to smile. 'We want to go back up, you see. We want a place where we can live together and grow vegetables and keep animals. This place doesn't really exist; we've invented it, but it's become sort of real. We call it Skylight.'

'Skylight?'

'Yes.'

A confusion of emotions assailed Hare. One was sadness. He admired the way the Diggers lived: tolerant, considerate, humorous, self-respecting. And now the young of this strange but apparently successful experiment wanted to abandon it, and go back to the place where all the old mistakes would again be made. At the same time he was moved by their vision. Painfully naive (and how could it not be?) it had beauty. And hunger.

'It doesn't exist, you say?'

'No, but one day it will.' This was Fitz, jaw squared. 'We're going up anyway.'

There was a tension in the room.

'Do you know anything about growing vegetables?' Hare asked, in an attempt to lighten it.

'We've got enough books on the subject,' said Fitz, and Hare remembered the fears about the destruction of agriculture which had been one of the reasons for stocking the tunnels. 'We've got seed in sealed containers, we've got tools, we've got fertiliser. We've got tractors as well, but we're not expecting too much from those.'

'And when you say that one day Skylight will exist – '

'We will create it,' said Fitz.

Hare looked into the boy's eyes. They were angry, sincere and proud.

'Where do you think you will get the land?' Hare asked gently.

Fitz smiled. 'We shall take it,' he said.

It is a primary requirement of any manufactured threat that it should command universal public credence. Of threats that meet this criterion, the threat to the environment may be singled out as both genuine and serious. Unfotunately it cannot be considered for our purposes, since in the nature of the case it cannot be combined with an appeal to patriotism.

International terrorism would appear to hold possibilities. The problem in this case is the difficulty of presenting a terrorist attack in such a way that it is seen as an attack on the State but not by another state. It is known that terrorists cannot operate without resources which normally only a state has at its disposal. On the other hand, a terrorist organisation powerful enough to operate independently would in effect be a rogue state, and would revive notions of war.

Finally, the problems of orchestrating a terrorist campaign of unlimited duration which, for the whole of that duration, could be prevented from having undesirable repercussions are, we conclude, insuperable.

Internal terrorism holds out more promise but is more directly dangerous. A government nourishing this viper does not know where it will bite. Nonetheless, there is no doubt that an urban guerilla group striking unpredictably at buildings and public figures, sowing confusion and fear, provides an internal enemy against which the population could, at will, be rallied.

Here again, the problem is of maintaining the threat for a long period; although in this case the difficulty is likely to be explaining the failure of the police, over a long period, to eliminate it.

In spite of this, we consider that a version of the internal threat holds out the best solution to the problems government will face, and we recommend that a further study along these lines be immediately put in hand. Attention should be given to devising a threat which, while clearly seen to menace society, is for some reason beyond the capacity of the normal forces of law and order to combat.

Hare sat motionless. He had before him the explanation of the Zone. It was an invention, a nightmare fabricated to frighten a population which might otherwise prove ungovernable into believing itself under siege by something demonic.

The vastness of the deception astonished him. He wondered who in the Council knew the truth, for surely someone must? But how could you know the truth about the Zone and keep it to yourself? The temptation to hint that you knew what no-one else knew, that you had knowledge which would turn their world upside-down, must be a torment.

Then, thinking about it, he knew it was not so. They hugged their knowledge to them like treasure. It made them like gods.

He read on, the last few pages.

The enemy against which every government will shortly have to defend itself, now that it cannot risk defending itself against another government, is its own people. Government must look to itself without confusion as to where its responsibilities lie. Its responsibility is to preserve the State as a governable entity, and to do that it must preserve itself.

With this in view, we suggest consideration be given to refurbishing the network of tunnels and underground storage chambers constructed many years ago for use in wartime as a government shelter against aerial bombardment. The network contains office and living accommodation, water supply and its own power. It is well stocked with basic foodstuffs. Over the past twenty years machinery and other equipment has been taken down to the storage chambers (also, in perhaps misplaced zeal, most of the collection of the Metropolitan Art Gallery, in place of which copies have been hung).

The object was to preserve a nucleus of equipment with which to rebuild the country after a war. Stocking and all but the most basic maintenance ceased two years ago, when it was finally admitted that not only was another war exceedingly unlikely but that if it did occur any society established in the aftermath would be so primitive that it would be unable to make use of modern equipment.

The fact that the tunnels are useless for their original purpose should not lead to their being abandoned, for they would provide an ideal underground headquarters for a government beleaguered by civil strife. The aim, however, should be to produce a policy of psychological management which will make use of the tunnels unnecessary. In this, modern electronic methods of surveillance and record-keeping will be of great assistance.

With the removal of the greatest single factor that has made the state manageable, and the necessity of finding other ways of managing it, the need for government to be several steps ahead of its population is more crucial than ever and will increase as the methods government resorts to become more complex. For not only must these strategies be planned overall so that in detail they do not conflict, not only must they be kept flexible to respond to unforeseen conditions, but at every stage they must be kept secret.

If the population suspects the scale of the deception that has been practised on it, there will be such a revulsion of popular feeling that no government will survive it and no *system* of government will be possible for a period which cannot be predicted. In the supervening period of anarchy, human society will slide into a barbarism from which it may not again emerge. In that darkness one gleam of hope may be discerned: that out of anarchy may arise warring groups and out of warring groups a series of nation states will once again develop. These nation states will presumably find themselves in time at the stage of history which we have reached, confronted by a choice between chaos and annihilation. The doubtful benefits of this prospect should not encourage government to be lax in its duty, which is to maintain, for as long as possible, the *status quo*.

At some time in the future, the problems of national coherence which to us appear insoluble may be solved, *if social conditions permit*. It is the job of government to maintain society in a condition in which decisions can still be taken and in which nothing has become irrevocable. If, in the circumstances, this means indoctrinating the population with a completely fictitious picture of the world it is living in, that is what must be done. The same has been done for millennia, with much less at stake.

'You have to think of the drawings as a sort of dream,' Al said when Hare next asked him about Skylight. 'It won't be like that for a long time; if it ever is.'

'You'll have to learn to build,' said Hare, looking at the village in the mural. 'You'll have to build as well as you paint.'

Al grinned. 'We'll learn. But there are houses there already, which we can live in for the time being.'

Hare was startled. He realised he should be taking this conversation seriously. 'You have a site in mind?' he asked.

'Oh yes,' said Al. 'One of the tunnels comes right out into the middle of it. It's quite a big area, and it's *completely deserted*.'

'What?' said Hare.

'Nobody lives there,' said Fitz. 'Well, almost nobody. It's all just empty houses and gardens full of weeds.'

Hare made a connection. 'Is that the site?' he asked, pointing to the part of the mural which showed the tumble-down houses and cramped little streets.

'Yes,' said Al, pleased. 'Do you know it?'

'It's familiar,' said Hare. 'Where is it?'

Fitz could only describe how to get there through the network of tunnels, but when he talked about the appearance of the area, Hare knew it was Morristown.

'They're going to build on it,' Hare said. 'It's a Company scheme. You can't go there. You'll be turned off straight away.'

'We're going there,' said Fitz. 'It's ours.'

'They'll evict you,' said Hare. 'The police will evict you. With extreme roughness.'

None of The Bag said anything.

'Look,' said Hare, beginning to feel very anxious. 'I know it's a fine idea, going back and having a village and growing things, but they won't let you. You have to do it their way. Why don't you just go back and live quietly like the marginals? In a place nobody else wants?'

'The marginals!' Dido was scornful. 'That's not a life. Searching through dustbins, pretending not to exist. That's degrading.'

'The whole point of Skylight is that it's *ours*,' Al explained. 'It's like our own little country. It's . . .'

Fitz said, 'Why should we ask their permission to breathe?'

'But,' said Hare, 'what else can you do? What else can the marginals do? They're too strong for you.'

Their eyes accused him.

Dido got up and walked over to a bed in the far corner. She knelt down and, with some tugging, brought a shallow crate out from underneath it. She fished under the sacking which covered the crate and pulled something out.

In her hands, green with mould and rust-pitted, was a rifle.

182

11

'Don't you see,' said Hare a few days later, rubbing with steel wool at a rifle on his knees, 'that if you go up there with these things you're playing straight into the Government's hands? The author of the Report would have loved it.'

'This isn't a revolution,' said Dido. 'We aren't an urban guerilla group, whatever that is. All we want is somewhere to live.'

He could not get through to them that taking possession of somewhere to live at gunpoint was revolution. Even if it wasn't, the police were not likely to weigh the distinction finely before they opened fire.

Fitz said, '*Any* action we take they can use for their propaganda. If we worry about that, we'll never do anything.'

'Right,' said Al. He was fiddling with the bolt on one of the rifles. Nearly all of them had stuck solid and The Bag had spent many hours cleaning and oiling them, and poring over the training manual which had been packed in the crate. They had not yet ventured to load them, although they had found the ammunition. Hare was almost as apprehensive about the damage they might inflict on themselves when they started practising as about what was likely to happen to them if they ever got out of the tunnels.

He had tried in vain to dissuade them from what could

only be a hopeless venture. He had explained that the site they intended to occupy, however long it had been derelict, was earmarked for something, to which Fitz had replied scornfully, 'We know that: they've earmarked the whole world. Well, they can't have it.' He had pointed out that they could not hope to defend their territory with eighty-year-old rifles against a mechanised police force armed, at the very least, with more sophisticated firearms. The Bag were not listening. They knew almost nothing about either fighting or the police, Hare realised. They had found the rifles among the hundreds of crates that littered the tunnels, and they had seemed like a gift or a sign.

'And what do you suggest?' said Al. 'That we sit here for the rest of our lives because we're afraid?'

Hare could not understand at first why the older Diggers did not interfere.

'It's their right,' said Tapper, and would not be drawn further on the subject.

Danny said, 'We bore children and we brought them up in these tunnels. They didn't ask for that, it was what *we* wanted. It's completely unnatural: they're human beings, not badgers. Now they're growing up and they want to live as human beings should live. The least we can do is allow them to try.'

'But they will be going out there with guns,' said Hare.

'Yes. To defend themselves.'

'They are going to seize land that doesn't belong to them, and defend it by force.'

'They believe it does belong to them. They want justice.'

'Do you think justice can be bought with a rifle?'

'What I think has no bearing on the matter. They think so. Many other people have thought so in the past, and perhaps it's true.'

'But they will be killed,' said Hare.

Danny turned away.

184

It was after this conversation that Tapper told Hare that Fitz was Danny's son.

The ammunition was wrapped in oilcloth, in a crate labelled 'Lupin seed: Handle with Extreme Care'. The Bag carried the crate into the middle of the dormitory and inspected its contents with interest. Hundreds of small pointy-nosed objects half-encased in a brass sleeve.

'So those are bullets,' said Fitz. 'Why does the manual call them rounds?'

'They make a round hole,' said Hare.

The Bag had invited him to be present at their first practice session. There was discussion about a target: at first they were going to pin a piece of paper on the wall and shoot at that, but Hare said the bullets would bounce off the wall in unpredictable directions and might kill a few of them, so they fetched a packing case, filled it with sugar and drew a large circle in red paint on the outside. They positioned the packing case at one end of the dormitory. Then they pushed the beds back to the walls to give themselves plenty of space, and went into a huddle over the manual again.

'It looks as if you feed the bullets into one of these metal cases, and then slot it into this bit at the bottom,' said Al. He did so, and then looked at the rifle in surprise, as if he had not really expected the procedure to work.

'Well, that seems simple enough,' said Fitz, and picked up the rifle. He brought it up to his shoulder and took aim at the packing case.

'No, you're supposed to lie down,' said Al.

'We shan't be lying down up there,' said Fitz, and pulled the trigger.

Nothing happened.

'Perhaps it isn't cocked,' said Al.

'You really are a pain sometimes,' said Fitz, and gave it back to him.

185

Al, holding the rifle carefully, took up a prone position on the floor facing the target. He did something to the bolt of the rifle, took aim and squeezed the trigger. Nothing happened. He squeezed it again, an expression of perplexity crossing his face. Again, nothing happened.

Fitz grinned, and stepped forward with hand outstretched.

Al was fiddling with the bolt again. He got the breech open and for a moment they all saw clearly the bullet snug in its chamber, and then the breech had slammed shut, the rifle kicked in Al's hands and there was a deafening bang. Fitz flung himself backwards as the bullet hurtled past him and buried itself in somebody's mattress.

Al laid the rifle down. He was white. He and Fitz stared at each other.

'Perhaps not so simple,' said Hare.

Detective Koberg hated the dark. As a child . . .

He shuddered and pressed on behind the narrow beam of light.

Only anger could have brought him here. Jacobs had spoken of tunnels. Sewers, more like, thought Koberg. There would be rats and spiders and other foul things. If he lost his way he would never . . . He brought a shutter down on that thought. It was impossible for him to lose his way. There was a direct route from the entrance by which he had come in to the storage room which he needed to find; it was only two hundred yards and there were no passages leading off.

At least, that was what Jacobs had said. He might have been lying.

As he followed the beam of torchlight along the tunnel, trying not to see the shadow on the walls, this idea, that Jacobs had been lying, grew in Koberg's mind. He tried to think sensibly about it. Why should Jacobs have lied? Jacobs had not imagined he, Koberg, would come here looking for the canisters. Of course not. But . . .

Sweat broke out on the back of his neck. Wouldn't it be the perfect way to get rid of him? Once in the tunnels he would never be found; no-one knew about these tunnels, Jacobs had said.

In his mind he heard Jacobs's round, fruity laugh.

That was it. Why else should Jacobs have told him about the tunnels, told him he had put the canisters there, if he did not want Koberg to go in there and look for them? It would be a stupid thing to do, to give away such information without a reason.

Except that Jacobs did talk too much after a few drinks. Koberg's lip wrinkled. He never drank too much.

Forcing himself to walk at a steady pace while his heart pounded in terror, he then realised that Jacobs had told him what he had done with the canisters before he had started putting the pressure on Jacobs. At that time, Jacobs would have had no reason to get rid of him.

Yes, he would. Koberg tripped over an unevenness in the ground and just caught himself in time. He started to shake. Jacobs would want to get rid of him *before* Koberg attempted to blackmail him. It wasn't blackmail, of course, but Jacobs would think it was.

He stood supporting himself with one hand against the wall of the tunnel, trying to control his heart rate. This was no good. If he couldn't get a grip on himself he'd better go back straight away, before he started seeing things that weren't there.

The wall of the tunnel was rough to his hand, and reassuringly solid. Shining the torch on it, he saw that it was brick; the walls had been built, then, not hacked out of the stone by some disgusting race of dwarves in the distant past. Koberg tried to remember what Jacobs had said about the tunnels, but was unable to, because he had not understood it at the time. They must have been here for centuries.

Suppose they were no longer safe? After all this time you could expect roofs to cave in. Ahead, the passage might be blocked, parts of the wall might have given way; trying to find his way past the obstruction he might get lost. The roof might fall on him just as he walked underneath it . . .

Detective Koberg rested his head on his arm, and heard the pulsing of his blood. It told him that he was alive and alone.

He swore into the darkness. The word was cut off and curiously deadened. He shouted, all the obscenities and blasphemies he could think of, until he had filled the space ahead of him with his hatred. Then he began to walk forward once more.

It was not possible to keep Al's near-miss quiet, and that evening in the dining hall the tensions broke surface.

'Perhaps that will serve to show you the folly of the whole idea,' said Joe to Fitz, who was prevented from answering by the speed with which Dido intervened.

'If *you* thought it was a *good* idea we'd have something to worry about,' she said acidly and, as Joe flushed with anger, she went on, 'What upsets you? The fact that we have guns or just the fact that we don't want to go on living the way you do any longer?'

'The fact that you are resorting to violence,' said Tapper quietly.

'Look, it's self-defence,' said Leah. 'We won't use them first. It's like a warning.'

'Don't you understand that to carry a gun is a form of violence?' said Tapper. 'If you wave it at somebody you are using it, whether you fire it or not.'

Most of The Bag, after thought, accepted this, but it did not deter them.

'*They*'re violent,' said Al. 'Why should *we* be squeamish?'

'Yes, have you seen the rifles the police carry?' said Fitz with something like enthusiasm. 'They must be a lot more powerful than ours. They don't even look like ours.'

'That is hardly a good reason for confronting the police,' remarked Hare, but no-one heard him.

'It's precisely because their society is founded on violence that we don't live in their society,' Danny said.

Fitz shrugged. 'Well, you can do what you like, we'll make our own decisions. We've done it your way long enough.'

'All violence can do, all it has ever done, is provoke more violence,' said Tapper.

'Violence is the only thing they'll listen to,' said Fitz. 'If they cared about justice, if they cared about people, would the marginals have to live out of dustbins? There wouldn't be any marginals. There wouldn't be *us*. They want it that way. They want people with nothing. And you accept it. In spite of the fact that one of the results of it is that you're living down here in the dark on mouldy food that might poison you any day. And you pretend to be happy here because you haven't the courage to do anything else!'

There was a profound silence. Finally Danny said, 'Fitz, we really are happy here. We aren't pretending.'

'Then they've won, haven't they,' said Fitz, 'if they can make people think they're happy living in a tunnel underground? If they can do that, they can do anything.'

Nothing further was said for a few minutes.

Hare then said, with a certain desperation, 'None of you seems to have thought about what is actually going to happen when you come out of the tunnel with your guns and take over these empty buildings.'

'Tell us what's going to happen, Hare,' drawled Pug.

'If there are people about they'll call the police,' said Hare. 'If there's no-one about, the police will find you soon enough. They have armoured vehicles, short-wave radios . . .

189

they're equipᵖed to deal with a major uprising. That is what they're *for*.'

'Indeed,' said Danny, 'they have never been much good for anything else.'

'If there are people about,' said Fitz, 'we shall ask them to leave. Then we shall settle in and wait for the police. When they come, we shall try to explain to them what we're doing — '

'Do we have to take the rifles?' said Leah suddenly.

'Oh my God!' said Fitz. 'Have you been asleep for the past few weeks?'

'But think about it,' insisted Danny. 'Do you have to take the rifles? Or are you just taking them because you've found them?'

'Of course we're taking them because we've found them!' howled Fitz. 'It would be utterly stupid *not* to take them now we've found them!'

The argument continued, getting nowhere.

When Detective Koberg was four, his twelve-year-old brother had shut him in the cellar and left him there all day.

The cellar was pitch dark: there was a light switch but he was too small to reach it. The shapes came and went, sometimes almost touching him. There was no sound, except the sounds he was making. When, six hours later, he was found by his gin-fuddled mother, he was silent and rigid. He did not speak for two days.

When Detective Koberg was fourteen, he had jumped his brother in an alleyway and, assisted by three other boys, kicked him unconscious. His brother had lost the sight of an eye.

Detective Koberg walked slowly and carefully along the tunnel, holding down his fear as if it were an animal that might buck and throw him. He had not been prepared for

190

the panic that rose in him as he set off down the dark passageway, and felt humiliated.

Feeling humiliated made him angry, and he was angry already. Anger was his only comfort as he pursued the narrow torchbeam along the narrow tube of darkness.

Jacobs had insulted him. Nobody had spoken like that to Koberg since he had joined the force: it was a shock, and made him feel insecure, because it meant that an invisible barrier which he had felt protected him now protected him no longer. Together with his troubles with the credit company, it contributed to an oppressive sensation of vulnerability and a conviction that a growing number of people, for reasons he could not understand, wished him harm. He had a sense of some menace that had escaped his calculations lurking behind the enemies whose names he knew. Knew to weariness. Day after day, night after night, he pushed them round in his mind like pieces on a chessboard.

But it was Jacobs he hated the most. Hated more than the new sergeant, who was now on his back daily, more than the gorilla from the loan company, who had taken to hanging about in the street outside his flat. They were both on his level in some sense: he understood them. Jacobs was different. Jacobs was not on his level, but he had pretended to be. And Koberg, flattered, and with his ambition touched, had not seen through the pretence, and so to his anger at Jacobs' betrayal was added another humiliation, for he prided himself on knowing what people really were.

Jacobs had been very nice to him. He had bought him dinner, stood him drinks in a club (Koberg wished he belonged to a club), and arranged for a crate of expensive wine (Koberg thought it was expensive: the label was ornate) to be delivered to his flat. He had talked to Koberg about the work he did for the Company, his responsibilities, the necessity of sometimes evading the letter of the law in obedience to what he called a higher law, and other serious matters. Occasionally he had stopped talking about serious matters and started telling jokes, which startled Koberg at first, particularly as they were very dirty jokes.

It had been balm to Koberg – not the money spent on him (though that was important), but being treated as an equal. Jacobs had been respectful about Koberg's special knowledge and skills, the courage that must be required of a police officer . . . Koberg's mouth twisted. Flannel, all of it. Jacobs had wanted him to do a job – a job Jacobs was afraid to dirty his own hands with. When it was done, Jacobs had dropped him. He had been brusque when Koberg repeatedly telephoned asking for a meeting, had put him off with one excuse and another, finally had spoken to him with open contempt and made him see how he had secretly regarded Koberg all along, although it had not been politic to say so. He had even, for a moment, made Koberg share his, Jacobs's, perception of him, and for that unendurable shaft of insight Koberg was going to destroy him.

He had made his plans. The canisters were the only direct proof of his story, and the first thing he had to do was check that the proof existed. Knowing it was possible that he might meet with an accident in the tunnels, or that Jacobs might try to stop him telling what he knew, he had put it all in a letter which he had left with a neighbour. The letter was to be taken to the police if he had not claimed it back within ten days. Koberg intended to have his revenge even if he did not live to see it.

Revenge would be exquisite. It scarcely bothered him at the moment that it would leave him with a great deal of explaining to do himself. He had reached the point of thinking that he was not much to blame for what had happened. He had been following orders. He had been told to co-operate with Jacobs and he had co-operated. It was not his fault if . . . No, it was not his fault at all.

The door in the wall appeared unexpectedly. It was

barred, but he lifted the bar and it opened at once. Inside it seemed even darker, if that was possible. He flashed the torch around the space.

Nothing. Had Jacobs tricked him?

The beam of light caught something that glinted. He lowered the torch a little. Yes.

They were hefty, the canisters. They came up to his waist and were a couple of feet across, with a rim at the top to facilitate handling. He put down the torch and manoeuvred one out of its line and across the floor. It was as much as he could do to lift it. He supposed Jacobs would have been able to roll them and manhandle them most of the way. Even so, he would have had to carry them at some point. He flashed the torch over them, counting. Eleven. Eleven canisters and two large crates. Thirteen journeys down the tunnel and back, in the dark, each time with a bastard like that. He felt a reluctant respect for Jacobs, and kicked angrily at the canister to get rid of the feeling. Then he turned and walked out of the cavern.

It was as he stood replacing the bar that out of the corner of his eye he caught a gleam of light. To the right of him, further up the tunnel. That was against all probability. It was also against all commonsense to start walking in that direction, when his way back was clear and lay in the opposite direction. Nevertheless he did start walking towards it, partly out of curiosity and partly because he could not turn his back on light and walk into darkness. After a few steps he realised that there might be another, nearer, entrance to the tunnels than the one he had come in by, and that it might admit daylight. If there was, it would be sensible to make his exit by it.

The light did not look like daylight, however. It did not have the cold, reassuring ordinariness of daylight. It had an unsteady quality, and it was bluish. Detective Koberg might not have progressed very far in the force, but it was not for lack of observation.

The light became brighter.

He switched off his torch – he could see the walls of the tunnel without it now – and began to move cautiously, keeping to the side. There wasn't much point, because in that confined space he could not have escaped being seen if there had been anyone there to see him, but adopting the procedures he had been taught gave him more confidence.

The light was coming from overhead lights fixed to the ceiling of the tunnel.

Koberg's mouth opened in astonishment. In this prehistoric place there was electricity, and it *worked*?

At first he tried to dismiss it as a sort of fluke. Then he realised that no fluke would account for it, and that it was impossible. His knees began to shake. The light became more terrifying than the darkness.

He saw them then, at last. The shapes that had been hovering on the edge of his imagination. Grotesquely fringed and tattered, the whites of their eyes staring, clustering round him with little cries, half-bat half-human. He pulled out his gun and shot wildly towards the twittering and the bat-stench.

In the dining hall, the argument between The Bag and the other Diggers was on its third circuit and showing signs of exhaustion when the wounded man appeared.

He stood in the doorway holding his right arm at an unnatural angle. There was a spreading red stain on it. His face was chalk-white. He walked forward and collapsed on the floor.

After a moment's paralysis, six people leapt forward to help him. 'He's been hurt,' said somebody in bewilderment.

'Bandages,' said Danny, but Al had already gone for them. They lifted him on to one of the tables and began to cut his clothes away from the wound. Someone tied a strip of cloth round his arm as a tourniquet. Nobody spoke: there was nothing useful to be said.

Then the others came through the doorway.

They were silent and shocked. Three, wounded, were being helped by others. One was being carried by his friends. They brought him to the nearest of the tables and laid him on it. His chest was soaked in blood.

'What happened?' said Danny harshly.

The doorway was thronged with silent Diggers. As Hare watched, they began to push one of their number forward – roughly, Hare saw with surprise. The man resisted. After a series of struggles he was ejected and stood alone, frightened but still defiant. Not a Digger: the clothes were dirty but not ragged. He was young. And surely . . . Hare knew the face, and felt a surge of hatred without knowing why, and puzzling over this caused him to miss the clue. It did not, by this stage, look much like a uniform.

But Tapper's eyes were clearer. 'God,' said Tapper, 'it's a milkman!'

The young policeman was pushed forward by the crowd until he was forced up against the table on which the Digger with the chest wound lay. Someone tried to make him lower his head, bow down to the wounded man; he turned and lashed out with his fist and was immediately grabbed by half a dozen Diggers who held his arms behind his back.

'What's happened?' demanded Danny again.

The policeman swung round with a fleeting expression of viciousness which Hare intuitively understood: he despised women and would not be interrogated by one. Hare recognised him then. He was the policeman who had given evidence at the Inquiry. Hare even remembered the name: Koberg.

One of the Diggers came forward and placed a police hand-gun on the table. Danny's eyes rested on it.

'Did you shoot these people?' she said.

Koberg's chin came up and he said nothing.

'What were you doing in the tunnels?'

'That's my business,' said Koberg.

'You *are* a policeman?'

Koberg sneered.

'Look,' said Danny, 'you're going to have to tell us sooner or later. You can't get out of here on your own, so you're here until we let you go. And there are hundreds of us and one of you.'

Koberg said, 'I'm not afraid of a lot of stinking bats.'

'Is that what you think we are?' mused Danny. 'Is that why you tried to kill these people? You thought they were not human?'

Koberg did not answer.

'Why did you do it?' persisted Danny. 'What are you doing here at all?'

'You can do what you like with me,' announced Koberg. 'There's plenty who know where I am and will come looking. They'll clean this place up, get the smell of bat-shit out of it.'

Hare thought: Several hundred people who won't resort to bullying will be unable to extract the truth from one lying little bully who would have no hesitation in torturing any of them.

'Your name's Koberg, isn't it?' he said.

The effect was surprising. Koberg paled, and made a shaky attempt at nonchalance.

'Maybe it is, maybe it isn't.'

'Of course it is,' said Hare. 'I know about you. How's your friend Jacobs?'

As he said this, he thought it was a stupid thing to say, but it hit something. Shock appeared on the policeman's face. Hare pushed further.

'Did Jacobs send you down here?'

196

The result was astonishing. The young policeman gasped, stared at him (he did not, of course, recognise Hare, who by now looked like all the other Diggers), and said weakly, 'Oh. So you know about it then.'

'We know quite a lot,' said Hare.

'So you were expecting me,' said Koberg. He appeared to be thinking furiously. In a tone of almost hysterical bitterness he said, 'He set me up. It was a trick. I knew it was. He told you to ambush me.'

No-one moved. In the stillness Koberg glanced around suspiciously. He said, 'The canisters. The canisters are real, aren't they?'

'Oh yes,' Hare reassured him. 'The canisters are real.'

'What's in them then?'

'What did he tell you was in them?' parried Hare.

'Chemicals.'

'They're full of sand,' said Hare. 'The canisters with the chemicals are somewhere else.'

'What did he want to lie about that for?'

'Presumably he doesn't want anyone knowing where they are,' said Hare, beginning to feel he could keep this up indefinitely.

Koberg was staring around him. 'Who are you people?' he demanded. 'You don't – you don't *live* here, do you?'

The Diggers exchanged glances. It was clear that they could not let the policeman go, now that he knew of their existence. There was an unbroken semicircle of people standing behind him, blocking any move he might make towards the door. But what were they going to do with him? He would be a confounded nuisance, thought Hare.

On the other hand, he might have uses. Hare walked down the side of the table and gingerly, in case it did something unexpected, picked up Koberg's gun.

12

It was so easy to say things. Hadn't people once believed a devil could live on your tongue? There was a devil on his, Jacobs thought.

Koberg was serious. For a week after he had stalked white-faced out of the bar, Jacobs had heard nothing from him and had begun to believe that Koberg would do nothing to pursue his demand for money. Then had come the latest telephone call. Koberg had a taste for terse sentences and meaningful silences. 'Koberg here,' the voice had said as Jacobs lifted the receiver. 'I haven't forgotten. This is just to let you know.' Here had followed a meaningful silence. 'Forget the transfer,' Koberg had then said. 'Just the cash. You've got ten days. I'll be in touch.'

Jacobs could still hear the click as the receiver was put down.

At first the call had simply numbed him: his brain refused to deal with it. After a day of going through his work like an automaton, he had pulled himself together and tried to think.

The idea of paying Koberg the money he dismissed out of hand. He did not have it; if he borrowed it he might find it was only the first instalment; but, over and beyond this, the thought of giving in to Koberg's blackmail filled him with such disgust that he thought he would rather face the consequences. He considered what the consequences were likely to be.

Koberg would say that Jacobs had incited him to murder and to the framing of false evidence against a Company employee. Jacobs weighed up his chances of refuting these charges. There were of course no witnesses to any of the conversations he had had with Koberg. He now saw that he had been too expansive in these conversations, both given away too much and promised too much; for Koberg's greed had been whetted by these attentions, and just as it had been fully aroused they had stopped. That had been stupid, but Jacobs could not afford to go on wining and dining the young dandy. And, although cursing himself for mishandling the situation, Jacobs could not see that he had had a choice: Koberg's support had to be bought because it could not be commanded – Jacobs was, after all, an employee of the Company, not an officer of the force, however closely the two at times worked together.

Had worked together. Jacobs's mind flew back to his conversation with Mr Terry. There lay the factor that overshadowed everything: a few months ago, if this situation had arisen, he would have appealed to the highest authority in the Company and confessed to a mistake made as a result of excessive zeal; and the highest authority, confident of being able to hold off pertinent enquiries from the Council and knowing that Jacobs had been serving its best interests, would almost certainly have protected him. If, now, he appealed to that authority, he was likely to find himself turned over to the full power of a newly-purged police force vigorous with righteousness and intent on demonstrating its complete independence of the Company. In the changed circumstances, the Company would risk more by trying to protect him than it would by handing him over as a sacrifice to the new regime.

Yet, surely . . . Jacobs's brain was hypnotised by the vision of Detective Koberg in the witness box, telling the truth for the first time in his miserable life, and it found difficulty in focusing on anything else. Surely, if the Company let Jacobs face interrogation, things would come out that could not possibly be in its interests? The truth about the illegal manufactures would be impossible to suppress. Questioned about the dockets, he would have to explain that it was normal procedure for him to remove incriminating material, and the full extent of the Company's illicit operations and systematic cover-up of them over the years would stand revealed.

Investigations would be set in motion which would uncover facts which probably even Jacobs himself did not dream of. Fifty years and more of evasion of the law: not haphazard, not opportunist (though sometimes that as well), but planned, deliberate and thorough. Necessary, Jacobs believed, and so did those who gave him his orders. Necessitated by the fact that law must reflect an ideal state of affairs and the world was not an ideal state of affairs but had to be run on its own terms. Laws were for ordinary people: those who ran things could not afford to obey them. It was in the interests of the State that they defied the laws of the State. Once, the men in the Council had understood that. But now, for decades past, no-one in the Council had understood it, and the responsibility of doing what was odious in order that the good might be safeguarded had devolved solely on the shoulders of the Company; and there were times when Jacobs felt the burden had devolved solely on him – on him the crimes, the deaths and the lies, on his own shoulders. There was a kind of nobility in it and he did not seek to put it down, but it was very heavy.

All this would come out, in the appalled, uncomprehending gaze of the innocent. Jacobs knew about the innocent: they made other people do their killing, and turned very nasty when shown a corpse.

But it would all come out, and the tremors would leave

little standing. The Company could not want that? Because, once interrogated, he would have to tell.

Or did he mean that he would tell those to whom he appealed that, once interrogated, he would have to tell?

Jacobs made a wry face. That was blackmail.

Or was it? He would merely be pointing out that his interrogation would have certain unavoidable effects. Jacobs tried to imagine himself saying 'certain unavoidable effects' to Mr Lucy, but his imagination faltered.

The question of evidence was crucial: he must try to concentrate on it. If the Company thought Koberg could prove his accusations it was presumably more likely to hand Jacobs over to the police than if it thought the accusations stood no chance of being substantiated. And what evidence was there? The only concrete evidence for any of it was the cache of illicit chemicals in the tunnels, and Koberg was not likely to get his uniform dirty going to look for them. Jacobs had put nothing in writing, naturally. It was possible that Koberg had planted a witness in the pub for their last meeting, but he did not believe that Koberg thought that far ahead. No, the strongest factor in favour of Koberg's story was that he would have no sane motive for making it up.

Koberg was himself a policeman, of course. Jacobs recognised this obvious fact with rather a shock. The police would naturally incline to believe one of their own.

Yet Jacobs had a feeling that Koberg was not liked by his colleagues.

If the police had recently been purged of officers like Koberg, it was indeed possible that they would be biased *against* Koberg's story.

But then, for the same reason they would be biased against Jacobs.

Jacobs put his head in his hands. His need for a drink was tormenting.

Perhaps it was the other way round; perhaps the Company

was more likely to hand Jacobs over if it thought Koberg could *not* prove his accusations, so that the trial could turn into a vindication of Universal Goods?

Jacobs stared unseeingly at the window. His head felt as if it would split.

Koberg had given him ten days, and this was the third.

He opened the drawer of his desk and brought out a bottle and a glass.

It was impossible to lock Koberg up because nowhere locked. However, it looked as though he had taken at face value Danny's remark that he would be unable to find his way out of the tunnels unaided. He did not seem particularly interested in trying to escape. He was left alone in a room for some time, with guards outside, and whenever anyone looked in he was sitting rigidly against the wall, as if afraid to move. Hare thought he looked more frightened sitting there than he had in the dining hall with thirty angry Diggers around him. Perhaps he was afraid of being underground, but could cope with it as long as he was not alone?

Hare was not normally malicious, but he had a score to settle. He arranged for Koberg to be left alone for his first night in the tunnels. The policeman was put in an otherwise empty dormitory with a flask of water and a stump of candle.

In the morning Hare was the first to go in to see him. Koberg was curled up in the foetal position and had to be roughly shaken before he would rouse, although Hare was sure he was not sleeping. His face was pale, and blotched and dark-ringed beneath the eyes. The eyes . . . Hare was fascinated to see that the eyes were haunted like the eyes of someone awakened from nightmare. For at least half a minute, they did not seem to see Hare at all.

'Are you all right?' asked Hare, which was not in the least what he had intended to say.

'For God's sake let me out of here,' whispered Koberg.

Hare sat on the side of his bed, torn between revulsion and pity.

'Fucking bats,' wept Koberg, 'living in the dark. Let me out of here, I'm not a bat.' And then, when Hare continued to sit there stiffly, he screamed, 'I can't stand the dark!'

Hare retreated. He went away for ten minutes, leaving his torch, to give Koberg time to recover. When he went back, Koberg said sullenly, 'All right, what are you going to do with me?'

Hare had made up his mind about that. He gave Koberg breakfast (Koberg refused to eat it) then took him through well-lit corridors to The Bag's dormitory. The rifles were piled on a bed. The Bag sat around talking and trimming each other's hair. A silence fell as Hare and Koberg came in, and many pairs of eyes fixed on the policeman with curiosity and dislike.

Koberg glanced around, and his gaze fell on the rifles. His eyes widened. 'You rob a museum?' he said.

They watched him. He walked to the pile of rifles and as he looked down at them the tautness of his face relaxed. He picked up a rifle and inspected it, handling it in the way some people handle animals – respectful and interested.

'Manual bolt-action,' he said, so quietly they could hardly catch it. Then, 'They're not loaded?'

'Some of them are,' said Pug, cleaning his fingernails.

'*What?*' Koberg snapped back the bolt and extracted a bullet from the breech. Then he took out the magazine, fed the bullet into it and tossed the magazine on to the bed.

'You should never leave firearms lying around loaded,' he said. 'And as for leaving them lying around when you don't know whether they're loaded or not – what are you trying to do, kill each other?'

He fitted the rifle stock to his shoulder, took aim at the target on the packing case and squeezed the trigger. He smiled. 'All right if you've got all day,' he said. 'What are you going to be shooting? Elephants?'

They looked at him with incomprehension.

'The target,' said Koberg. 'It's about twenty times the size it ought to be.'

'How big should it be?' faltered Al.

Koberg held up his right hand, and with the first finger of his left hand traced a circle round the palm.

'A bit smaller than that,' he said.

They stared at the palm of his hand.

Fitz said, 'And we should be able to hit that?'

'You should be able to hit the centre of that from the end of the room,' said Koberg. 'At least nine times out of ten.'

They pondered. The conclusion was obvious, however unwelcome.

Fitz said, 'Will you teach us to shoot?'

'What do I get out of it?' said Koberg.

'You get out of here,' said Hare.

'Deal,' said Koberg.

Hare's reasoning was pragmatic.

He had not joined in the debate in the dining hall because he had never been sure where he stood on the question of violence. He deplored it, agreed with Tapper that it provoked more violence, but could not rid himself of the feeling that in some circumstances it was justified, and he knew that there were circumstances in which he would resort to it.

However, in the present situation all this was irrelevant because The Bag had made up their minds and no amount of argument would dissuade them. They were going to arm themselves with rifles and go out to claim their birthright. The problem therefore resolved itself into how to prevent them from killing themselves with antiquated rifles which they did not know how to use.

Now, by an extraordinary piece of luck, the Diggers had

captured a firearms expert. If he could be persuaded to teach The Bag to shoot, they would be able to give some account of themselves against the police and might hold the police off long enough to make their escape. For a dizzy moment he even wondered if they might succeed in holding onto their bit of land: perhaps they could bargain with the Government? He caught himself up sharply at this point: The Bag's optimism was eroding his own grasp on reality.

At the very least, he thought, it would be salutary for The Bag to be in contact with a policeman and to see what firearms could do. It might change their minds where argument could not. That this was a forlorn hope should have occurred to him, because Koberg had shown them on the evening of his arrival what firearms could do, and it had made not the slightest difference.

Koberg was meticulous. He made his pupils paint a line across the floor and shoot from behind it, and ordered everyone who wasn't shooting to stay well behind the line. He made targets with numbered circles so they could reckon up their score. He taught them to squeeze the trigger without jerking the barrel and to hold their breath when firing. After a few days, with the more promising ones, he started teaching them how to shoot from cover.

Hare was surprised that Koberg took his assignment so seriously. He had expected a display of resentment and sullenness. It took him some time to realise that Koberg liked his role.

Koberg was scathing about the rifles. He referred to them as 'your antiques' and talked a lot about his own police rifle, from which it seemed to cause him pain to be separated. He was even ruder about the ammunition, and in this his dislike appeared to be well founded because it did have a habit of jamming in the breech and failing to fire. Koberg said it was dangerous and might explode in the firing chamber, but The

Bag said, well, if it did it did, and went on shooting. They were getting quite good.

Hare, watching them, thought it looked enjoyable. He did not see why opposition to the general plan should prevent him from acquiring a skill.

He took a rifle from the row against the wall and weighed it in his hands. It was heavy and satisfying.

Naturally, Koberg wanted to know where the rifles had come from and why The Bag wanted to learn to use them. Equally naturally, no-one told him. However, the secret could not be kept for ever, Hare thought. In time Koberg would piece bits together and make a coherent story (he was, after all, a policeman). Or someone would just get careless and blurt it out.

Once out of the tunnels Koberg would tell everything he knew, and for that reason he could not be allowed freedom until The Bag had showed themselves; once they had, the most dangerous piece of intelligence would already be public. But Koberg would still have the information he had gleaned within the first hour of his arrival in the tunnels. The information, that was, about the Diggers' existence.

Hare wondered if the Diggers realised how imperilled they were.

They could shoot Koberg, of course. That was what anyone else would do. But then there would be no point in anything.

Fortunately Koberg was not too importunate with his questions. Perhaps he had already guessed what was going on, because from time to time he gave a knowing smile.

Hare found his dislike of Koberg lessening. It had received its first dent when Hare found him in a state of terror on the first morning. He could not forgive Koberg for shooting at the Diggers, but he thought he could understand it: Koberg was, after all, trained to react quickly, and the Diggers' sudden appearance must have thrown him into panic. And Koberg was almost human in the training sessions.

Hare was learning to shoot. He scored high on his first attempt and made a hopeless mess of his next two. 'Often happens,' said Koberg. 'It'll come.' Hare doubted that, but he did manage to hit the centre of the target with a frequency that surprised him, although no-one else was much impressed by it. Al never missed, and would have spent all his time lying on his stomach with a rifle in his hands if they had let him.

In a relaxed moment, Hare broached a subject which was never far from his mind.

'Have you ever wondered why I recognised you?' he asked.

Koberg looked at him suspiciously. 'I thought it was to do with Jacobs.'

He uttered the name with venom, and Hare wondered what falling-out of thieves had occurred.

'In a way it was,' said Hare. 'Do you remember giving evidence at a tribunal at which Jacobs was putting the case for the Company? The defendant was a man called Hare? Yes, I see you do.' For Koberg's face had instantly become alert. 'I was the defendant,' said Hare. 'I'm Hare.'

For a moment, Koberg obviously couldn't believe it. He searched Hare's face. Then, to Hare's alarm, his features assumed an expression of intense anger.

'You?' exclaimed Koberg. '*You*?'

It was extraordinary, thought Hare: as if he had done something to harm Koberg, rather than the other way round.

'That's right. I joined the marginals when I lost my job, and then I came down here.'

'Marginals? Then you came down here? But who are you then, all you lot? I mean, whose side are you on? I thought you were something to do with the Company. Jacobs said there was a plot.'

Hare could not make head or tail of what he was saying, so ignored it.

'What I want to know,' he persisted, 'is what was that tribunal all about? Why was I fitted up for something I hadn't done? You gave false evidence.'

'Good God, how should I know?' said Koberg disgustedly. 'It happens all the time.'

Hare got angry. 'I don't care whether it happens all the time. I want to know why it happened to me. You went to my flat, and pretended that you'd found a docket there which wasn't there. Why go to such trouble? I wasn't important.'

''Course you weren't,' said Koberg. 'It was Jacobs. You pulled his chestnuts out of the fire. Pity: they should've roasted a bit longer.'

'What chestnuts?'

'Well, it was him that removed the dockets, wasn't it?'

'*He* removed the dockets?'

''Course he did. They were incriminating, because of what the factory was manufacturing. Then he had this big cover-up job to do, when the fact the dockets weren't there was discovered. That's where you came in.'

Hare tried to think.

'The dockets were to do with something illegal that one of the Company's factories was manufacturing?'

'Yes.'

'What was it manufacturing?'

'But I thought you *knew* about that,' said Koberg, staring at him. 'It's what the canisters are, the ones I was looking for. The Company's been making that stuff for years. There's really going to be some fun when the whistle blows.'

Hare could find nothing to say. Koberg went on, 'Jacobs is playing a very deep game, and he thinks he'll win. He wants people put out of the way if they're a nuisance and then he thinks he doesn't have to pay for the service. He believes he's going to the top, Mr High-and-Mighty Jacobs, where he won't have to pay his debts.'

'You mean he wanted me put out of the way?' said Hare.

'Nah.' Koberg was scornful. He made the motion of cutting his throat with an imaginary knife. 'Put out of the way for good. It was an old guy, a bookseller or something. Jacobs wanted the building, it was some scheme or other.'

His voice trailed off, uninterested. Afer a few moments Hare said in a small, dry voice, 'What happened to this bookseller?'

'House burnt down,' said Koberg, and sniggered. 'Very inflammable, all that paper.'

A long time seemed to elapse. Then Hare said, 'Did you do that?'

Koberg went on the defensive. 'He was leaning on me, I had orders . . .'

He broke off in surprise as Hare pushed past him.

Out in the tunnels, Hare began walking towards the nearest exit. It was the early hours of the morning when he stepped out into the streets. The city was at the point where life had most withdrawn from it. The houses and shops slumbered. Once or twice a lorry droned past on a main road. Hare kept to the sidestreets, where not even a prowling cat crossed his path.

He walked for two hours, and at the end of that time a number of things of which he had had only a theoretical understanding had become as real to him as his own body. The streets through which he walked, the city and all who lived in it, were in the grip of a complex evil. It was possible to attach labels to this evil and call it the Company or the Government, but that was misleading because another Company and another Government would be of the same nature. The evil was inherent in their very structure; anything which assumed the same structure would thereby take on the evil.

And what was evil in the structure was that it was a structure for controlling. The Report had spelt it out with complete clarity: the Government's supreme task was 'to preserve the State as a governable entity'. The convoluted plotting of Jacobs on behalf of the Company had been essentially for the same end: to preserve the Company intact.

Hare stood in the shadows of the sleeping city and contemplated the ruin that was caused by the desire to control the future; the chaos that flowed ceaselessly from the defence of order. Yet the gigantic effort was not self-defeating: the ruin was in human terms, and human casualties were unimportant. The machine itself ground on. And yet what was this machine? It did not exist. It was simply people. There were people who by resigning their humanity had become like parts of a machine.

And they knew what they were doing. Jacobs knew, Koberg knew. The author of the Report had known, and had assumed his readers would know. They were not innocent: they had chosen.

The Diggers were wrong in their pacifism, Hare thought. Anything that could be done to diminish that inhuman empire should be done.

Detective Koberg was starting to enjoy himself.

Once he had realised that the weird people living in this horrible place were not going to kill him, and would not even leave him alone in the dark if he was polite to them, he relaxed and began to size up the situation. It was not all bad. True, he was in effect a prisoner, there was a total lack of amusements in the place, the sanitary arrangements were disgusting and the food was unbelievable. On the other hand, if he played his cards right, he would not be here much longer, and meanwhile there was something to be said for being no longer under the eye of the gorilla from the loan company. Nor was that all.

To his surprise, Detective Koberg found his contempt for his captors mixed with a sort of sympathy. Once he had worked out who they were – not, as he'd first thought, something to do with the plot Jacobs had mentioned, but just a different sort of marginals, planning a half-baked revolution – he felt that he understood what they wanted, and that it was not very different from what he wanted. It seemed to him that they hated the same people. He too knew the desire to seize what was his, to burn and destroy. Indeed it came upon him sometimes with such ferocity that he hardly knew what to do with himself.

He instructed The Bag in the use of the Noah's Ark firearms they had, and he enjoyed that because he always enjoyed anything to do with guns. They did what he told them, and he liked that, too. He had grasped the fact that they wouldn't take orders; but they would obey instructions because they wanted to learn, and he thought that if you were clever you would be able to get them to do pretty well what you wanted.

If it wasn't for the ridiculous way they looked, with their flapping rags and bits of bloodstained paper on their chins, he almost wouldn't mind joining them. Well, leading them would be more like it. Koberg's pulse quickened. His own little band.

If it wasn't for the ridiculous way they looked, and for the fact that they were doomed to failure. Because, however many there were of them – and he hadn't worked out what the older ones intended to do – the antique weapons they carried would be useless. They would be a danger to those who carried them. He could see his pupils, lying prone or crouched behind rubble or resting barrels on a windowsill as he had taught them, fighting with jammed cartridges while a police marksman prepared to pick them off.

It was then he remembered the canisters. Hare had been

bluffing him at the time of his capture. They would not be full of sand at all.

The Bag were clustered round a bed peering at something when Hare went into the dormitory for target practice. He nudged his way through.

Laid out on the mattress were several dozen metallic-looking black spheres about the size of an orange. A few of The Bag had picked them up and were handling them nervously.

'Whatever you do, don't drop them!' Koberg was saying.

Hare picked one up. It was even heavier than it looked. There were notches on it as if it had to be fitted into something. Between the notches was a die-stamped skull. Hare weighed it on his palm. It felt ugly.

'What are they?' he asked.

'Gas grenades,' said Koberg. 'They were in the canisters you said were full of sand.' He held one up, turning it as if it were a rare gem. 'They explode on impact, releasing the gas. What happens next depends on what mixture the gas is. They've been experimenting with this stuff for years; some of it kills you stone dead and some of it just gives you a bad time. I don't know what's in these but the skull probably means it's the lethal kind. There are some sealed canisters for use with a spray, but that's not so handy for your purposes.'

Hare put the grenade carefully back on the mattress.

'What do you mean,' he asked, 'by "our purposes"?'

The Bag looked sheepish.

'We told him what we're going to do,' Dido said.

Hare didn't see that it made much difference. Koberg, however, appeared to be building a great deal on it.

'Now that you've told me what you want to do I can really help you,' he said. 'The rifles are kids' stuff compared to this. With the rifles – well, you might hold out for a while,

212

but with this you're in the big time. No-one is going to argue with these.'

He held the grenade before them again, like a salesman, or a priest.

The Bag looked at the grenade, and then at Koberg, with the watchful but fascinated expressions of children in front of a conjurer.

'What makes them so much better than the rifles?' asked Fitz.

'Kill a lot more people,' grinned Koberg. 'Hundreds at a time. Like flies.'

A look of revulsion crossed the faces of many of his audience.

'I'm not sure I want to kill hundreds of people like flies,' said Al.

Koberg glanced round and realised his mistake.

'Ah well, you see,' he said quickly, 'you won't have to. That's the beauty of it. You've got something so powerful that the mere threat of it's enough.'

They looked interested. He followed it up.

'In fact you are much less likely to have to use these than you would be to have to use the rifles.'

'But if we do use them we'll kill hundreds of people like flies,' said Al.

'But you won't *have* to use them,' said Koberg. 'That's what I'm telling you. The point of them is that you won't have to use them.'

'That's crazy,' objected Dido.

'It's perfectly logical,' said Fitz. 'You just aren't listening.'

'It's you who aren't listening,' said Dido. 'What he's saying is that we can't afford to use them. They're only useful as a threat.'

'So?'

'Suppose the people we're trying to threaten know that?'

'How should they?' said Fitz angrily.

Some of the older Diggers had come into the room, Tapper and Danny among them. They looked searchingly at the grenades and then at Koberg, but said nothing.

'If we *should* want to use them,' said Fitz, '*how* would we use them?'

'They're designed to be fired from a launcher, but you can throw them,' said Koberg. 'They've got this nice little loop here, you see, which you can use to hang them from your belt.'

'Where did these things come from?' asked Tapper with distaste.

'Oh, the Company made them for the police,' said Koberg. 'I was looking for them when you found me.'

'And who do you propose to throw them at?' asked Tapper.

'Concentrations of enemy personnel, any buildings or structures you want to flush the enemy out of . . .' Koberg appeared to be quoting something.

'Who's the enemy?' said Danny.

'Depends,' said Koberg, 'doesn't it? In this case it's likely to be the police.'

They all stared at him. He seemed unconscious that he had said anything strange.

After a while someone said, 'But you've just told us that this gas will kill people like flies.'

'Yes,' said Koberg. 'Bullets can kill people too, if you get them in the right place.'

'But,' said Leah, '*you*'re a policeman.'

Koberg looked taken aback for a moment, then embarrassed. 'Just take it that I've come round to your way of thinking,' he said.

There was a stunned silence. Then:

'You want to *join* us?' said Fitz.

'Well,' said Koberg. 'Let's just say, I'll help you and you help me.'

214

'Help you in what way?' asked Hare sharply.

Koberg looked at him with dislike, and said, 'A little project of my own which a couple of you can help me with. We can talk about it later. Not too much to ask, is it, in return for these?'

They studied him, standing there with his eyes hard and bright, holding out to them the globe of gas which they would not have to use.

Dido, who had been thoughtful for some time, said suddenly, 'If that gas is lethal to them it's lethal to us.'

'Ah,' said Koberg, and looked pleased. 'There are protective masks to go with it.' He fished inside a crate and brought out something rubbery which he began to put over his face. They watched in growing horror as his face became that of a malformed animal, with monstrous blind eyes, snout and a perforated disc where the mouth should be.

There was silence for a few moments. Then Al said, 'I'm not wearing that.'

'Nor am I,' said Dido, and someone else said, 'And I'm not throwing one of those things, either.'

'For heaven's sake,' said Fitz, 'it's the answer to the problem. It's a fantastic piece of luck. What's the matter with you?'

There was a murmur of agreement from the group of boys who were usually clustered around Pug. Pug took out his penknife and began an excavation of a thumbnail.

'Fitz is right: it would be crazy to turn this down,' he said.

'But it's horrible!' said Al.

'If I may express an opinion, I think it's disgusting and inhuman,' Tapper said. 'It doesn't even look human.'

'You may not express an opinion in this room, to which you were not invited,' said Fitz.

'I'm sorry, but some things are too important for one to wait to be invited,' said Danny.

'I wondered when you'd discover that,' said Fitz.

215

'If *I* may express an opinion,' put in Koberg, 'you seem to think there's a difference between killing someone with a bullet and killing them with gas. There isn't. Dead is dead.'

'There's a difference between fighting and murder,' said Joe. 'Why can't they use their rifles?'

'Oh, the rifles are all right now, are they?' sneered Fitz.

'They're all right because they're no good,' said Pug. 'They don't shoot properly.' He turned to Koberg. 'Isn't that what you are saying?'

'The ammunition's off,' said Koberg. 'It jams, it misfires, you can't rely on it.'

'I'd rather rely on it than on those things,' said Al.

'But the rifles will just get you killed,' persisted Koberg. 'While you're fiddling about with them the police will wipe you out. You'd be better off unarmed: there's a chance you might not be fired on, then. The police have automatic weapons. Don't you understand what that means? They can *spray* bullets, several hundred a minute. Those rifles are slow to reload, they aren't accurate –'

'I can hit the centre of the target with mine from the other end of the room,' said Hare.

'I expect you can, lying down comfortably and taking quarter of an hour to aim it,' said Koberg.

'Suppose we take the rifles and are prepared to use the grenades if we have to,' suggested someone in Pug's group.

'But if the rifles are no good we *will* have to, so we might as well use the grenades in the first place and save ourselves getting killed,' said Pug.

'*Use* them!' exclaimed Danny. 'A few minutes ago the whole point of them was that they wouldn't be used! What's happening to you? Has he poisoned your brains?'

'Shut up, Danny,' said Fitz between his teeth.

Leah said, 'I do think if we used the grenades at all it would have to be in self-defence.'

'But by that time we'll be *dead*,' said Pug.

'Look, do you want weapons that work or don't you?' shouted Koberg.

'I think I'd rather have ones that didn't,' said Al, white-faced, 'if that's what it means.'

At this the argument became ferocious. Fitz, Pug and about twenty others insisted that those who supported Al could not simply back out of the agreed plan because they disliked the new weapons, that if they did so they would be betraying The Bag, and that if they chose to fight alongside the others with weapons that were a liability, that would also be letting their comrades down. At which Al and his supporters became very angry indeed and said that if you had to turn your back on everything you believed in in order to fight for something, there was no point in fighting for it.

Koberg listened, his small cold eyes darting over them, his face flushed. He was in a state of considerable excitement, Hare saw. He really wanted The Bag to accept his gruesome offering; he really wanted them to put grotesque masks on their faces and go out to lob killer gas at policemen. The policemen who for years had been Koberg's colleagues.

Hare wondered at the furniture of Koberg's mind. He had assumed that Koberg, if allowed out of the tunnels, would at once give them away to the authorities; but now, seeing the flush of fever on the young man's face, he knew that Koberg wanted something different. He was not sane, Hare realised, and saw with a chill that the madness was infectious, for The Bag, still arguing, were dividing into groups of those who did and those who did not agree to the adoption of the grenades, and the first group was the larger.

13

They were barmy, Koberg thought. All that fuss over a bit of gas. It was very hard to please some people: he might have got on better if he'd said the stuff didn't work.

However, they had come round in the end. Not all of them, but then he didn't need all of them: he didn't need more than two or three. What happened to the rest was their own concern. They didn't have much chance, but then they would have had even less of a chance without him. They ought to be grateful.

His own plans were laid. Everything had fallen into place quite suddenly, when he prised open the first canister and saw what it contained. Here was power. Never again would he have such an opportunity. He owed it to himself to take it.

It would be a quick strike and a quick getaway. Koberg knew what was in the police armouries, and he didn't intend to be at the wrong end of it.

In the end, opinion among The Bag was roughly two to one in favour of the grenades. Since those who disapproved of them could not, in logic, be part of a group which was using them, this meant that Al and his group were barred from taking part in the occupation of Skylight.

Al was bitter. He refused to speak to Fitz or any of Fitz's group. The rift within The Bag widened daily. Al and his friends moved to another dormitory. Hare saw all this with a sadness sharpened by the knowledge of his own part in it. He wished profoundly that he had never interfered.

'Don't blame yourself,' Danny said. 'There's something inevitable about it. It became inevitable as soon as they found the rifles. We should have hidden them better.'

'*You* should have hidden them?' said Hare.

'We've known for years they were there. We should have thrown them into the burial pit,' said Danny. 'The trouble is, we aren't used to throwing things away.'

There was a terrible sadness among the older Diggers, too. They expressed a forced optimism about The Bag's chances, but they knew that their own way of life was coming to an end. They did not want their children to try to keep the secret of the tunnels under the various methods of interrogation the police might use. They would have to go back and live as marginals. The Bag seemed not to have grasped the implications, and to expect the older Diggers to carry on as usual.

In the few days following the debate over the gas, a decision gradually crystallised in the minds of the older Diggers to do something to support The Bag. Something peaceful, naturally, but something that might usefully divert the attention of the police while The Bag were taking possession of their territory. It was enough simply to show themselves, they decided; they would emerge from the tunnels and walk in procession through the centre of the city.

'When do we go?' said Fitz, who was looking very tense.

There was a feeling that it should be as soon as possible.

'Something's up,' Ezra said as Angel came into the kitchen.

They did not often see each other in the mornings, because Angel had usually gone to bed by the time Ezra came down. On this occasion, Angel had been chased by a policeman, which delayed him, and Ezra had had a sleepless night.

'What kind of something?' asked Angel.

'Diggers,' said Ezra.

It took a moment for this to penetrate Angel's preoccupation. Then he sat down.

'What are they doing?'

'God knows,' said Ezra. 'God knows what they *think* they're doing. Coming out into the open – some sort of demonstration.'

'When?'

'Today.'

'But what on earth for? They've never come out. It'll change everything.'

'Yes,' said Ezra heavily, 'I fear it will.'

Angel studied him. His mood was uncharacteristic.

'There's something you aren't telling me,' he said.

Ezra shrugged. 'I can hardly believe it, but it must be true because otherwise the demonstration doesn't make sense. Some of them are coming out armed.'

'What?'

'It seems they have some sort of secret weapon.'

'They're going to blow up the Council?'

'It's not a matter for joking, Angel.'

'I'm sorry,' said Angel. 'Of course it isn't. Only I can't believe it either.'

They sat at the table in a thoughtful silence for a few minutes. Then Angel said, 'What do they hope to gain?'

'Their birthright. The young ones want to come back up and live.'

'Oh.' Angel took a deep breath. 'I see.'

'Well, perhaps it's understandable. But to do it this way makes no sense at all.'

'Probably not.'

'And will put all marginals in very grave danger.'

Angel looked at him. Ezra's face was drawn with sleeplessness and worry. 'I see,' Angel said again.

220

Ezra flared up at him. 'It's not myself. I'm not a coward.'

'I know,' said Angel.

'I feel I have a responsibility. This house – '

Ezra flung his hands out, indicating the scope of his burden. It turned into a gesture of despair as he buried his face in them.

'Considering the other people who live in this house,' said Angel, 'you probably do have a responsibility.'

'And so,' said Ezra, '*do they.*'

There was a pause.

Angel said, 'You mean the Diggers have no right to do this because of the effect it will have on us?'

'Yes. It would be a different matter if they had some chance of success.'

'Would it?'

'You presumably think they do have a right.'

'There will always be marginals,' said Angel. '*They* need us, they need us to be visible. The Zone isn't enough by itself. Life may not be pleasant for a time, but in the long run we're safe.'

'I don't want to see lynchings,' said Ezra. 'Nor do I want to be lynched. I suppose I am a coward.'

'If you like,' said Angel. 'I don't know what the word means. Courage, cowardice. It's a lot of nonsense. Sometimes people are one thing and sometimes they're the other. What does it matter anyway? It's not as if brave people always do useful things. They can be a terrible liability.'

Ezra smiled.

'But yes,' said Angel, 'I do think the Diggers have a right.'

'Ah.'

'They have a right to live decently. They have a right to claim that right. We don't have a right to expect them to put our safety before their needs.'

'Do they have a right to claim their rights by force?'

'I think we've been here before,' said Angel.

221

'We have. I thought you opposed violence against the State on the grounds that it was illogical.'

'Yes. Sometimes I think one thing and sometimes I think the other. This morning I think the other.'

'It doesn't seem to me to be the sort of subject one can be frivolous about,' observed Ezra.

'I'm not being frivolous. I'm trying to be honest. It's very difficult, Ezra. I envy you your certainty that the use of force is always wrong.'

'It's the essence of the system we deplore.'

'I know. But suppose it's the only way of overcoming the system we deplore?'

'In time power decays.'

'And we shall all be dead. Which doesn't matter, but suppose everyone else who cares is dead as well? Power doesn't just stifle opposition, it stifles the ability to think in opposition. And suppose power *can* only be fought with power, Ezra, and that some kinds of power are worse than others, and that what goes on out there – ' he jerked his head at the door ' – is a particularly vicious kind?'

'You would kill for that?'

'Me?' Angel laughed. 'Goodness, hardly my style.' His voice became serious. 'You do know that there are different forms of violence, don't you?'

'Meaning?'

'You don't have to kill people. You can just deprive them of hope so they kill themselves. I grew up in the ghettos.'

'I know,' said Ezra.

The silence returned.

Finally Ezra said, 'Well, we shan't agree. I respect your views.'

'Thank you,' said Angel. 'I think you're all right, too, Ezra, in spite of being so lamentably strait-laced and serious.'

They smiled at each other. Angel went out.

*

222

The Diggers made their way into the city through an entrance deep in the shadows of a railway arch. All of them were there, except a few who had stayed behind to look after the children. They filed through the narrow opening with many nervous glances, the hesitant ones encouraged by their friends. Some had not visited the surface for years, and in their thoughts it had become not quite real.

They stood in the empty roadway, shading their eyes from the sun, while the procession formed. They had chosen an area likely to be deserted, a dingy common used unofficially as a waste dump, but a group of men pushing a broken-down car saw them and stopped to gape.

The procession moved off. It was colourful: in the bright light the Diggers' bizarre rags took on a poetic quality. They walked down a street of small and ill-kept houses also transfigured by the sunlight, dazzling on window panes and car roofs.

A man standing on the opposite pavement stared at the procession, then spat in the gutter.

The Diggers kept walking roughly north-east, towards the bridge that led to the city centre. The slum area in which they had come out was on the edge of the expanding commercial district. The transition from one to the other was abrupt: you crossed a major road and were in a different world.

The Diggers began to cross the road. Cars screamed to a halt, swerved violently; pedestrians scuttled into doorways, or if there was no doorway pressed themselves against the wall. A few people gesticulated angrily before disappearing into the fortress-like bank buildings that lined the road.

So far they had seen no policemen.

'At least the citizenry haven't thrown anything yet,' said Danny. 'Have you noticed that some marginals have joined us?'

Glancing behind, Hare saw a number of faces which were

223

undoubtedly friendly but which he did not recognise. It lifted his spirits.

A few minutes later they were on the bridge. Hare wished they had thought more carefully about this because, although the pavement was of a generous width, the procession took up all the room and those on the inside were squeezed against the stone balustrade. However, there didn't seem to be any other pedestrians on the bridge. The traffic was thin, as well.

Too thin.

Hare stepped into the roadway with a sudden suspicion, and instantly leapt back to safety. Swinging into the lower end of the bridge behind the tail of the procession came the white motorbikes of the police. They roared past the procession, two abreast, deafening and choking the demonstrators. At the far end of the bridge they divided, wheeling off to left and right, presumably to wait. About a minute after they had disappeared from view, another wave of motorcycles came past, and then a third. After that, no more. No ordinary traffic. There were now only Diggers on the bridge.

Hare stepped out onto the street again and looked behind him. The southern end of the bridge had been sealed off. A line of white vans was strung across it. In front of the vans stood a row of policemen, feet apart in relaxed stance, each holding a riot stick.

Hare's heart began to thud.

Everyone in the procession had realised, with the passage of the motorbikes, that there was danger. They walked on, in what had become an oppressive silence save for the steady tramp of feet. A few voices tried to start a song, but could not overcome the silence. They walked on towards the northern end of the bridge.

At which a cordon of white-helmeted policemen now stood.

Steps faltered. People behind bumped into the ones ahead,

who had stopped. People turned round and tried to go back, not realising that the southern exit was also blocked, and blundered into those at the back who were trying to get away from the policemen behind them.

From both ends of the bridge, the line of white uniforms began to advance.

Hare could see it all, could see what would happen. He shouted, but shouts only intensified the panic. He knew they would start to climb up onto the stone parapet and jump into the river: anything to get away from those wickedly long riot sticks. But the river at that point was shallow and treacherous with mud. It was not possible to jump into the silty water from a height of twenty feet and hope to swim. Hare heard the screams of those who had jumped and were drowning in the mud. They mingled with other screams from the bridge. The riot sticks descended in rhythm. People were staggering, clutching their heads, while red oozed between their fingers. Those who had not been hit were running in bewilderment from one side of the bridge to the other, in the gradually narrowing space between the two ranks of police. Hare had seen trapped mice behave in the same way.

He had once seen a trapped mouse in desperation fling itself straight at its tormentor, who, astonished at such unmouselike behaviour, let it get away.

Hare's brain felt very clear. He did a rapid estimate of the number of police: about eighty, not more. The police had been taken by surprise. There were nearly three hundred demonstrators. The eighty were divided into two. It must be done now, while the two lines of police were still quite widely separated and before reinforcements arrived.

For some reason they followed him: perhaps they had made the same calculation. For a long time the police didn't fire: the mouse was right. The first shot, a hot dry sound like snapping bone, ripped out when they were almost on the line of white uniforms. Hare kept running. He expected to die. Part of his mind was in agreement with dying. It saw that his life had been a muddle, that things would get worse and not better, that he would never be able to solve anything, and that here, now, in this small space of passionate action, was a redemption into some sort of meaning. This part of his mind remained calm and directed him forward. The other part of his mind was terrified and gibbering, and he ignored it.

He was facing a wall of perspex. The eyes behind the visors were cold like metal. There was something strange about the faces: a distortion. As he closed his own eyes, put up his arms to protect his head and allowed himself to be carried forward like a battering ram by the surge of the crowd behind, he realised what the distortion was: fear.

He was being crushed. He seemed to be hanging, not standing, held up by the two forces he was caught between. Passive, he prayed only that he would be spared the pain that degrades – the pulped eyeball, the smashed groin. Then all at once there was nothing holding him up and he fell – squarely on hands and knees, scarcely hurt at all, but winded.

The crowd was running again, quite a way ahead of him, and there was exultant shouting. He set himself to catch up. There were a lot of faces he did not recognise now. He found himself after a few minutes' effort in the midst of a mob of laughing, cheering, skipping marginals.

One of the marginals was Angel.

Hare flung an arm round him.

'Well!' said Angel. 'Fancy meeting you here. It's naughty of you, Hare, not to come back to see us. We've missed you.'

'I'm sorry. I've been busy,' said Hare.

'You don't say,' said Angel. 'Was this your idea?'

They looked around them. On all sides rose the glass palaces.

*

Fitz's group stepped out into the sunlight, and stared round in bewilderment. The houses had gone.

For a moment Fitz thought they had come out of the wrong exit, although his brain told him that such a mistake was not possible. He was frightened. The whole thing was frightening enough without finding yourself in the wrong place.

Then, walking over the torn and flattened earth, he understood. It was not the wrong place. Hare had told them something was going to be built here. Well, in the short time since he had last visited the site, work had started.

He wanted to cry. It was so unfair: after all the planning and preparation there were no houses, there would be no Skylight.

'Have you seen the fence?' said Dido.

He hadn't noticed it. He looked at it now. A high fence made out of some sheet material – metal, plastic? It glinted in the light. It completely enclosed the large area in which they stood, an area the size of which he could not estimate except by saying that it was several times as big as the dining hall in the tunnels.

It had been put up, he presumed, to protect the trenches.

Only now did he register what had been done on the site. Deep trenches criss-crossed it in a grid pattern. Curiosity overcoming his depression, Fitz walked to one and looked down into it. He saw a wall of earth, rich brown in colour but flecked with the white and grey of small stones and shells. A soft wall compressed by the bite of metal, and in places still shiny where the metal had smoothed it. Worms wriggled in the earth. And at the bottom were more worms – fat ones, blue and white and orange ones, pipes to carry something or other.

He went over to another trench and found pillars of concrete standing in it.

This was interesting. Perhaps it didn't matter so much, he

227

thought, that the houses had been knocked down. There were still a few walls and half-demolished buildings here and there on the edges of the site, where they had come in: couldn't they live in those? He must talk to the rest of the group about it. They were all wandering about, looking into the trenches.

He watched Dido for a while. She did not agree with this – not with the grenade business – but she had come because of him. He was at the same time touched and irritated. It seemed to give him an extra burden of responsibility when already he had enough.

Shifting his gaze, he saw a box-like thing attached to the fence at head-height. In fact there were many of them, set at regular intervals along it. He tried to imagine what they were for, but all he could think of was that the workmen put their sandwiches in them to keep them away from insects. The surface was full of incomprehensible things: usually it excited him.

He had to decide what to do. Were they going to stay here? They had come to claim it and it seemed feeble to go back just because it was no longer in the same state as before. They must make another plan.

He was getting a headache.

He began walking along the side of the trenches. The intricacy and logic of their layout fascinated him. The grenade knocked against his hips. He had forgotten it for a moment. In fact he had almost forgotten what they were doing here.

His headache was quite bad. He sat down at the side of a trench because he thought it might help him think, and his eyes followed the travelling of the blue, white and orange pipes. So clever, so pretty.

All of a sudden they were not pretty at all but made him think of intestines, and he wanted to vomit. He got up unsteadily and started walking again. He did not know

228

where he was going but it was important to move; it seemed to control what was happening in his head.

Dido came towards him like a sleepwalker.

'What's the matter with you?' he said sharply.

'Fitz, there's something wrong here,' Dido said. 'We ought to go back.'

'Don't be silly, we aren't going back.'

The effort of speaking coherently made him nauseous once more; after a moment's strenuous effort to contain himself, he surrendered and vomited on the ground.

'*Fitz!*' Dido tugged at his arm.

He lost the rest of what she was saying: the words disappeared from his mind as soon as he heard them. He waved her away, and then forgot about her.

Soon he realised that the way to stop the fissioning and flickering in his brain was to jump into the trenches and walk along them, and that was what he did. He followed the logic of the pipes, and it did not let him down. He walked and walked, and always blue followed blue, white white and orange orange; and he met others who were weaving their own paths between the walls, and in some cases sitting down, as in the end he did, and waiting.

Waiting.

Hare didn't see who threw the first stone: there was a loud crack, and above him a window starred. The cheering rose in a wave, and almost at once windows were shattering all along the road. There was no shortage of ammunition: kerbstones, paving stones, traffic signs and flower tubs were being prised out, broken up and sent through the air. Angel, whooping with delight, had found a scaffolding pole and was systematically breaking all the ground-floor windows of a newspaper office. From the upper floors, the ashen faces of the newspaper staff looked down on the riot.

'Print this!' whooped Angel.

Until that moment, Hare had thought himself not the kind of person who would ever give way to impulsive violence. Now, with dramatic suddenness, it overtook him. He hated, fully and passionately, for the first time in his life, and what he hated was all around him. It was the Company, with its endlessly-ramifying interests, which would kill if those interests were threatened; it was the featureless conspirator in the quiet rooms, where truth was never considered and controllability was all.

He threw stones with a savage joy. Every stone was hurled with all his strength: it was a tiny blow against Leviathan. He ran, cheered, exulted and smashed, in a sort of drunkenness and an ecstatic comradeship with the ragged folk around him.

He had heard the gunshots for several minutes before he registered what they were. Then, running down an alley in the direction of the sound, he saw Al and his friends shooting at car tyres with their rifles. Al was wild-eyed, and had a streak of blood down his face.

'Where are the milkmen?' said Al.

Where, indeed, were they?

'Lend me your rifle for a minute,' said Hare.

He swung it in an arc, taking in the many windows of an insurance company. Insurance! Insure against loss, against accident and natural catastrophes, against political dissent and social unrest and the mutability of the world. Ensure that nothing ever changes, or that if it does the change will not affect you. Preserve. Preserve yourself.

There was a face at the end of the rifle barrel, small but distinct. Hare's finger was covering the trigger. The face looked at him.

Hare looked at the face, and was arrested by its expression. There was fear, but also something else. A contempt which, Hare knew, exactly mirrored his own. That man, thought Hare, sees me in precisely the same way as I see him. If I kill him, I am only doing what he has known all along I will do to him. There is no difference between my hatred for him and his for me, between my conviction of rightness and his. And since that is so, how can I act on my own passionate feeling, when it is all the same thing?

He lowered the rifle and gave it back to Al.

They were in an open space from which radiated several streets, and one side of which was occupied by the former art gallery, now a government department. A wide, shallow flight of steps rose from the street to the building's entrance. Many marginals and Diggers had gravitated to this area from the neighbouring streets and were congregating on the lower steps. Angel had climbed part of the way up a pillar at the top of the flight.

Hare made his way over to him. In the bright sunlight Angel's pale skin seemed translucent. He was pointing over the heads of the crowd.

Then Hare saw the tanks.

By two-thirty on the afternoon of the tenth day, Jacobs was near collapse.

He had not heard again from Koberg, but there was no reason why he should. Koberg had delivered his ultimatum, and would act on it as soon as the tenth day had expired.

Or slightly earlier. Koberg had telephoned him on the morning of the Wednesday before last: it had been the first call Jacobs received when he got into the office. This was Friday. If Koberg wanted to be sure of getting hold of Jacobs, he would have to do it before Jacobs left the office for the weekend. It was less than ten days: but a man who took to blackmail like a duck to water was not likely to be scrupulous over a few hours.

The call from Koberg could come at any moment. Jacobs's palms sweated.

He could bluff, he supposed. But Koberg would see

through it. And what would be the point? At some stage soon he would have to say that he did not intend to pay the money, and Koberg's revenge would be all the more vicious if he had been lied to.

All morning the sound of the telephone buzzing in his secretary's office had made him nervous, although it was always his personal line, which did not go through the switchboard, that Koberg used. So far that telephone had rung four times today. It had not rung since lunch. Jacobs knew that when next it rang he would not have the courage to answer it.

He must disconnect it. Otherwise his secretary would hear it ringing and come in. And find him sitting there looking at it.

He moved to disconnect it and then realised that, if Koberg was unable to get through on that line, he would simply ring the switchboard, in which case his secretary and anyone in the switchboard room who felt like it would also be able to hear the conversation.

He could simply tell his secretary that he was leaving early, and go home. Would Koberg be able to reach him there? Of course he would. Koberg was a policeman. In despair Jacobs contemplated his own cowardice, and knew that even if he escaped Koberg's call at the office he could not bear a weekend spent in this torment of uncertainty.

There was only one thing to do. He had known all week that there was only one thing to do.

He reached for the white telephone.

Koberg had run into trouble.

He had picked this bank with care. It was in an unmodern-ised building in a narrow one-way street and it had a roomy entrance with a conventional door. It was in the business sector and handled large transactions, but at this time of day it would be quiet.

The plan was for Koberg and one other person to burst into the bank and demand the money, while two more colleagues outside prevented anyone from entering, and also commandeered a passing car. The boy called Pug and two of his friends had volunteered, and Koberg was to drop them later at a place from which they could get back to the tunnels.

It was a simple plan, and in Koberg's experience simple plans worked best, particularly when you were relying on amateurs. There was no reason why this plan should not have worked, if the layout of the entrance hadn't been changed.

The side-hinged door had been replaced by a heavy steel-and-glass revolving door. A lot of businesses were installing them: they looked impressive and could be electronically locked in position – thus closing the entrance – by the touch of a button somewhere inside the premises.

Koberg and Pug, pulling masks over their heads, got inside the bank and someone locked the door.

Pug's friends, who had been jittery from the start, realised from Pug's frantic gestures through the glass that something was wrong, and took off.

Koberg reckoned he still had a chance. The grenade was in his fist, and a terrified cashier began thrusting money into a sack for him. Angrily Koberg gestured for more speed, more money. He demanded that they open the door, but his voice through the mask was muffled and they pretended not to understand, and of course he couldn't remove the mask because then he would not be able to throw the grenade.

There was a buzzing in his ears. He shook his head to get rid of it, and then knew what it was. The alarm had been activated.

Furious, he grabbed the money with one hand and lobbed the grenade into the back of the room with the other. He didn't know what was in it, but it served them right anyway.

233

He picked up a chair and smashed it through the street window. Then he turned to Pug, but the boy was standing by the wall shivering and was obviously no use for anything. Koberg would have to find his own car.

He poked his head through the hole in the glass. Six policemen were jumping out of a white van and taking cover behind it.

The little grey tanks advanced from several directions on the crowd. There were nine of them, and within a minute of their appearance at the end of the streets which led to the square they had fanned out to encircle the crowd, who were trapped on the steps of the government building.

A hush descended as the crowd watched the approach of the strange vehicles.

There was something insect-like about them. They were about the size of a large car but higher-roofed, and they were high-slung with a sort of beak at the front. They had no windows, only a single slit where the driver's head would be. They were made of flat sheet metal apparently bolted together, and this utilitarian design was for some reason very frightening. However, what gave them their peculiar menace was the wide, fluted gun barrel mounted at the top. As they approached, the barrel swivelled in this direction and that in horrible suggestion of an antenna.

Hare recognised them as the vehicles he had seen coming out of a Company warehouse yard.

They advanced steadily. The slowness was part of the terror. Signs of panic now appeared among the crowd. People were pushing and jostling, but without clear purpose, for there was nowhere to go except back, back up the steps where they were even more exposed.

The little tanks came on. Those unpleasantly wide mouths had, Hare now saw, a sort of mesh arrangement just before the aperture. Were there people inside the things, or were they just machines? One could not ask a machine for mercy.

The crowd was now tightly surrounded. Angel was clinging to the pillar a short distance from Hare; he was pointing again and shouting something, but Hare could not make out what it was partly because of the noise of the approaching tanks and partly because his brain had ceased functioning. Dread had settled on him like a cloak.

The tanks stopped.

There was a long, long moment.

Then one of the tanks raised its proboscis and aimed it straight at Angel, who seemed unable to move. There was a rustling sound, and out of the mouth of the thing came a long tongue of flame, which engulfed Angel and withdrew, and Angel toppled forward shrieking with his clothes on fire.

Half a dozen people flung themselves on the smoking body to extinguish the flames. By the time Hare got to him, Angel's eyes were closed. He looked dead. Shock, Hare thought vaguely, and glanced around: at any moment there might be a panic-stricken stampede. With help, he lifted Angel and held him in his arms like a child.

Hare realised then that the whole crowd was screaming.

Things were confused after that. Hare found he was carrying Angel through the streets. He walked without direction, from time to time putting Angel down to rest.

He laid him down gently, for the sixth or seventh time, on a low wall on which were growing tiny ferns and mosses. He was glad of them, for Angel's sake, and he also liked the wall, which was a real stone wall and not concrete. Then he saw that it was the wall bounding a churchyard. Inside the churchyard were green hummocks, tufted and riotous with tall grasses and wild flowers. Headstones leaned. Grey slate, white granite. Lettering softened by rain, the graves blurred, the bodies too, beneath. Fittingly, he supposed. Better the earth than the fire.

A priest was coming out of the church and down the path towards him. This was impossible, there were no priests left; or was that another lie, and did they live on, carefully, like mice? The priest had a faded look like an old photograph. He knelt on the wall beside Angel and took the charred wrist in his hand. He said to Hare, 'He is dead.'

Hare nodded. Then the priest said something else, which Hare didn't catch because at that moment he heard shouting and the rattling fire of automatic weapons. Instinctively he covered his ears. Seconds later, a strong feeling that he was not finished with the day's events seized him. With an obscure sense of duty, he said goodbye to Angel and began walking towards the noise.

At the end of a long street, he turned a corner into a narrow thoroughfare where a police van was parked, and recoiled in disgust.

Crawling towards him was a figure he barely recognised as human, its white uniform fouled with vomit and blood. It was crawling in a peculiar way, like a toy whose mechanism has been slowed down. Its head turned slowly in this direction and that, with a motion he had only seen before in a tortoise.

With a thrill of horror, he saw that there were five more crawling figures behind it, making their slow and dying progress up the street, all doing the same tortoise-movement with their heads.

As Hare watched, the first figure collapsed and its body contracted in a muscular spasm. The spasm passed, but was succeeded by another, and another. At the end of the longest and most violent of the series, the body gave a single jerk that almost lifted it into the air, and lay still in a pool of filth.

From further down the road Hare heard Koberg's voice, subjected to some grotesque distortion, demanding more money, a safe-conduct, more money.

A small grey tank passed him at speed, heading for the scene. It was followed by a line of police vans.

'What are we going to do?' said Danny.

Her right arm had been paralysed by a blow from a riot stick. She was listless, but it was not from pain. Those who had managed to make their way back to the tunnels as the police flooded into the city centre were all in much the same state. They crowded together, shocked and exhausted, in one of the dormitories, making intermittent attempts to comfort one another and the subdued children. Al sat with his arms round Dido, who could not stop shivering. No-one else from Fitz's group had returned.

'All we can do is stay here and hope they forget about us,' muttered Tapper.

'Idiot, why should they forget about us?' said Danny wearily. 'They know where we are now.'

Of course they did. The tunnels had been a refuge for so long that it was difficult to grasp that they were a refuge no longer. Miserably the Diggers huddled in what had been their home, and one by one they realised that if this underground network was no longer safe, then it was the opposite thing – a trap.

'Can we block the tunnels?' asked Hare.

'Too many,' said Danny. 'There are dozens of entrances.'

'We could block the most obvious ones.'

'They're likely to use the least obvious ones.'

Hare chewed his knuckles. 'If they have a map . . .'

'If they have a map of the tunnels they'll be able to find their way through once they get inside. But if they don't have a map it won't stop them coming in if they want to. They'll have searchlights, they'll have – '

'God knows what they'll have,' said Tapper.

237

They thought for a moment about what the police might have.

'But at least we're on our own territory,' said Al. 'That must give us an advantage.'

'It would if they just came in with guns and searchlights,' said Hare. 'But suppose . . .'

Danny said, 'All they need to do is find the ventilating system and switch it off. We'd suffocate. Let's hope they don't think of it.'

There was dead silence. Hare pulled himself together. 'We need two plans,' he said. 'A defence plan and an evacuation plan. We need the evacuation plan first.'

'How can we make an evacuation plan when we don't know which direction they'll be coming from?' said Danny.

'Isn't there a direction they *couldn't* come from?' Hare said. 'Or that they would never choose?'

He saw Danny's brow crease with the effort of thought. Finally she made a hopeless gesture and laughed. 'Only the Zone,' she said.

The air seemed to become chill.

'The Zone,' repeated Hare.

'I'd rather give myself up,' said the cellist. He was holding his cello with one hand and dabbing at the cut on his forehead with the other. He looked very ready to give himself up. Several Diggers around him grunted agreement.

'You won't get anyone to go there,' said Danny.

Hare said, 'You mean to tell me there is an exit from these tunnels into the Zone?'

'Of course there is,' said Danny. 'There are exits to every point in the city, so naturally there's one into the Zone. The network goes right underneath it.'

Naturally. Why hadn't he thought of it? The underground rail system went under it, so the tunnels would.

'How far away is it?'

'Not that far from here. About a mile and a half.'

238

'And you've never been there?' he said.

'Into the Zone?' the cellist laughed. 'D'you think we're crazy?'

'But there's nothing there!' protested Hare.

'Who told you that?'

'Ezra,' he remembered.

'That's what the marginals think,' said Danny. 'But they're wrong. There is something there, and it's dangerous.'

'What is it?'

'We don't know. Diggers used to live in that part of the tunnels, before they worked out where it was. They got ill, some of them died. We don't go there now.'

Hare was silent, thinking. The stories he had been brought up on were lies concocted by the Council and its accomplices. That fact had come as such a liberation to him that he fought hard against accepting that there really might be something in the Zone to be afraid of. Yet the Diggers' faces were haunted, as if they had been reminded of a past horror.

'What sort of illness?' he asked.

'I didn't see it, it was before I came here,' said Danny. 'You should ask the older ones.' But the older Diggers showed no interest in replying: they merely shook their heads.

'It wasn't one illness in particular,' said Danny. 'That was what frightened them. They just got *ill*. Abscesses, diarrhoea, hair falling out, haemorrhages, difficulty in breathing . . . oh, all sorts of things. And they died . . . well, they just seem to have wasted away and died. As if they'd caught death, rather than a sickness.'

Hare struggled to get the conversation back to a rational footing.

'But the thing that made them ill might have been actually in the tunnels; perhaps buried there because it was dangerous? Like some sort of poison. It doesn't mean the Zone itself is poisoned.'

'Funny coincidence, though, isn't it?' said the cellist.

'How long,' Hare persisted, 'did they live there before they became ill?'

Danny shrugged, then winced. 'I don't know. Does it matter?'

'Yes, if it means we could go through that part of the tunnels safely as long as we don't linger in it.'

The air in the cavern had suddenly become heavy. There was a sweetish taste in Hare's mouth. Some of the Diggers had started coughing.

'But you're assuming what it is is inanimate,' said Danny. 'Suppose – '

She could get no further, but clutched her chest.

Something clicked audibly in Hare's brain. He dived at the huddle of children on the floor and pushed them towards the far end of the dormitory, shouting over his shoulder, 'Get out of here, it's the gas!'

They ran and stumbled down the tunnel. The air in the next passageway was clear: perhaps it would take some time for the gas to percolate through the network.

Ahead of them the tunnel forked. Danny pointed.

'It's that way.'

No-one asked where they were going. There was no choice.

14

'What a stupid man you are,' said Mr Lucy dispassionately.

Jacobs bowed his head. He had been through the worst afternoon of his life and it was not over yet.

'You have bungled everything,' said Mr Lucy. 'You have taken unnecessary risks and exposed the Company to goodness knows what hazards, both legal and political; you have taken into your confidence an amoral little rat from the police force who should never have been the recipient of any confidence at all and who has predictably betrayed you; and now you are attempting to blackmail me.'

Jacobs's lips contorted into a sickly smile. 'If I am interrogated, there will be certain unavoidable effects . . .'

Mr Lucy threw back his head and laughed. It was a clear, bone china laugh, and it made Jacobs feel like a cracked cup from the staff canteen.

'Anyone less naive, Jacobs, would see what he was trying to do. Have you never thought of yourself as naive? I suppose not. It accounts largely for your usefulness.'

He pressed the tips of his fingers together and waited for Jacobs to speak. Jacobs preferred not to.

'I admit you have done some good work,' Mr Lucy continued. 'Whatever your faults, it must be said that you have served what you believed to be the Company's interests unswervingly. You have been loyal, yes. We value that. One must accept the connection between loyalty and naivety.

Sometimes one wishes one could adjust the borderline between them a little.'

He gazed at the window, which it was not possible to see through because the blinds had been pulled down. They were always pulled down when Jacobs was in this room.

He would not be in this room again.

'However, you have never understood what the Company's interests are,' said Mr Lucy. 'If you had, you would not have made such a stupid mistake as to put yourself at the mercy of a policeman. You have assumed throughout that the Company's interests are antagonistic to those of the Council. They are not. The two sets of interests are complementary. The two organisations need each other.' He leaned forward slightly with a smile on his thin lips. 'The Company is a commercial organisation, Jacobs. It cannot govern, or legislate, or police. All it can do is make and sell things. And that is precisely what a government cannot do, and what it *must* have done for it.'

Jacobs did not understand. He was not even sure that Mr Lucy was addressing him. If there was one thing Jacobs knew about himself, it was that he was not naive.

'There are good reasons why this should not always have been obvious to you,' continued Mr Lucy, 'but I would have thought you would grasp the general principle. However, there we are.' His glance raked Jacobs up and down as if gauging the commonness of the clay of which Jacobs was made: very common. 'Many years ago the Company took over a function of the Government which the Government, for certain reasons, was no longer able to perform. The possession of that function brought with it a great deal of power, and such influence as the Company has in political matters is largely due to it.'

Jacobs could not help himself. 'What function is that?'

Mr Lucy flicked his fingers in contempt. 'My dear Jacobs,

don't you know what we manufacture? Of course you do. You've spent half your adult life concealing it.'

'You mean that the riot control agents and the prohibited . . . That the Council . . .' Jacobs was bewildered.

'What a literal mind you have,' said Mr Lucy. 'A function delegated may be forgotten. It certainly will be, if it is more convenient to forget it. Then it can be disowned.'

Jacobs saw light. 'We have continued manufacturing equipment for the police because it is in fact needed for security even if the Council chooses not to acknowledge it.'

Mr Lucy sighed. 'If you wish. Yes, we do that. That is part of what we do, and it is part of what the Council does not wish to know about, although – ' his eyebrows lifted ' – in the light of present events they may be less reluctant to know about it. No, I am referring to something much larger in scope, almost abstract in a sense. Some fifty years ago the Company, which was then of comparatively minor import- ance, took on a major economic role; one might even say *the* major economic role. I do not wish to be more specific, except to say that nothing that happens in this organisation, however bizarre it seems, is accidental. And some of it must have seemed bizarre even to you, Jacobs. Warehouses of rotting goods, and so on. Hmm?'

Jacobs was not interested. He was preoccupied by the 'must have'. His service to the Company was in the past tense.

'Well, never mind. The point – and of course you missed it – is that the friction between the Company and the Council is the friction between partners, not the friction between rivals. There is no rival to the Company. How could there be? No-one else can do what it does, and it is not fitted to do anything else.'

'But,' said Jacobs who no longer had anything to lose and was also beginning to get angry, 'there is a conspiracy.'

'Indeed?' said Mr Lucy. 'A conspiracy to do what?' He

243

toyed with a glass paperweight on his desk. It was the only thing on his desk, apart from a telephone.

'To replace the existing Council, I presume.'

'An interesting idea. And how is this to be done?'

'The police have the means,' said Jacobs, 'and we have supplied them.'

'Certainly they do, and we have, but it seems to have escaped your attention that the Council *has* been replaced, and without any of the excitement you suggest. You have met Mr Terry?'

'Oh yes,' said Jacobs.

'An excellent fellow. Most energetic. Don't you agree?'

Jacobs ignored this. 'There was a lot of secrecy over Drawbridge,' he persisted.

'Drawbridge!' Mr Lucy again gave his disquieting laugh. 'Drawbridge is part of your plot, is it? Jacobs, Drawbridge is part of something of which you have no conception. I will not tire your brain by saying more.'

He let a few seconds pass. Traffic droned in the street far below.

'There is no conspiracy,' said Mr Lucy. 'A small number of policemen may have developed ideas incompatible with their duty and been relieved of their posts, but that is all. A certain slackness may have crept into Company practice, particularly as regards relations with the police, but that is at an end. And to make clear that it is at an end, I shall take no steps to protect you from any investigation put in hand by the police or demanded by the Council.'

Jacobs was desperate. With consummate stupidity he played his card again, because it was his only card. 'Mr Lucy, I know things about this organisation which . . .'

'You know nothing,' interrupted Mr Lucy. 'If you did know something you wouldn't have the wit to know what it meant. You haven't even the intelligence to see that the value of what you do know has been completely changed by what is happening out there.' He pointed, oddly, not to the window but to one of the walls. 'There's a revolution going on. It's a silly piddling revolution, but that doesn't matter. It amply justifies all the equipment the police aren't supposed to have. Do you imagine the Council will complain about riot control agents now?' He stared with contempt into Jacobs's eyes. 'You may go and clear your desk,' he said.

Jacobs, after a moment, turned and left the room.

When he had gone, Mr Lucy sat for a few minutes toying with his paperweight. It was a rare one. He collected them.

He understood why Jacobs had taken the policeman into his confidence. Being in possession of information such as Jacobs possessed (and some of it was important, although he had belittled it) was isolating. It could weigh heavy. One longed to talk about it to someone, from a variety of motives, one of which was the desire to see what such knowledge looked like to a normal human being. Allied to this, but more dangerous, was the desire to impress, to silence. He himself had been tempted, out of sheer irritation, to tell Jacobs the truth about the 'conspiracy': how nicely it had been handled, the Company extending just enough encouragement to the dissident officers to ensure a boost in weapons sales but not enough to commit itself politically, for the Company was always neutral, it would always wait to see which way the cat jumped . . .

A game, yes, but a necessary one.

Fortunately, militating against this temptation to tell was the even stronger desire to keep one's knowledge secret, not because it was supposed to be secret but because there was nothing so seductive and heady in the world as secret knowledge. Poor Jacobs: his downfall had been that he was not seduced by secrets. But then, a man not seduced by them does not deserve them.

Secrets, games. All save one, the biggest one. In a sense that was a game too, but no-one had found the way to play it. Mr Lucy stood up and walked to the window, and pulled up the blind. A summer evening.

Hare and the Diggers walked through the last section of tunnel.

As they neared the exit they had come to big brick-lined rooms once used for storage and for living in. There was an air of desolation here. Hare saw bed frames and a child's doll, children's drawings, a chipped enamel bowl with a shoe in it.

They they were walking down a lane of concrete. On either side rose smooth brown-grey walls, lit by strong lights that cast an orange glow. A large circle was incised in the cement wall, and in the middle of the circle was a sign: 'STRICTLY NO ENTRY'.

It was a door, but there was no visible means of opening it.

Hare found his skin clammy with sweat. He glanced at Danny, who met his eyes fleetingly and looked away. No-one had spoken since they entered the area.

Then they were there. It was much too soon: he wanted to protest. He wanted to stay in the tunnels. Anything was better than what waited at the top of this absurdly simple flight of concrete steps, winding in a spiral from where they stood.

For some reason the others seemed to expect him to go first. Hare set his foot on the bottom step. He would not have been greatly surprised if the staircase had convulsed or howled or done some other demonic thing. It accepted his tread as any other staircase would have done. He walked up it with trembling legs, and behind him walked the Diggers.

He was at the top. He was standing on a square platform of concrete, looking at a door. Actually, two doors, the larger door being wide like the door to a warehouse, while

246

set into it was a small one just big enough for one person to go through.

Both doors would be locked, Hare thought. They would have to go back, thank God they could get no further, he should have realised all along that it would not be possible to get through into the Zone. His eye fell on a key hanging from a hook in the large door.

Hare felt his heart thumping in his ribs. The key was the key to the small door: it could not be anything else.

Danny looked at it, and at him, and said, 'Well?'

He took the key, turned it in the lock and tried the door. It did not move.

Danny reached across him, turning the key in the other direction with her left hand, and pushed the door. 'It was already open,' she said.

There was nothing for it. He was there in the doorway, and the door was open. Hare stepped out into the Zone.

The sky was a clear violet-blue from which the light was gradually being withdrawn. In it hung reefs and bars of gold. The sun, near setting, blazed red and gold in his dazzled eyes.

He began to walk forward, vaguely aware of the others filing through the door behind him.

The first thing he saw was the towers.

Tall and skeletal, they were invisible against the sun. Only when he shaded his eyes could he see them. A slender scaffolding, tapered towards the top. He had an impression of spiders. At the top, he fancied, were eyes. Eyes on stalks. Black and probing, perhaps with human eyes behind them, but he thought not.

Dropping his gaze from the towers, he saw the wire, and that he was very close to it.

There were miles of it. And it was not plain wire, the kind used to keep chickens in and footballs out, wire you could come to an accommodation with, could even, possibly, climb. This was murdering wire. It was piercing, flesh-tearing wire, wire that would cut you to the bone if you touched it with a bare hand. Strand after strand of it, nerve-taut, rose to well over human height, and then at the top it reached outwards and broke into a disgusting exuberance of curls and coils and hoops as if unwilling to come to an end.

That was just the first fence. There were . . . Hare could not count them. They zigzagged and ran into each other in a crazy manner so that he could not work out any possible way through them: a maze of fences, a deadly riddle in wire.

He had a sudden feeling he was being watched. He swung round, but saw only the Diggers, who were staring, not at him, but at the towers.

He walked further.

Inside the fence (the outer fence, that was) the ground had once been asphalted, but weeds had broken through and now the surface was interrupted by clumps of tall waving grasses and thousands of brilliant dandelions.

Something glowed red on his left.

He turned his head swiftly. A glint. Metal? More like glass. A smallish square thing, absurdly domestic: an electric fire. No, it wasn't. The red was too pink, unearthly somehow, and was that colour only when looked at in one particular direction, being otherwise colourless like water. Hare studied this water-fire thing standing on the edge of a wilderness of weeds and asphalt, and wondered if it was the watcher. Then he noticed another, and another. There was a line of them, all along the outer fence.

With the shadows of the tall spidery towers falling across him in the evening sunlight, Hare was afraid with a cold fear he had never felt before. And now he saw the last thing. Gazing through the wire he saw, far in the distance, domes of concrete like the shells of hideous eggs half-buried in the ground, and he heard faintly the high, chill pulsing that had once come to his ears as he stood by the wall of the Zone.

He turned away, full of dread, and found himself facing a strange figure who had been standing close behind him. It was a woman in ragged clothes, with long grey-streaked hair and a wild look about her. She was not one of the Diggers, he knew that at once by the creased and weatherbeaten brownness of her skin. She grasped his wrist. He drew back, a little frightened, trying to avoid the penetrating gaze of her eyes. She's insane, he thought.

Then she smiled, a smile that tugged painfully at forgotten parts of him and that was not insane at all, and he knew he had found his wife.

He could not react at first: he froze instead. He was not ready. There were all those years between them, stillborn. He stood there mute. But she was still holding his wrist, quite gently.

'Do you live here?' he said at last.

'Yes,' she said.

'What is this place?'

'The centre,' she said. Her voice had a strained quality, like something unused.

'The centre?' Hare tried again. 'What is it for?'

'The weapon,' she said.

'Is that the weapon?' Hare pointed to the concrete shells.

'It's all the weapon,' she said. 'The place is the weapon, the weapon is the place.'

'I don't understand,' said Hare.

She said, 'Climb a tree.'

She *was* mad. But then he saw that there were trees, sycamores, which had sprouted here and there, and that some of them were quite tall.

Presumably she wanted him to look at something. There was of course no other way one could get a general view of the Zone.

He chose a tree and started to climb. His limbs protested: he had not done this since boyhood. Nevertheless, one did not quite forget how. Eventually he reached a fork, fairly high, on which he could rest. He parted the boughs and looked out.

Once you had seen it, it was obvious. Immediately below him, bare and cancerous where the trees and grasses had not reclaimed it, stretched the Zone. Around its perimeter ran the wall, which was only the outermost of a series of roughly concentric barriers, most of them wire, which protected – ultimately – the concrete shells. The shells were thus the centre of the whole system. But not the centre solely of the Zone. For the Zone – and this and this only was the reason why maps could not be made and why traffic was forced on endless detours and everything possible was done to confuse a sense of direction – the Zone was the centre of the city. The city stretched around him on all sides, for as far as he could see, a vast, untidy, innocent jumble of houses and streets, workplaces, scrapyards and cinemas; held at bay, ruled and dispossessed by the thing at its centre, which it could not touch, which was sealed off from it like an infected organ, like a forbidden thought, like evil.

He descended the tree with care. The Diggers had gathered round and were looking at him expectantly.

'We are the only people here,' said Hare. 'We are probably safe from the police, though we may not be safe from other things. Perhaps we can live here. Perhaps we can make it – '

'Whole,' said someone. The voice had a strained quality, as if not often used.

In his room high above the city traffic Mr Lucy sat late. He had no particular reason to sit here: he had a comfortable home to go to, and everyone else except the janitor had left the building hours ago. Something kept him here. The truth was that his comfortable home bored him, and only in this room was he completely himself and all he could be.

The room also had, undeniably, a fine view. One could even say that it had the finest view in the city. He smiled at this little joke. And it was certainly a fine evening.

He walked to the window. Lights were coming on in the houses. His gaze drifted upward, to the dark line of the wall, and stopped there. What he saw was impossible. It was a trick of the fading light. But Mr Lucy had keen eyesight and it was not easily misled.

Quickly he went to his desk. He fetched the binoculars and trained them on the dark line near the upper edge of the cityscape before him.

It was true. There were people in the Zone.

His mind whirled. At first he was near to panic. They were the marginals, of course, or whatever rubbish had today come out into the streets and been dealt with by the police. Now they had got into the sanctum. *They had to be got out.* No, it was too late for that. They had to be silenced.

But no-one would go in there to do it. The police would not go in there whatever orders they were given, and whatever they were threatened with.

And, of course, they must not. The police must not go in there. For the same reason that the marginals, or whoever was in there, must be eliminated – that no-one could be allowed to see what was in the Zone and survive. If the truth came out, the whole elaborate edifice of belief would collapse. Years, decades of work by his predecessors, not to mention his own . . . And the chaos that would ensue! More than anything, the justification of his life was that it kept chaos at bay.

What was to be done? He raced through the possibilities, running his hand almost fiercely over the smooth contours of his paperweight. Gradually he calmed. He began to think clearly.

At the end of half an hour he was content. Nothing need be done after all. The land was poisoned, they would die.

Even if they did not, and found their way back with their tale to the city, they would not be believed. Meanwhile, they could stay there. And that, after some thought, pleased him. For every citizen of the great city spread out before him believed the Zone to be inhabited by a species of foul, filthy half-human beings; and now it was. A prophecy had been fulfilled.

Mr Lucy chuckled. He always preferred to tell the truth if he could.